Praise for *The Slummer*

2021 READERS' FAVORITE 5-Star Review ★★★★★
"The prose is stellar, filled with terrific descriptions and strong imagery, and the plot so skillfully crafted that it transforms the tale into a page-turner."

"This is the first running book I've read that I think, wow this is like peeking into my brain and my way of thinking. I will be reading it again and again."
CHRIS SOLINSKY, Former American Record Holder - 10,000 m (26:59.60)

"Lace up for a powerful story of commitment, loss, aspiration and an unlikely challenger of systematic oppression."
ANDY SCHMITZ, 3x US Olympic Coach - Triathlon

"*The Slummer's* inspiring story pits the indomitable spirit of a runner against economic disparity and genetic engineering in a believable, dystopian tomorrow."
JONATHAN BEVERLY, Editor in Chief - *PodiumRunner*

"A futuristic take on the simplest of sports. I couldn't help but lace up my shoes and go for a run."
DEREK GRIFFITHS, *Colorado Runner Magazine*

"Well written, there is a message of oppression, hope and determination. Is this where we are headed in spite of all the talk of affirmative action? Thought-provoking and one of those reads that leaves a mark."
Tome Tender Book Blog

THE SLUMMER
Quarters Till Death

THE SLUMMER
Quarters Till Death

GEOFFREY SIMPSON

Published by

BarkingBoxer Press
The Future of Sports Fiction

The Slummer: Quarters Till Death / by Geoffrey Simpson — 1 ed.
Published in the USA by BarkingBoxer Press LLC
Sheridan, Wyoming

© 2021 by Geoffrey Simpson
Cover Design © 2021 by Geoffrey Simpson
Interior Design © Geoffrey Simpson
Author Photograph by Andreas Redekop
First Printing, 2021

www.geoffrey-simpson.com

All rights reserved. No part of this book may be reproduced or used in any manner without the express written permission of the publisher except for the use of brief quotations in a book review.

This is a work of fiction. Names, characters, businesses, places, events and incidents are either the products of the author's imagination or used in a fictitious manner. Any resemblance to actual persons, living or dead, or actual events is purely coincidental.

Issued in print and electronic formats
ISBN 978-3-9822801-0-3 (pbk)
ISBN 978-3-9822801-1-0 (ebook)

Library of Congress Control Number: 2020924932

FIC038000	FICTION / Sports
FIC028110	FICTION / Science Fiction / Genetic Engineering
FIC055000	FICTION / Dystopian

Dedicated to my parents and sister who understand exactly where this story is coming from.

tal·ent /ˈtalənt/ n.

natural ability or aptitude in a special field:
a talent for running

Chapter One

"Hardest part about running is lacing up the shoes," Benjamin Brandt whispered to himself as he double knotted his trainers on the top step of his apartment building. It was an old saying that had become a sort of mantra before hard workouts and long runs. The irony was that running was the easiest part of his life. It was the *only* thing Benjamin looked forward to.

The dark, uneven streets required tactical maneuvering as his feet rhythmically paced through the neighborhoods on Cleveland's east side. Just shy of 5:15 a.m., the moon was still up, and not much stirred besides an unsuspecting raccoon rummaging through the overfilled trash cans. Partiers on East Thirty-Ninth Street seemed unaware that dawn was around the corner. Bass pumped into the darkness, no doubt infuriating the neighbors. He did not wish to tangle with this crowd, nor did the sleepless nearby residents.

Rule number one: Don't put yourself in harm's way. A good rule to live by anywhere, but in the ghetto, it required frequent practice.

In this neighborhood, the party wasn't some drunken college kids celebrating the end of the school year. This was the slums, and their gathering had nothing to do with moving on and moving up. Every square foot of the East Side was someone's territory. This was theirs. Everyone else just minded their own business.

Benjamin sucked in the damp air. He felt alive. A deep and enriching cycle of breathing repeated as his body processed the natural resources.

At nineteen, Ben looked as a runner should. With his long legs, thin bones, and smooth stride, he was as ready as any gazelle to dodge the predators in his midst. His skin tone was a soft brown created by the accumulated genes of his family's generational melting pot. The same was true for his dark hair, which he trimmed tight on the sides with some mess on top. His eyes were bright and wide with a greenish-yellow tint occasionally shifting to a blue, especially on cold winter days. All of this was a gift from nature. A body constructed by the very essence of genes traveling down through the generations. Ben, by every measure known, was a "natural birth," as were his parents, grandparents, and ancestors before him. Whatever this complex mixture was, it made him a natural-born runner.

This was one of the rare days every year Ben truly looked forward to. Christmas and his birthday were mere footnotes on the calendar by comparison. It was Saturday, June 26, 2083, and today was the US Track and Field Championship. This year promised to be quite a show.

Three of the most ferocious distance runners in US history were going up against each other for the title. His personal favorite was a younger up-and-coming runner, who was ready to challenge the older, more experienced order. Ben knew that this year's 5000-meter race would be worthy of songs being written about it.

One of the toughest and most experienced competitors on the national stage was Archer Sinclair—a cold, calculating machine by every report. Even his personality was bound to a methodical sense of control. His training regimen was revered by the most capable of runners.

Eric Richardson, the second of the older two, seemed to be less concerned about his competition than he was about his ultra-wealthy father's expectations. The pride was embroidered in their exceptional family name and, of course, ongoing bragging rights surrounding their elitism. Eric was the conversation piece his father could boast about at his weekly snooker games, a good diversion from his family's ill-run business, which was hemorrhaging their fortune.

It was Cyrus Cray, Ben's favorite, who had the wild personality to match his competitiveness. Long blondish hair bobbed in the wind, free from the elite's conservatism. He spoke in brazen statements and referred to the older guys as fossilizing with each lap of the oval. He intended to relieve them from their burdens of the national title and said so on national television.

Whether this was the year Cyrus took the top step of the podium or not, he was certainly going to force them to fight to the agonizing end for it. His motives were fame and glory, and he was hungry for both.

Ben looked at his own striding feet. The silver shimmer of his shoes glistened in the setting moonlight. Between the old leather patches in his insoles, the bonding agent he'd secretly borrowed from work, and the duct tape he'd used to bind it all together, it was clear he'd grown up on the other side of the tracks from his running heroes.

The unsurmountable reality was that his patchwork shoes were the least of his concerns. Even though Ben closed out nearly 120 miles per week, not just running but doing intensity training, he would still never compete at the national level. Along with 17 percent of the American population, Ben was referred to as a "slummer." The term had once meant someone from the upper class who chose to spend the night in the slums for fun, to do some drugs or find a low-class partner for a one-night stand—someone who was a thrill seeker at best. But in some twisted irony, the divide between middle class and poverty had widened to a point where there were two distinct social hierarchies. A slummer had zero opportunity to rise, and someone who dabbled downward found themselves ostracized.

Over the past half century, the world had accomplished some of the greatest technological achievements toward enriching the health and longevity of the human species. Things that were once long-feared causes of suffering and death, such as cancers and rare diseases, were now only concerns of the slummers.

At first, the medical community, which had been overrun by the geneticists, focused on major health concerns. Immunization against the most notorious viruses, not by vaccination shots, but rather by making small adjustments in DNA coding at the insemination stage.

Investment in genetic engineering grew exponentially, drawing funds and donations away from other previously well-funded charities, for MS, heart disease, Alzheimer's, various kinds of cancers—the list was as endless as the tears. Businesses keen on improving their long-term engineering competencies bought into exclusive programs offered only to their own employees, at least those planning to have children. Insurance companies bet on the reduction of claims. Governments nationalized the initiatives to gain an inch in global supremacy.

It all flowed into a single river of cash. The product was priceless and knew no bounds. The self-feeding financial vortex had created the most lucrative industry the world had ever seen. As a result, a century's worth of progress in DNA coding occurred in mere decades.

Choosing a boy or girl was child's play. This was not just socially acceptable, but to not choose your child's gender became taboo and was an indication of a low social standing. Popular selection of either a girl or boy would oscillate in waves. The government would even offer incentive programs if there were too few boys or girls at one time or another to balance the mix.

As gene manipulation progressed, new doors opened up a myriad of options. Parents now had endless features to select, to ensure the very best for their little Jane or Johnny. Height and hair color were technologically simplistic.

Many advancements were not even optional. The Budget package included a list of more than thirty improvements, like a basic IQ booster, 20/10 vision, critical immunizations, and so on. However, if parents had saved a little extra cash, they could pick some more advantageous traits to set their children apart from the evolving general population. The advanced IQ booster was a good investment, which was included in the Budget+ plan. This also came with 20/5 vision and strength profiles for improved general fitness.

It was the wealthy who really got to play with the genetic machine. The price of the services was not related to the cost, as the selectable options were simply programmed into their equipment. The value was the exclusivity that the feature offered. Mr. and Mrs. Fantastic who dreamed of little Jane becoming the next president would need to start their shopping list here.

Ben, on the opposite end of the spectrum, was a slummer. A natural birth. His genetics came from his family and the spin of the roulette wheel.

Breaking the silence of the early morning was the sound of flies buzzing in masses down the alley to his right. It wasn't the first dead body Ben had seen during his predawn runs. Since he was the earliest one out on the streets in the ghetto, he was also the first one to see the remnants of the night predators. Usually the body would be pulled off the street by loved ones within a day, but once he had seen one lay in an abandoned lot for more than a week. The smell could turn your stomach at fifty paces. This one was still fresh.

In the world of elites, occasionally families could no longer keep up with the financial pace. The wiser ones chose to not have children at all. Those who dared to have a natural birth also chose, inadvertently, to send their kid to the slums. No genetic papers meant no work, and down the spiral he or she would tumble. It was an insurance issue, and a natural birth was forbidden in a company's policy except for those jobs that were deemed "low risk." What that meant, exactly, was anybody's guess. Perhaps it was a kind way of regulating social-class distancing.

The gap between the impoverished and the middle class grew slowly at first and more rapidly within a single generation as social acceptance of genome editing took hold. It wasn't just money and opportunity any longer; the human race was in its earliest stages of dividing. Insurance documentation aside, genetic engineering was creating an enhanced version of the human species, and distinguished doctors predicted that within another hundred years, the division would be statistically notable. Others predicted the shift far sooner. As an athlete, Ben could already recognize the split.

Being a second-tier citizen had taken on an entirely new meaning. The lowest levels of the workforce were no longer protected by the unions or government regulations. These rights were only reserved for the middle class and upward. Slummers had no money, and those with no money had no rights. Voting had been long since revoked.

East Thirty-Fifth Street was Ben's least favorite stretch to traverse on his morning run. Two dogs resided within a few doors from each other. These weren't your ordinary cuddly house pets that wagged their tails when their owners returned home or greeted girl scouts with cheerful woofs. These animals were the security systems of the poor. The best-known method of encouraging the local gangs to move one house up or down the street for tagging, theft, or old-fashioned entertainment.

One of the two beasts, with a mouthful of snarled teeth, Ben was quite sure was a direct descendent of the gray wolf.

The first house was coming up on the left. The more docile of the two dogs, a mangy Belgian Shepherd, resided there. Only once he had escaped when the owner forgot to close the gate. He was more interested in his newfound freedom than chomping a bite from Ben's hamstring muscle. He lived behind a chain link fence, which pulled across the driveway on a pair of wheels. It was a two-story house with distressed yellow siding but appeared nearly gray in the moonlight. Peeled white paint adorned the window trimming. The front lawn had several patches of greenish weeds but was mostly a dust bowl. No sign of the dog this morning. *Must be sleeping around back*, Ben thought.

Two doors down was the more significant threat. Wolfdog, or whatever breed it had really been, was a savage. Fables could be created surrounding this animal's persona. He slept with his nose pressed against the chain link fence. This morning, he was awake and snorting through the mesh. Blasts of angry mist projected from his snout. Teeth began to show.

Ben was already on the other side, as far as he could go. He ran on the dilapidated sidewalk, which contained more overgrown weeds and protruding tree roots than actual cement. Wolfdog popped his front feet up onto the chest-high fence and let out an alarming single bark. His tail showed no sign of wagging. From behind him, Ben could hear the Belgian Shepherd come alive. Footsteps with long claws scrambled across the driveway. He, too, started barking. Wolfdog's duty to protect his home and alert the others was in full effect.

Ben always had a twisted hope that Wolfdog would escape and give chase. He daydreamed of leading the animal ten miles out of the way, until he could no longer stand. That is, if Ben didn't get bit before he reached the end of the street.

Ben didn't make eye contact with the animal, not daring to realize his fantasy today, and sped effortlessly toward his quieter destination along the Cuyahoga River.

***

The sign read *Towpath Trail at Scranton Flats*. The path began along the river, tucked within an industrial zone, with a view of the Cleveland skyline. The post-World War One art deco truss bridge, coincidentally named Hope Memorial Bridge, stretched over the river and trail a few hundred yards down. It was the link from the poverty-stricken East Side and the uplifting West Side. For a city known for its bridges, this was Ben's favorite, with the towering carved stone guardians on either side.

He found solitude within the processing plants early on this Saturday morning. Concrete and gravel suppliers were well positioned, with easy access to Lake Erie. During the weekdays, barges came and went through these waters by the minute, but for now, all was quiet.

Ben eased over to the side of the truck-worn road by the river, where he stopped to stretch before his workout.

An old brick firehouse stood to the left, with the American flag hanging in the still air. With the looming excitement of the championships, Ben decided to revel in a 5000-meter tempo run.

He spread his legs out in an inverted *V*. Stretched out his hamstrings from side to side as the sun broke into the hazy horizon. The warm reddish-orange glow made even the ugly run-down industrial area a place of beauty.

The finish line marker had been established with his white T-shirt, which he'd already stripped off and tossed carelessly to the ground. His lean six-pack gleamed in the light as he punched out two stride-outs, then returned. Ben stepped up to his shirt with his right foot forward and his right index finger prepared to press the start button on his watch. A gentle breeze carried scents of dead fish and other foul odors of a more undiscernible nature from the river. With his eyes closed, he inhaled deeply, envisioning he was lined up on the track at Hayward Field for the National Championship.

After two rapid exhales, his eyes opened. He simultaneously pushed off from the line and depressed the watch's start button. Toned muscles rippled into action.

The pace gradually increased until he found his target speed. He knew exactly how fast he was going based on feel alone. A dust trail, illuminated by the sunrise, followed him along the dilapidated pavement into the distance.

Ben was alone with his fantasy. Side by side with the lead pack consisting of Cyrus, Eric, and Archer. Archer being the tallest of the three, with legs undoubtedly designed to help him become a distance runner. Together, Ben held stride as he passed the mile marker. He didn't dare look at his watch. A self-imposed rule he had somehow adopted from something he had read years before.

The burn presented itself for the first time as he neared the turn-around point—mile and a half. He felt strong and made it there sooner than expected. It was going to be a good split. The 180-degree turn robbed him of his momentum. A burst of energy was necessary to bring him back to full speed. The sun cast his own long shadow beside him, which had a slight lead. Ben glanced at it, cast a sneer, and said, "Oh, you wanna race?"

The shadow didn't know what was to come as Ben put on a blistering surge. The river arched to the right, which pushed the shadow farther behind him. It was not the first time he'd chased his shadow along this stretch of the muddy Cuyahoga. Every time—in the morning, anyway—he was victorious.

Two miles in the bag, but now he needed to compose himself. The lactic acid was attempting a hostile takeover. His willpower needed to fight this battle. He regained control of his breathing. Thumbs rhythmically tapped his hips with smooth low hands. No side to side swing in the shoulders.

Half mile to go; he had to finish hard. He squeezed his eyes shut for a mere second, envisioning his favorite, Cyrus, putting on a bold move on the backstretch. Ben chased him toward the white T-shirt lying in the dust ahead. He pushed with a grunt, letting an obscenity slip through his lips, as if it would unburden him of the overwhelming hurt. Flying down the road at a speed reserved for only the most prestigious carnivores on the

African Savannah. He couldn't be the prey. He was too ferocious.

At the exact moment he passed his T-shirt, he squeezed the button of his wristwatch, which didn't return the typical audible response. Gliding to a stop, he knew that it had finally kicked the bucket. Ben looked at his battered black plastic watch, a blue line framing the digital display. Blank. The battery was dead again. It didn't matter, though—he couldn't possibly feel more alive.

Chapter Two

Ben resided in a tiny, dreary south-facing apartment with just one window by the front door. Natural light struggled to penetrate across the room, despite its narrowness. It was clustered together with another fifty or so units, and all of those were infested by either rats or cockroaches or both. Living standards were grim, and many units lacked running water. In those units that did have water, it usually had a yellow tint and smelled of sulfur. The authorities said it was safe to drink, and the smell was something everyone was used to. His street had seven more buildings of the same design, all of them built within the same year, and all of them controlled by the Cleveland Housing Authority.

Ben carried a covered aluminum cooking pot around the corner of his building through the tall weeds, then down a small dirt path leading from his street to the next. The street behind his building was entirely different to his own. It was packed with small double-story homes with postage-stamp-size front lawns and narrow driveways leading to single-car garages in the back. Many of the garages were rented out as small apartments, at least until the housing authorities performed their random inspections. Most of the homes were covered in graffiti with trash tangled in the scattered weeds and dead shrubs ornamenting the front steps.

The nicest home was the fourth house on the left from the cut-through path. His girlfriend, Maya Ramirez, who was one year younger than him, survived there with her dad. She always took extra care of the yard, as it was a good way to get out of the house yet stay near her father. In the slums, because of the city's strict control over housing, most people lived with their parents even after they were married. Others ended up in Tent City. Maya had an additional reason—to keep her father alive. Without him and his second income, she would have been off to the tents, where surviving required an advanced degree in street wisdom with a healthy dose of luck.

He hopped up the three crumbled concrete steps, then cheerfully offered the secret knock of rap-rap-rap and proceeded inside without pause. The entrance opened directly into the living room, where Maya lounged with one leg tucked beneath her, the other stretched out to the footstool. The soft light coming from the window cast a shadow along her toned legs. Maya was probably the only other runner in the Cleveland slums. At least the only one who caught Ben's attention.

"Hey, is it on already?" Ben said as he slid onto the faded blue couch beside her. He had lost track of time. It didn't really matter that his watch was broken; Ben was habitually late.

She gave him a sultry look, and said, "You had a good run this morning, didn't you?"

"Perfect, seriously ... You know, the sunrise, cool breeze along the river. I started at Scranton." His thoughts momentarily channeled back to the deep fresh breaths of air and the smell of fish. The feeling of a good run always stayed with him throughout the entire day. "Stupid watch died."

"Again?" Maya said, then covered her mouth with her hand to shield a smile. "Told you. Those batteries are going to cost more than a new watch."

He scrunched his brows together and placed the pot of noodles beside him. Ben didn't have two quarters to scratch together, let alone twenty bucks to waste on a watch. "I think I'm gonna run on feel for a while. Who needs to know how fast I'm running, anyway? It's not like anyone knows what my times mean."

"What ya bring? Oh, is that your famous mac 'n cheese?" She leaned over him, peering at the covered pot.

"Yeah, sort of. I didn't have any cheese."

He lifted the lid, allowing her to see his concoction. Steam billowed out, and a drip of hot condensed water dripped on his bare leg. It didn't go unnoticed, but he avoided squealing like a child.

"Um, that's just noodles with chopped hot dogs."

He raised his left eyebrow. "Er, I got some butter in there, too."

"Yummy." She shook her head, sticking her tongue out like she had been poisoned, and reached for the remote control. "Channel nine," she whispered while searching for the championships. "Ah, just in time, it's the opening stories . . . I love these."

Ben nodded in agreement. He loved everything about the elite runners and was constantly looking to learn more about them, especially their training regimes.

They always watched the races at Maya's house, since Ben's family, which consisted of him, his father, and his brother, Daniel, hadn't had a TV since he was a kid. Things like bread and noodles were higher on the Brandt family shopping list than a television, and even those grew scarce from time to time.

"Your dad home?"

She patted him on his knee. "Nope, off into the world somewhere."

Ben sighed in relief. That was great news.

The TV host, Samantha Bell, was synonymous with track and field. Her deep backstories of the athletes ratcheted everything up a notch and enriched the viewers' enthusiasm for the runners' accomplishments. She was stunning, charismatic, and held a torch for the sport like no other.

Her own older brother had once been a national-caliber pole vaulter. He'd died in a car accident years earlier after coming back from the bar with seven or eight more drinks in him than he should have had. His fate was one that even the most advanced geneticists couldn't entirely avoid, especially if the parents had selected the sports package.

In early models, alcoholism had been nearly eliminated by switching off a few triggers that led to addiction. The

Budget package included the anti-addiction coding, which was best for society at large. What they learned, however, was that those same addiction triggers were required by elite athletes to excel. The triggers facilitated obsession, and only an obsessed athlete could be a competitive athlete. So, for an additional fee of course, parents could purchase the addiction strain in the sports package. Naturally, a warning label came with this option, since the occasional athlete, like Samantha Bell's brother, became a cautionary tale. Still, no parents believed it would be *their* kids who ended up on the coroner's cold stainless-steel table.

"It is a special occasion this year," Samantha said through the TV. "We mark the tenth consecutive year since the Prefontaine Classic at Hayward Field in Eugene, Oregon, became the National Championship for US Track and Field."

Ben was on the edge of his seat, holding Maya's hand. She was enthusiastic, however significantly more relaxed about the event than he was. She enjoyed watching it as much as she enjoyed watching him enjoying it.

"I would like to take you away from the track activities for a moment and introduce you to a much-talked-about rising star who will compete in the highly anticipated 5000 meters at 6:00 EST." Her radiant TV smile sparked a curiosity as she faded into a collage of video clips from throughout the season.

The race announcer howled throughout the final hundred meters of a race from earlier in the season. Eric Richardson, a former Volunteer, charged home for a sizeable win at his hometown stadium during the Sea Ray

Relays. The next clip showed the final lap, where Eric Richardson battled Archer Sinclair to a grisly end, and Archer won by a half stride. Two more videos flashed on the screen, showing their back-and-forth victories throughout the season.

Samantha reappeared as a new race scene slid into the upper-right corner. "And now it is time to show you the triple threat. An athlete who has been climbing through the ranks all season. The youngest athlete in decades, at the fragile age of nineteen, to be a legitimate contender for the national title. It is my distinct pleasure to introduce you to the youngest champion of the Penn Relays, Cyrus Cray."

The film transitioned from the corner to full screen as the official race announcer cried out the step-by-step status of the final eight hundred meters of the race where Cyrus strategically managed his more senior-level competition. He kicked in the final three hundred meters, melting the track's surface, and obliterated the veterans.

A still photo of Cyrus crossing the finish line, with blazing hair and a wild expression, covered the screen. A calm and collected voice began telling the thirty-minute life story of Cyrus Cray, accompanied by photos and videos.

Ben's heart throbbed. He had been following Cyrus's running career over the past several years. They were the exact same age, and it was a dream come true that Cyrus would be the choice for this year's profile.

"You got a man crush, don't you?" Maya said as she poked Ben rather firmly below the ribs.

He squirmed away, grabbed her by the ankles, then pulled her feet toward him. "I got a crush all right."

As Maya giggled, Ben continued to pull her closer, inch by inch, until he could effectively plant a sizeable zerbert on her now-bare stomach.

She squealed, then said, "You're such a fan boy."

"Sure am," he said, followed by a faux-seductive wink.

A commercial came onto the screen, attempting to sell an advanced sports package at the DNA clinic.

Ben laughed. "What do you think, should we start saving up for our kids so that they can run in the championship? You know, we can buy them what they need to make us proud."

"Yeah, let me do some math . . . Okay, I got it. If we both save 90 percent of our incomes, it will take us . . ." She squeezed her eyes shut and scratched her chin, pretending to calculate. "Exactly 7,423 years . . . Um, and three months before we can start a family."

"Gosh, at that age, I am not sure I could keep up with him . . . especially if he is as fast as they advertise."

"Her," she said as she pinched Ben. "I want to buy a girl."

"*She* will be a wonderful athlete." He then mumbled under his breath, "Anything like Mom, she'll drive me nuts."

She punched him hard enough in the shoulder that his muscle would remember the collision for ten minutes.

As he rubbed his arm, they cuddled back into each other.

The 5000-meter race was about to begin as the top competitors were individually announced. They each raised their hands on cue to receive well-deserved roaring applause.

The 5000 had gained in popularity over the past several years and was considered one of the most famed of all track events. The deep and fierce competition, combined with the strategic element, had earned it an unrivaled fanbase.

Ben was beside himself. After twelve months waiting for this moment, he stared at the television as the running gods got called to the line. Within a fraction of a second, the starter cannon shot from the infield. Their muscles blasted into motion as they catapulted from the white line.

Ben and Maya talked strategy, key moves, and getting boxed in, and made bets on who would be crowned champion. There was nonstop chatter for the twelve and a half minutes of fast-paced action. In the final stretch, it was Eric and Archer gunning for the finish line. Ben's favorite, Cyrus, faded back to fifth place, behind two others from the field of runners who all yearned for a place on the podium.

"Blast," Ben said as he jumped from the couch.

"Ha ha!" Maya shouted. She shot both hands in the air as her favorite, Eric, charged over the finish line for the national title. "Two years in a row. Deal with that," she taunted.

Ben simply smiled. No matter the outcome and despite the fact that his favorite runner had struggled, this annual championship race was what kept him alive. It was the very spirit that inspired him, not just to keep up his own running, but to momentarily rise above the dismal life that he trudged through day after day. The faint streaks of light burrowing through the cracks that kept him from total darkness.

Chapter Three

Hundreds of people lined up at the razor wire–topped fence stretching halfway down Broadway Ave. He slid his badge across the scanner beside the security guard at the turnstile, which released the lock so he could enter. Crossing the large and mostly barren parking lot, Ben added in short bursts of running to reduce the time it took to reach the front doors. He was already late and, unlike in a workout, shaving off a few seconds wouldn't amount to much.

The red block letters bolted to the rooftop extended the front of the already impressive towering building, which dominated three city blocks, up another twenty feet. The factory could be seen from two highways and represented a significant part of the region. AluMag Foundry was Ben's place of employment and was one of the largest employers in the ghetto. He flipped his wrist, which looked naked without a watch. The brighter space on his arm left his imagination to predict exactly how late he really was. This wasn't the first time he had charged across the lot under similar circumstances. He pulled hard on the door of the workers' entrance at the front.

His morning run, which pulled him to his feet at 5:00 a.m. without hesitation, had been too good to conclude. After a brisk five miles, he felt great. The air was clean, the solitude was welcome. As the loop wrapped back toward his apartment, he decided that he had time to squeeze in an extra mile . . . or two. He figured he had the extra twelve minutes. He figured wrong.

Besides the gruff, oversize security guard standing beside the metal detector, he was alone in the workers' entrance. To avoid the long queue of workers, which could lead all the way back to the exterior turnstile entrance, many employees would arrive thirty minutes early. More in tune with Ben's timeliness, he would often arrive just as the bell tolled.

"Keys, wallet, anything in your pockets. In the basket," the security guard said to Ben. His tone was flat, and his blank expression told the story. This fellow slummer had been standing there every day, repeating this sentence every minute of every morning for at least ten years, long before Ben started his job more than five years ago, at the ripe age of fourteen.

Ben didn't know his name, despite the fact that it was printed on a metal badge on his uniform. He really didn't care.

The only exciting days for the guard were when someone forgot a knife in their pocket and had to be ejected from the building. Not just for the day. The person would be permanently removed from the premises. No tolerance for rule violations. Ben didn't have a knife ... couldn't afford one. Since Ben was the last employee to arrive, the guard's day was doomed to be a boring one.

Ben entered the changing room, where his personal protective equipment resided, and bumped into his brother, Daniel, who was already heading to the floor. He had apparently been hanging behind until the last minute looking for a chance to chastise Ben. It had become a hobby of his to ensure the younger Brandt boy knew his place. Today, he found the opportunity he longed for.

"Tick tock, little brother," he said. "Late again ... Dad's gonna kill ya if you get kicked to the street."

Ben turned sideways to clear himself between his brother and the doorway. Eyes locked through the entire encounter. "Worry about yourself, jerk. I'm not gonna lose my job."

The changing room was a soft green, with a dozen rows of lockers and wooden benches between. The benches wobbled, and several had been removed. The bolt holes in the floor and a square brown mark where the foot had once protected the dirt from the mop were all that remained. He twisted the dial of his combination lock. The room was empty, and his brother had already vanished onto the factory floor.

He geared up with steel-toed boots, hard helmet, and a company-branded shirt, all company owned and not allowed off the premises.

AluMag Foundry was one of the largest metal foundries in the country. Two thousand five hundred employees working three shifts, including weekends. They primarily serviced the aerospace industry with metal castings and were coming up on their fifty-year anniversary. Their name was a thinly veiled cover for aluminum and magnesium. Their exploitation of slummers as paid slaves was just as thinly veiled.

He burst out of the locker room onto the factory floor, still buttoning his shirt. His eyes shifted to the oversize clock on the wall to see what the damage was. It ticked forward to 6:04. *This is gonna suck.*

Mr. Peterson, his line supervisor, eyeballed him as Ben approached their Short Interval Control meeting, which was held at the beginning of every shift. His boss's number one rule: punctuality. No tolerance for rule violation.

Ben tiptoed to the back of the group. He looked down at his old brown leather steel-toed boots. A sign of his submission. Boss-man liked that.

Mr. Peterson was at the bottom of the elite society. He was a genetically enhanced person who had a chip on his shoulder—not one made from silicon, but of the emotional baggage sort. He never really blended into society. People like Mr. Peterson were the hands who held the whip, the bridge to the have-nots, allowing the more traditional middle class to avoid having to interface with the slummers. A duty detested by most elites, but this guy loved to show off his unearned dominance over the less fortunate. As they say, crap rolls downhill, and Mr. Peterson certainly had a big ol' shovel with plenty rolling upon him to pass on down the line.

"Brandt," he said. Deeper voice than normal, which the workers secretly joked about once they were back in the safety of their homes. "Where the hell you been?"

"Sorry, sir. It won't happen again, sir." Eyes fixated on his shoes. He realized that he needed to clean his shoes—they were filthy—and didn't need more trouble coming his way.

"Don't make promises, you pond scum. This month you've already been late . . ." He lifted his clipboard and flipped the page. His eyebrows raised. "Four times."

"Sorry, sir. I'll do better."

"That some kinda record for a slummer? I thought you people should just be thankful for a job?" He jabbed his finger toward the front of the building. "I got a hundred people waiting outside to take your job. Don't you get that, boy? Wanna live in a tent?"

Ben remained silent, hoping this conversation would move on. Silence and patience were key life skills of a slummer. Loudmouths lived in tents. Guys who lived in tents stood outside the gates *hoping* for work.

"So, can't get outta bed in time anymore. Isn't the paycheck inspiration enough to get outta bed? Put some food on that table for your little slummer babies."

I got no babies, you ignoramus.

The coworker who stood to the right of Ben, a scrawny guy who looked as if he would collapse in a puff of wind, was a well-known brownnoser. Beaker was what everyone called him. However, Ben had no idea what his real name was. Beaker had developed a strategy that was perfectly tailored for Mr. Peterson. His intention was to whittle down the competition on the job floor by tattletaling about everyone else's faults, true or otherwise, to ensure he kept his quality-inspector position in prime standing. His voice echoed sighs around the audience. "Oh, Ben was up all right—he was *running.*"

With his head down, Ben glanced toward his coworker. *Asshole. Just happy to be eating from the trough.*

Mr. Peterson raised only his left eyebrow this time. "Running? What, was . . . was somebody chasing you? A dog perhaps?"

No dogs today, sir. Ben hoped his smirk was unnoticeable.

"I'm speaking to you, Brandt. Was someone chasing you?"

He inhaled, acknowledging that the skill of silence would no longer be his best tactic. "No, sir. I'm a better worker if I get some fresh air in the morning."

Ben was pleased with his rebuttal.

Mr. Peterson shifted his weight to the other foot, evidently unsatisfied at the competent response, glanced at the clock, and proceeded with the morning meeting as planned. He, too, was on a schedule. The production manager would have his hide if he fell behind the daily orders. Ben had cost the company four minutes, which he wouldn't get paid for anyway. Mr. Peterson took an additional four minutes from twenty guys to show everyone that he was the man.

After the meeting, Ben proceeded to his workstation, which he regretfully shared with his brother. Although his dad had more respect among the workers and was stationed in another one of Mr. Peterson's teams, all three Brandt men received equal pay, as did every other slummer.

Daniel leaned in close to Ben as he approached. "You stupid or something?"

He huffed, then whispered into his brother's ear. "They would surely fire me if I jumped around his neck and tapped him out. A double win in the short term, now that I think about it."

"No wonder Dad can't stand you. Get your crap together for the family, you selfish, spoiled jerk."

Ben hissed through his teeth, "At least I'm not some enslaved sheep trapped within the walls of conformity."

Daniel laughed, but his eyes glared. "Maybe they shear my wool, but you're the one who's gonna go to the butcher. You like mutton, Ben?"

Ben grabbed the two-handled end of the crucible, and his brother grabbed the pivot.

They worked in the small parts side of the plant. Insert the crucible into the furnace to melt the magnesium, then pour it into the high-pressure die-casting molds. Today they had an order for some aerospace parts, but they were never told what they were. Ben thought they looked like overdesigned ice-cream scoops. According to the aerospace contracts, slummers were not allowed to know what the products were being used for. Security risk if information ever leaked out to spies or the like. Even in the non-aerospace wing, they still kept the slummers in the dark. Need-to-know, and slummers only needed a job, not knowledge, they figured. Opinions were not appreciated around the factory, and with less information, the less of an opinion someone could have.

As Mr. Peterson walked by their workstation, they clamped their mouths shut and worked efficiently in silence. Glaring at each other. Brotherly love.

The furnace kicked the workstation's temperature up ten to twenty degrees above the ambient. In the winter it was a sweet relief from the bitter cold outside, as well as from their death-warmed-over apartment. July was something else altogether. Ben heard his coworkers saying the other day that this was going to be the hottest week on record. He didn't know if that was the case, but it was blistering under the noon sun. Already, he was dripping sweat. The air could be wrung.

Years ago, there had been automated machines that did this work with minimal human support. Especially the more dangerous stuff, like pouring magnesium. Mag had the tendency to ignite if the temperatures were not tightly controlled.

Everything changed because of the war in Europe. Still raging today, eight years since its inception. Promised money from the government to the factory in support of the military was a far cry from received money. AluMag, and many others like it, struggled to get by. Expensive machinery with costly maintenance in exchange for cheap labor was an easy decision. For years the European situation was simply called "a conflict," but three years ago, they officially defined it as a third world war. America had mostly stayed at arm's length, as they had their own issues to deal with, but the military was ramping up just in case. Funny how humans never learned.

Resegregation had begun well before the conflict, but the transition put rocket boosters on the divide. Ben knew—all slummers knew—that their willingness to work for less than the cost of a machine was why they slaved in these unfit jobs. The peak of human decency had come and gone—a fad that sounded good on paper but didn't fit into the design of people with power. It never had.

Just 20 percent of slummers had reliable jobs. Another twenty lived day to day with the more volatile contract work, which would frequently dry up for months at a time. The ones who were least fortunate, the clear majority of the slummers, had no real income. They either lived with people who did have incomes or lived in Tent City. A place that was synonymous with desperation. The lowest rung of human existence.

***

Ben spent his lunch breaks, when it wasn't raining, at the furthest corner of the AluMag property, sitting beneath a half-dead maple tree. From the edge of the crumbling parking lot to the tree was more than thirty yards and filled with a patchwork of weeds, grass, and bare dirt. Usually it was overgrown, but somebody had come in a few days ago and hacked it all down, and now the remnants lay like hay.

"Oh, come on," Ben whispered to himself when he noticed his brother walking over. There was a reason he was sitting alone below the tree—to be alone. He raised his voice and said, "Go away."

Daniel smiled, enjoying his disobedient act. "Mom would have been so disappointed in you."

Ben rose to his feet. His fists instinctively clenched, knuckles slowly growing white as the blood went elsewhere. Ben typically shielded himself in a cloud of humor while being challenged, but not with his brother.

His brother inspired an ugly side of his anger to emerge. Words never worked, only a well-landed fist. "Don't bring Mom into this."

"What, you gonna swing at me?" Daniel shook his head side to side. "I'd squash you like a bug."

"Mom is the only one who would have believed in me. She wasn't hopping along after the *man*."

"How would you know? You never even met her. She sacrificed her life to bring . . . to bring *you* into this world. Dad must hate you more than anyone. Don't you think?"

Ben stepped forward, and although he was several inches shorter than his older and much thicker brother, he puffed up and went nose to nose. Fighting was cause for immediate dismissal. Neither of them concerned themselves with consequences at that moment.

"What are you two doing?" said a voice in a sharp whisper, rapidly approaching.

Daniel snapped, "Dad, just trying to keep this boy on the ground."

"Go back to the benches," he replied to Daniel. Their father's scowl was unrestrained and wild.

Ben sighed and spun on his heel to look away.

"Ben, this isn't working. I heard the supervisors talking just now. They got you on a short leash . . . We can't lose your income."

Daniel said over his shoulder, as he strolled back toward the factory kicking away the hay, "That's what I was trying to tell him."

Ben turned back toward his father, who looked into his eyes. A half smile pulled up his left cheek, then he winked. "Brothers."

Ben released a huff just short of a laugh. "Sorry, Dad. I'm gonna fix this."

"I know you will, Ben." He patted him firmly on the shoulder. "I know this isn't easy. Heck, it isn't easy for anyone. You gotta be more like your brother if you're gonna survive in this world."

Ben glared at his dad. The idea of being like his brother repulsed him. *Act like a sniveling rodent?* Ben's expression spoke volumes.

"Okay, not exactly like your brother."

Ben looked back to the mob of factory workers eating their vending machine sandwiches with their heads hanging, lifeless. *Slaves.*

"And Ben, this running in the morning?" He moved in close to secure eye contact. "Everyone is talking about you like some fool . . . You gotta stop."

Chapter Four

An old ironwood grew beside the path that meandered between Ben and Maya's streets. The tree had been tagged with a marijuana leaf and was their designated meeting location for almost any event, particularly on Saturday mornings, when they met for their weekly run.

Ben pulled his right knee up to his chest, feeling his thigh muscles tighten. He held the position, then switched to the other side. He could smell the damp dirt moistened by morning dew. He felt good. Legs strong and enthused for one of his favorite workouts.

"Hey chump, ready to get yo self blasted?" chimed a sweet voice from the entrance to the path.

She was in good spirits, and the sound of her voice twisted a smile to his face. "What? You wanna throw down today, woman?"

Maya and Ben had been dating for more than two years,

run together for almost five, known each other for around fifteen, and spent a lifetime within a few hundred yards from each other in the slums. The place had changed over those years. Worsened. Darkened.

Ben met Maya for the first time beneath this very tree. It seemed larger back then. From a child's perspective, it grew to the clouds. A summer morning, no later than 9:00 a.m., she had been crying, nestled into the bushes, hiding from something, everything. She was just five or six at the time and had a bloody lip. Left cheek bright red. He remembered vividly because of her answer to his simple question: "What happened?" She whispered in a wavering voice, "I spilled his beer."

He had never known such fear as he had witnessed that day. Not before, nor after. He had become numb to it.

Maya joined Ben beside the tree, kicked an empty beer can out of the way, and began stretching with him.

"You hear about the Jacksons?" Maya asked.

"Your neighbors? No, what did he do now?"

Maya offered a halfhearted smile, acknowledging the blame to the deadbeat father, always shooting his mouth off. "Yeah, well, he lost his job at the sand pit. Guess he got in some kinda argument with the boss man. They threw him out, then reported him to the authorities."

Ben was more surprised by how long he had kept the job rather than the fact that he had lost it. "They gonna lose the house?"

She grimaced. "Already done. Housing authority came in and moved 'em out overnight."

Ben knew exactly what that meant. The slums had gotten so overcrowded that only the upstanding slummers were allowed in the housing. Consequently, Tent City was booming. It had almost overrun Industrial Valley at large, where multiple steel plants once operated. Two entirely separate social class systems had emerged. One for the elites, where Ben's boss, Mr. Peterson, firmly belonged on the lowest tier. And one for the slummers, where Mr. Jackson just found that lowest tier last night.

"What about Brian?"

She slouched and sighed, then looked him in the eyes, wrought with sadness. "Come on, let's get started."

They walked beside each other to the end of the path in the direction of Maya's house, then jogged down the middle of the crumbling road. The sidewalks were so overgrown and upheaved by ancient tree roots and repetitive freezing and thawing that it was more dangerous to run there than in the street. Nature was taking back what had once been its own. Storming the castle with a patience and persistence that humans could only succumb to. It was inevitable.

He didn't know Brian as well as she did. He did know that the boy was around twelve years old. He'd suffered a head trauma as a baby, which had caused irreversible brain damage. To think of the boy moving to Tent City was dismal. Most likely it would be the end of the road for him. He wouldn't make it through the winter. Tent City would eat him alive, as it did to so many, even those who were stronger and more capable than he. There was no real law in the ghetto beyond the housing authority and the gangs. However, in Tent City, even those didn't exist. A jungle of the most desperate humans, who were incapable or unwilling to conform to the hierarchy created by the elites.

There was little human decency left in Tent City. Being human there was more of a technicality than a quality.

***

They took their normal route to the metro parks, winding through the slums along East Fifty-Fifth Street to Harvard Ave., then toward the towpath along the Cuyahoga River. Just over four miles to the park entrance.

"Any news on the National Athletic Union? Did Woodard say anything about his plans to get the Olympics running again?" Ben asked, hoping to hear that the track and field giant, Harvey Woodard, had outmaneuvered the political reach of the ongoing war in Europe.

Since the war, which had by now outlasted every expert's speculation, was officially declared, international travel had been banned for all private citizens—including athletes. Harvey was the head of US Track and Field, who, through his own vanity, had made it the most profitable sport on American soil.

"Woodard," she replied while rolling her eyes. "Yeah, he was on the news yesterday. He said that they have been in negotiations with the US government as well as Germany, England, and France trying to allow athletes to travel again. He offered to host the Olympics in the US to reduce the risk of Turkey or Russia screwing around again. Of course, he just wants total control of it all."

"Wouldn't it be great to see our guys go head to head against the world? Not a single international race since the

European Union collapsed, what ten years ago? Those guys are posting times as good as anyone."

"Absolutely. But I get kinda tired watching Woodard make it all about himself. It almost wouldn't be worth it to see him gloat about his success."

Ben looked over to her. Maya's gaze was off in the distance, in thought. He was of a different opinion. Woodard could gloat all he wanted as long as Ben could watch international racing. "I wouldn't care if they change the name from the Olympics to the Woodard Games. It would still be the greatest show on earth."

She shrugged.

Ben thought about the world athletes racing against each other again, like in the old days, for a few minutes, then drifted back to something closer to home.

The story about Brian heading to Tent City scratched at Ben's stomach lining, twisting his guts. Ben recognized the heightened risk of losing his own job. The consequences of the added burden on his family and the uncertainty it would bring. They lived in what was declared as a three-income apartment, although they probably wouldn't lose it, since they were certainly not the only ones stretching the housing regulations. Maya and her father had maintained an entire house with two people just because her dad had some connections through his gambling ring.

Neither Ben nor his family had any connections. He couldn't risk getting noticed by the housing authorities. Similar to his boss, the housing board were the scum suckers of the upper society, and they loved to play games with the slummers. Wield their battle-ax for the simple joy of it. Best to not be on their radar.

Ben decided that he would apply more of an effort at AluMag to avoid termination. In cases like the Jacksons', termination was the beginning of a slow but expected extermination.

As they approached the entrance along Harvard Ave., Maya broke the silence. "What's the workout plan today?"

Her tone was uplifting again, and she clearly hadn't used their silence to fume internally about Woodard.

"Repeat miles. I was thinking five with a half mile jogging rest. Sound good?"

"Yeah, I mean, I'll do five repeat halves with quarters between, then we can meet back here."

Maya was a solid runner, but Ben wreaked havoc on the trails, covering significantly more distance than she. Their workouts were always scaled to ensure they finished around the same time.

Ben raised his eyebrows. Eyes wide and wild. "Ready? This is gonna be a bloody mess."

He let three bursts of air pulse from his mouth in rapid succession. He jumped a few times, testing the spring of his muscles, swung his arms in wide arcs, and touched his ear to his shoulder to stretch out his neck. He leaned forward and stepped his toe to the starting line—marked by a brown wooden sign with a map of the park behind glass. Next to the sign was a huge rusted metal wheel with spokes planted into the ground. Somehow it was intended to be a memento from the park's past, however Ben never really had an interest in what it signified.

He looked over at his running partner, who also pulled forward to the line. She looked amazing, he thought. Nodding to each other to confirm all systems go.

Ignition. They both launched off the mark.

Muscles pulsing like pistons, efficient, smooth. Ben was a well-oiled machine. Beneath the park's wooded canopy, the air was cool and refreshing. Each inhalation was nature's treat to his existence. A place where Ben could lose himself. For the moment, he could forget the slums. No mangy dogs. No peeling paint from the window frames of boarded-up homes that were unfit for human occupancy. No bodies discarded haphazardly in the alley, breeding maggots—well, beside the occasional chipmunk or mouse that had fallen victim to an owl's daggered talons.

The first two repeats were about control. Energy conservation. Usually he tried to stay at just under five minutes. Today he ran on feel as his watch lay upon his bedroom shelf, void of life. A graveyard of things too valuable to discard and too useless to use.

The towpath was frequented by joggers, bikers, and walkers strolling along. Although DNA markers were able to reduce the effects of obesity, leave it to the human race to override the gifts that had been given to them. At least these people attempted to work off the ultra-tasty, ultra-processed foods that satisfied their midnight cravings. Obesity was not a concern in the slums. It was a sign of privilege.

Ben had once seen a commercial about a company that produced treadmills and stationary bikes. They were complete with virtual reality, and the user could select one of a thousand trails and roads across the world to train on. There were even otherworldly trails on Mars or completely fictional places from your favorite movies and books. The scenario featured in the commercial allowed you to run through the Jurassic period among the highly curious dinosaurs. A few actually gave chase during the preprogrammed interval workouts.

The people on the towpath chose the real deal. Ben had never used a VR machine, nor had he ever seen one in person. He couldn't imagine that the fresh, cool air and the crumbling of cinders beneath his feet could ever be replaced by a machine. Perhaps these people felt the same; perhaps they were too poor or too cheap to buy one. Didn't matter; Ben was doing his own thing and loving it. He did consider that the dinosaurs would be cool, though.

One biker was oblivious to the high-speed machine that was approaching. Ben had no bell to announce his arrival, which meant quite frequently he scared the bejesus out of the unsuspecting. One trait that all of these trail users had in common was that they were exclusively from the elite class. No slummers here besides Ben and Maya. He was alone with his homemade clothes and duct-taped shoes. No hiding where he came from, and no illusion that he was welcome.

Toward the end of the first mile, his pace was in control and he felt phenomenal. He passed another biker heading in the same direction as he. Always a little sport in chasing down a bike. Once, he had seen a movie depicting a dog chasing a car. He couldn't remember the name or the point of the movie, but that sentiment had never been lost.

The biker was overweight but outfitted in the latest biking fashion. Pudge pushed against the overstressed skintight shirt, leaving some bare butt cheek to catch a draft down the dark and unsettling crack. Ben thought that if he dropped in a few nickels, he might ride a little faster.

Unfortunately, he didn't carry that kind of money to test the theory.

Crack Man, startled by Ben passing him in stealth mode, shouted, "Get outta here . . . slummer. Go back to your tent."

Ben smiled, then cut in ahead of him a little too early. The biker swerved and shouted more insults into the air. Despite their frequency, each comment from the elites wore on him. He pretended to act immune, but inside he was an emotional mess. On runs like this, though, his enthusiasm could compensate.

A moment later, the first repeat was done. He slowed into a half-mile jog recovery.

He listened carefully for Crack Man, who certainly had a bone to pick, but he never did cross paths with him again. Rarely did these encounters get physical. The elites, if nothing else, hated to touch slummers, as if they might get contaminated with the outrageous disease of natural conception.

The second repeat was quickly upon him. This time, he had a rolling start, allowing him to more efficiently arrive at his five-minute pace. A pace that was preprogrammed by repetition.

The park was mesmerizing, and despite the fact that he was gliding along the trail at a blistering pace, Ben absorbed all its natural beauty. The smell of the wooded park alone pulsed through his powerful lungs—rapid yet controlled. An inner peace can only be found when one finds themselves within nature, he believed.

As he sped by a group of unmindful walkers, grandmas who thought a pack of five wide was appropriate received the startle of their lives as he shouted, a little later than was courteous, "On your left."

They scrambled in every which way, nearly colliding with Ben. *Seems the word "left" was a bit confusing,* he thought.

Midway through the third interval, he passed beneath an abandoned trestle bridge high overhead. One of his favorite locations of this stretch of trail. A view into the past. A time when the blue-collar iron industry thrived in Cleveland. A time when an honest day's work afforded a life of comfort and respect. Long before DNA manipulation cultivated the high society. The bridge also signified the nearing of his turnaround point. He made a high-speed U-turn, which involved significant deceleration and a surge to push him back up to pace. For the first time, he had to start digging to maintain pace, but with only a half mile of the interval remaining, it was not a serious threat. The upcoming half-mile rest was welcomed to slow his rising heart rate. His body plotted an uprising against his casual abandonment of its initial warning signs of overexertion.

The fourth interval approached. Second to last, it was typically the deciding factor between a successful or failed workout. This was the one that hurt badly, and at the same time, there was still no end in sight. Ben whispered to himself, in his final steps toward the mile marker, "Control, focus, power."

His pace accelerated again into number four. His exertion level shifted from moderate to high. His calibration of speed also shifted into a more uncertain realm. Each stride cut deeper. Increasingly difficult, and he knew his pace was overcompensating. *Too fast.* He pushed through the mile marker, and despite not having a watch, he guessed he had tucked under four-forty. His lack of control was going to bite back in the final leg of the workout. His muscles had instigated a full-on riot with torches and pitchforks. He needed to ignore the consequences no matter what torture they bestowed upon him. The costs were all short-lived.

The rest was much too brief to disperse the rioters. He was still sucking air as the mile marker approached, his pulse rattling away. This time, he wasn't thinking of control, he was thinking of survival. A battle lay ahead.

His muscles screamed as he accelerated into the first ten yards. The first hundred yards promised a long agony, which he no longer thought he could endure. His thoughts encouraged him to call it quits. *Just jog back to the start.* There were no judges, no spectators. In fact, nobody but Maya would even know that he had cut his workout short. Nobody cared but him.

He maintained the breakneck pace while he considered bagging the final leg. A quarter of it was already finished, but he could feel the pace dragging, legs heavy and burning, gravity pulling him relentlessly. He surged back to pace, still undecided if he would cave to the rioters' wishes. He looked to his feet for reassurance. His legs screamed back in an unknown and ancient dialect, but the meaning was clear.

Ben was no slave to his pain. He was no slave to anybody or anything. He could not be controlled. His intellect, his heart, and his soul would decide if he would stop, not his legs. Besides, his legs weren't smart enough to know what is good for them. This pain and suffering were exactly what would make them stronger, despite their protests. If only they knew. He had to teach them.

He breached the halfway mark of the final interval. Slower than targeted, but not by much.

His legs were ill-informed that Ben thrived on their suffering, and despite considering stopping, tossing around the idea nonchalantly, at no time was there ever a chance that he actually would. He owned his pain. His rioters raged against him, but Ben was the fire-breathing dragon who would scorch them into charred bits. They never stood a chance.

With a quarter to go, Ben dug deep. He switched from pushing his legs to pushing his arms. Concentrating on his arms' pace, tapping his thumbs on his hips. Tap tap tap. Ever quicker. He flew toward the mile marker where Maya was waiting, stretching.

Ben blasted through the finish line at a pace that would rattle windows, like a rogue pilot might do to a control tower.

Maya cheered him on as a gust of wind blew by her.

He glided to a stop and circled back to her. Violently sucking air. Bent over, he placed his hands on his knees. His chest rose and deflated rapidly.

"Holy cow, that was insane," she said, looking at him with a sense of awe.

Ben lifted his head to look up at her. His smile gleamed through the panting breaths and dripping sweat.

He loved running.

Chapter Five

"Woah, that's way too much butter."

Ben had been charged with managing the garlic bread for their special dinner event. He sighed and looked toward his dad through the corner of his eye. "Yeah, but I like it with lots of butter."

His father looked at him in judgment, analyzing his careful work. "You think butter is free?"

"Really? It's butter."

He laid the kitchen knife on the counter and turned toward Ben, clearly prepared to discuss the financial implications of using too much butter.

Ben simply shrugged and began making the butter stretch. He knew this meal was already a splurge, one they could only afford a few times a year. They didn't take vacations or buy expensive things—or any non-necessity for that matter. With the few saved dollars they had collected together, they had the occasional feast. But by no means was it ever wasteful.

The apartment smelled brilliant. The lasagna in the oven promised something savory and comforting. His dad sautéed green beans with a clove of garlic. Both had been picked from their garden pots on the balcony, which was too brittle to stand on, but strong enough for a few plants.

Daniel and his girlfriend, Amy, would arrive momentarily. Maya was supposed to arrive in twenty minutes, after she took care of her dad. Ben knew that any estimate, with Maya's dad in the equation, was unpredictable.

"How long does the garlic bread need in the oven?"

His dad leaned over to inspect the redistribution of butter. He seemed satisfied with the results.

"Um, just a few minutes. We'll put it in once everyone has arrived, just before we eat."

Right on cue, his brother came in with Amy.

"Smells great," Daniel said as he kicked off his shoes by the door, letting them lay where they fell.

Shoes were not allowed in the house. Ben was told a long time ago that his mother insisted on shoes remaining by the door. Nineteen years later, without her presence, the rules of the house stood as a testament, a tribute to her everlasting leadership of the family.

Amy walked into the kitchen and gave Ben a hug, then did the same with his dad, but included a kiss on the cheek. "Can't wait. We brought some wine."

Amy was destined to be Daniel's wife and had already begun the integration process into their family. However, Daniel still hadn't proposed to her. He claimed he was saving money for a fancy ring, but for slummers, cheap aluminum drugstore rings were typically used in place of the elite's expensive golden or more exotic platinum bands. He wasn't holding out for someone better, but he was clearly dragging his feet. From Ben's perspective, anyone willing to marry his brother must be afforded zero opportunity to escape, and Amy was ten times what his brother deserved.

"Oh, that's a nice surprise," Dad replied, lifting the bottle to inspect the label.

Ben looked up from his garlic bread and immediately recognized the bottle, as it was one of three brands commonly sold in the slums. It was little more than the water that was used to clean out the barrels of the wine casks. But, he also knew, it was a generous gesture from Amy.

"How can I help, Pops?"

She always called him Pops. Ben could see that his dad liked it, too. Nobody in their family called him that. There was a noticeable pride in him that his boys were growing up. His family was expanding before his eyes, and despite the hardest days when Ben was young, there was finally something truly uplifting happening. At long last, the future was worth looking forward to.

Ben also liked having Amy around, for two reasons. One was that she was kindhearted and always interested in discussing new things. Two, his brother was much nicer to him when she was within listening distance. She'd probably dropped a frying pan on his head a few times after she heard how Daniel really treated his younger brother.

"My dear, my guest, please take a load off and let the boys take care of dinner tonight," Dad said as he turned to

Daniel. "Boy, set the table so this nice lady of yours doesn't have to eat with her hands."

Daniel rolled his eyes. "Yeah, yeah."

As he approached the kitchen, a double knock followed by a single one rapped on the door. Ben and Maya's secret knock.

"Oh, I'll get it," Daniel said, clearly desperate to get out of his table-setting duties.

He opened the door, and Maya entered in a light-white summer dress that showed off her toned and warm-bronze legs. She was radiant. A runner with angel's wings and a befitting smile.

"Hey," Ben said as he blew a kiss across the room. "Dad's got me as his apprentice today."

She smiled and winked back at him as she reached for a hug with Daniel, who appeared to be a bit too delighted by the embrace.

The girls, who were still getting to know each other, exchanged cordial hellos as Maya made her way to the kitchen. She smacked Ben on the butt as she walked by and bear-hugged his dad. "Hi, Mr. Brandt. How are you?"

"Oh dear, things are good. You know, we make the best of things here in the Brandt household."

She grinned and offered to help, as Amy had.

"Girls, can't you see the Brandt boys got things under control?" He raised his voice and sharpened the tone. "Daniel, back to the table setting."

Ben snorted to himself, then whispered under his breath, "Lazy fool."

This was rewarded with an all-too-common death stare. Siblings at their finest, brothers to the end.

***

In quick order, the finished meal was placed on the small white plastic table, typically used as cheap patio furniture. It was designed for four people, but with a corner stool straddling a table leg and some crowding around, they were able to squeeze the five of them in. Ben gladly took the stool between his dad and Maya. His father and the ladies obviously deserved normal seats, and he had no patience to listen to his brother whine.

The lasagna had been baked in a flimsy aluminum tray, which now doubled as the serving dish. This same tray had been used and cleaned a hundred times, offering a rustic character to the meal, thanks to the hard-to-clean edges. Beside it were the fresh sautéed green beans with garlic chunks and a plate of golden-brown and lightly buttered garlic bread. A hodgepodge of glasses and plastic cups, no two the same, sported the wine, which Amy had poured and divided evenly—the treat of the night.

Once the food was served, Ben's dad stood before the family, who were tightly circled around the feast. "Um, well, I just wanted to say something quick before we eat." He made eye contact with each of them, one after another. "Well, nights like these are a clear reminder that we don't spend enough time as a family. Maybe we can't afford nice dinners every week, but we don't need expensive meals for us to be together. You are all very important to me, and I know that independent of the occasional squabbles, you are all important to one another. Times are hard out there, which means it is the most important time for us to be strong together. Um, that's all, I guess." He offered an awkward smile. "I hope everyone enjoys the lasagna. I could never make it like Mom, but it is her very own recipe, passed down to her from her grandmother. Please, let us eat, enjoy, and take a moment to celebrate our family."

Nobody moved. After a long and awkward exchange of looks, they rolled into a laughter that none of them had enjoyed in a long time. Dad's effort to be profound was as entertaining as it was genuine.

Collectively they jumped into the food and began serving each other. The conversation dwindled to the necessities: "Pass the beans, please."

Pasta was a go-to meal at the Brandt house. Affordable and nonperishable were key specifications for the items on their shopping list. Somewhere along the line, they had some Italian in them from Great-Grandma's side, or something like that. Ben's family was the ultimate melting pot, so much so that they joked that they maintained DNA from every culture known to humankind. An exaggeration, of course, but without data, it was a convenient enough explanation, and truer than not. The composition of his genes had turned Ben into a beautiful yet unidentifiable mix of physical features. In the slums, this was the predominant way of things.

"So, Maya," Dad said, breaking the feasting trance, "how was your day?"

"Oh." She covered her mouth to swallow a forkful of green beans, which took longer than expected. Still chewing the last of it, trying to not prolong the pause, she said, "Good. Had a great run with Ben this morning."

Ben and Maya exchanged a smile. However, Ben was hoping they wouldn't discuss running tonight.

His dad inhaled deeply but remained silent.

"We were at the towpath in the Metroparks. The weather was absolutely perfect. I love those trails," she added, trying to fill the vacuum she had apparently created.

"You guys run together?" Amy asked, also picking up on the awkwardness.

"Um, yeah, sort of," she said. Maya sat up taller in her chair with a sense of pride. "We really just do the warm-up and cooldown together. I can't keep up with this beast."

"That's so cool." Amy looked at Daniel. "We should start running together or something."

Daniel glared at Ben, then looked back to Amy. "Running is for those being chased. Why on earth would I want to go running?"

Amy shrugged. "I don't know, for good health ... maybe to do something together."

He scoffed at the idea. "Ben is just wasting his life with that stuff ... no offense, Maya."

"Come on, let's not ruin dinner over this broken record," Dad added. "No need to get Ben all riled up about this foolish running stuff again."

Maya's mouth hung open as she looked toward Ben. He gave a casual shrug without wasting a breath. Ben was all too happy to move past the subject and return to the meal.

"With all due respect, Mr. Brandt," she said as she leaned forward. Ben sat between them on the small stool, feeling like a child. "Your son is something rare. He has more talent than I have ever seen from anyone in this neighborhood—in anything."

"Maybe so, but what good is running? He can't even put food on the table with it. If he chased some deer or something, now that would be worthy of his time."

Daniel laughed. Amy offered a halfhearted laugh, clearly trying to play the middle ground.

"Maya, don't worry, they can't understand," Ben said under his breath in an attempt to squash the conversation before it escalated.

She looked back and forth between the father and son. "No, Ben, it's important he understands what fabric you are cut from. It's important that he understands that his son is an absolute warrior. A shining star . . . a beacon of hope."

Amy raised her eyebrows. "Well, I think it's kinda neat. Do you win many races?"

Ben sighed. "I'm not allowed to race . . . they don't let slummers run in any events. Besides, they have entrance fees, which cost as much as a month's worth of food."

"Yeah, but tell them about St. Malachi," Maya added.

Ben scowled at Maya. He had explicitly decided to not tell them about the event . . . ever. Now the cat was out of the bag. He looked back to Amy across the table. "Well, St. Malachi—you know, down off Detroit Ave., past Irishtown? They're opening the annual five-mile race to slummers this year. Waiving the entrance fees for us and everything. It's some kind of outreach program."

Amy was absolutely into the conversation. "How far is five miles?"

Ben smiled in her ignorant enthusiasm. "It's like going from here to Edgewater Park."

"Oh," she said with wide eyes. "Is that a marathon?"

~ 52 ~

Maya couldn't choke back a laugh, and she shoved her hand to her face to conceal it.

Ben gave a calm and polite reply. "A marathon is 26.2 miles."

"Woah, that's insane."

"Kinda."

"You're gonna run this thing at St. Malachi?" Dad asked. His expression was stony.

"Yeah, Dad, it's on March 18, but I'm already training a bit for it. You know, I'm really excited about racing for the first time."

He pressed his lips and shook his head. "That's no place to be . . . Those elites are gonna cause a big ruckus about that . . . It's not gonna go good for you, son. Dangerous, even. Slummers don't mix with the elites—ever, Ben. I don't want you to go. I admit, I don't like your running, but this is serious stuff you're talking about now."

Ben looked him in the eye. "We'll see, Dad. Let's see how it goes first . . . Anyway, they are real runners, and I think they would have some respect for me."

His dad sighed. "Don't underestimate hatred. The source of it is so deeply engrained that they can't see what is right before their eyes."

Ben clenched his teeth and nodded in confirmation. He didn't agree to not go to the race, not exactly.

After dinner, the boys cleaned the dishes, then returned to the table for a rousing game of poker by candlelight. The deck was missing cards and was in such poor condition that several of them could be identified by missing corners and fold lines. They played into the night, as if they were high rollers on the Vegas Strip—without the trimmings.

Since it was already past 11:00 p.m. and late enough for it to be unsafe for Maya to walk alone, Ben walked her back to her house around the corner.

"I can't stand him. He can't tell me what I can or can't do. I'm nineteen. I'm gonna run that race." It had been hours since the discussion, but Ben had been holding on to it the entire night. Stewing in the background.

"Your dad loves you, Ben. No, he doesn't understand your running, but he is only worried about you."

"What? You don't want me to go, either?"

"No, that's not what I am saying." She shook her head quickly. "No. I am gonna go with you, stupid . . . I'm just saying that you got a great family. He's only trying to protect you . . . Don't lose sight of that."

As they walked up to her door, the lights were on inside.

"My dad's home," she said. Concern about what the situation would be inside washed over her.

Ben did everything possible to avoid going into their house when Maya's dad was home. He hated leaving her there with him, too.

"Ben, you don't have to do what your dad says, but also, don't burn the bridges with your dad in the process. You know . . ." She nodded toward her own front door. "You got something really great."

He knew exactly what she meant, and she was right. He also knew, somehow, that he was going to get her out of that place someday. He just wished she was willing to before it was too late. That house was a ticking time bomb.

They wrapped their arms around each other for a long while. The air was chilled; however, the shared warmth of the embrace was welcome and hard to leave.

She planted a kiss, smacked him on the butt, then pushed him backward. He stumbled down the steps.

He looked up at her, and she gave a quiet laugh, as did he.

She winked. "Love ya, stud."

He blew a kiss and returned into the night on wings.

Chapter Six

Ben opened the door to his apartment, and a squall of bitter-cold wind pushed it out of his hand, driving it into the wall. The doorknob reintroduced itself to the depression it had carved out over the years. He winced at the heavy thud. His dad and brother had been asleep, but whether they were now was anybody's guess. He jumped through the doorway and pulled it closed behind him. He was certainly not going to wait to find out. If they were still asleep, it didn't matter. If they had woken, Ben figured, they would appreciate some time to simmer down. He knew that he would.

December was the beginning of the end in Cleveland. Dark gray skies without any promise of letting up. On the east side, where Ben lived, was the Snowbelt that brought masses of precipitation, caused by Lake Erie. Some people called it "lake-effect snow." It didn't matter what it was called, it was synonymous with "don't go outside unless you must."

For a distance runner, it was a test, as was everything else. He trotted down the steps covered in several inches of fresh powder. He wore a pair of hole-ridden gray sweatpants, and a T-shirt beneath a long-sleeve shirt beneath an orange grungy sweatshirt with a hood. The Cleveland Browns logo was almost unrecognizable. The drawstrings were pulled tight, leaving just a small circular window for seeing and breathing. His hands were buried deep in an old pair of socks that were now makeshift gloves.

It was 7:00 a.m. Sunday morning. The sun was still securely hidden beneath the edge of the earth. Not much would change once the earth rotated, since a monster storm cell was pushing from the north over the lake. A blizzard squalled across the unsuspecting streets. It wasn't big fluffy snowflakes feathering down. This morning, nature offered small shards of ice, hurled through the air at slicing speeds.

A day without running was a day without purpose. A little snow, or a lot, would not prevent Ben from his purpose. A hundred and five days until his first race, and he figured that most of his competition would be sitting by their warm fires today. He, on the other hand, gained one more workout. It was like sand. Each grain added weight to the bag. Singularly, it amounted to nearly nothing. Collectively, it tilted the scale toward progress.

The external stairs of his apartment building were slippery and covered with snow, which ranged in depth from an inch to a foot. Nobody in his neighborhood owned a snow shovel, and if they had, they certainly wouldn't have entertained the idea of using it. There was no reason to brave the cold. No sense of pride to take care of the neighborhood.

"What the heck am I doing?" Ben whispered as he propelled himself into the white swirling storm. It was only a ruse. He knew exactly what he was doing.

There was no chance for a normal run, since the snow had amassed to more than a foot deep, and three times that on certain corners, where it had drifted.

High knees was the only way of traversing these conditions. He figured that the workout would have a similar effect to a never-ending hill workout. He did know for a fact that he would finish this run hardened. A tougher version of himself, both physically and mentally, would walk back up those same snow-covered steps. The footprints would still be there from the descent, but faded, and they would be replaced by the new footprints of a more powerful being.

It was an apocalyptic scene. One that was reminiscent of the next global ice age. In this city, they called it winter.

No humans or animals were out, just Ben. Everyone else was hunkered down in their apartments, the animals in warm burrows or under broken-down front porches. He couldn't imagine the suffering of those forced to reside in Tent City. Hundreds of people died every year because of storms like these. Ben wasn't going anywhere near that place today. Emotionally, he was a coward and couldn't handle what he might see. The suffering turned his stomach. His problems, his family's problems—they were already too much to tolerate. His shoulders were too weak to be burdened with more.

Besides, he decided he wouldn't stray too far from home in the adverse conditions, just in case he got stranded, injured, or stuck headfirst in a man-eating snow drift. Last thing he needed was to freeze to death by underestimating the storm. Death by running would certainly be the winning move for his brother. Proof to justify his anti-running movement. Checkmate.

The plan was to repeat a small circuit just under a mile. Each loop passed directly in front of his apartment, which meant at no point was he more than six hundred yards from home.

At first, he thought it was funny to see his own footsteps from the previous lap. Then he recognized how nonlinear they were. On the second round, he made a conscious effort to tighten his line, running next to his previous steps. The results were strangely rewarding. He laughed to himself as a mad scientist might after inventing an inconsequential invention only he could understand. Not many people would find pleasure in what he was doing right now. Ben, on the other hand, tasted freedom.

As he measured a few laps in this way, he played with the length of his stride. Goofing around with short steps as well as longer ones. Naturally, his pace quickened as he elongated the stride. Each lap was incrementally quicker, and he could measure it simply by his stride length.

Ben managed at least a dozen circuits, each time matting down a running track within the white blanket. Fresh snow slowly dissolved his oldest steps, but nature was no match as he retraced those same steps in an effort to maintain his trail. Distance runners always played little games to keep up the intrigue, to maintain the little sanity they had left. From an external perspective, nobody would consider what he was doing on that December morning remotely sane.

His thoughts drifted off toward the elite runners, to the very few who could understand what he was doing. However, they had the latest technologies available to them. Their equipment allowed them to train inside or out, irrespective of the weather conditions. All the elites had embedded chips to measure their vitals. But the athletes had the upgrades. They could track and graph everything imaginable. Resting heart rate increases could warn them of the necessity of an extra day's rest. Early warning of the flu gave them the chance to get ahead of it, to reduce the worst effects and shorten the duration. Each workout—hills, intervals, tempo runs, and long runs—had a desired resultant effect on the body's physiology. Their chips measured exactly these qualities and alerted the athlete if they were in the right zone for maximum effect. Even nutritional results were reported. Sodium, iron, pH levels. A full blood work-up was measured in real time, all day, every day.

What the chips didn't measure, Ben considered, was mental toughness. Was overtraining, running in blizzards, bringing your body obliviously to the brink of disaster and back again, going to make you tougher, harder? Was challenging your will to survive going to build character? In the final mile, when the wheels are falling off, was it your fitness that would bring you through, or was it a fire burning deep within your soul? Ben believed in the internal fire, and today he stoked it.

There was no official count that morning. His toes became extraordinarily numb. Too numb to be safe, he thought. Losing a toe to frostbite would certainly take him off his game. His estimate was that he had easily cleared thirty laps, probably in the neighborhood of twenty-five miles. His eyes burned from the unrelenting shards of ice dicing them all morning. He knew that under these conditions they had turned into a brilliant iceberg blue. He was proud of creating such a nice packed-down running track.

As he returned up the drafty steps to his apartment, having not seen a single person through this entire endeavor, he proudly thought, *I'm not sure that was very sane.* His grin resembled a madman's.

***

That afternoon, he braved the cold once more, but not as foolishly. He made his way to Maya's house. The snow subsided but left its mark on the city. White and pristine, it felt like it had gone through a deep cleaning cycle. The air was still bitter cold, and the streets remained empty. His own running track had nearly vanished as a sandcastle might return into the tide.

He was greeted at the door by Maya, who struck her finger across her lips to signal silence. Ben knew exactly what the point was and peered over her shoulder to scan the room. Lying in the armchair was her father. Ben knew that he wasn't sleeping. He was passed out from a morning of boozing in the living room—exactly where they wanted to watch the race.

She shrugged and invited him in. Ben's skin crawled at the sight of her dad as he passed.

The first televised indoor track and field event of the season was live. They had a tradition of hunkering down on her cold couch, buried beneath a warm yet hole-riddled blanket, and watching the legends compete in the fast-paced 3000 meters. Longer distances were reserved for the outdoor season.

She grabbed his hand, clearly seeing his apprehension, and towed him toward the couch. The TV was already on and was at the lowest audible level possible. The last thing they wanted was to wake the beast.

The famed reporter, Samantha Bell, came on the screen to provide one of her excellent profiles on another athlete who was in the spotlight this season.

Maya snuggled into Ben beneath the heavy blanket, cheek to cheek. She rolled her face toward his and whispered, "What an amazing job she must have. Traveling to every major track event around the country. I mean, seriously, she gets to meet these hot runner guys every week."

Ben twisted his face, then jokingly nodded in confirmation. However, Ben's dream job was slightly different. His was to meet Samantha Bell, as an athlete preparing for competition. The idea of her doing a profile about him was a dream like a child's fantasy about living on Mars.

This week's interview was with Damian Prince. He had been around for a few years now, and last season he had been crowned the fastest man on earth . . . ever. He'd been designed and manufactured for speed, straight out of the geneticist's lab. All legs, which looked more like industrial-strength pistons built atop a deep-earth mining machine.

Ben let out a light laugh. "I bet this guy would cause Michelangelo's *David* to run and hide beneath the bleachers."

All elites were enhanced at birth with intelligence, health, and a barrage of other fundamental features. Then there was another level, further boosted, that was reserved for wealthy families who wanted to further improve the traits of their patriarchs or matriarchs into the next generation. However, there was a distinct subset of the ultra-wealthy. So filthy rich, their greatest problem in life was sheer boredom. They were not only selecting optimum traits for their children to succeed in this ever-changing society, they were creating predefined champions who would be sent off to special schools without any real parental involvement. Designer athletes, designed for the sole purpose of profit.

This practice was technically illegal, but since the costs of creating such machines were astronomical, governments allowed the tip of the spear to participate. These families were above the law. In fact, because of their willingness to test out experimental configurations, which ultimately paved the way to better science, the government let the ropes fly in the wind. It was well known that Damian Prince was a handcrafted thoroughbred racehorse earning his owners—legally his parents—a nice sum in sponsorships and prizes. Their illegal practices were celebrated, as opposed to shunned.

The saddest part wasn't the existence of the parentless Damian Princes of the world, or his fellow competitors, who failed to win the championship because of him. It was those designer athletes whose DNA experiments went astray. It was known in the first few years if a child would develop, under close scientific supervision, into the investment their owners had purchased. If not, there were always church doorsteps throughout the slums, which would occasionally welcome a young visitor wrapped in a blanket within a cardboard box. A would-be mega-athlete cast into the pits of hell.

As Damian took to the starting line, there was no question. He was exactly what his daddy ordered—a cash machine. He was dark skinned, with silver hoop earrings in both ears, a shaved head, and a tattoo on the left side of his face that made him appear half man, half skeleton.

Only a fool would not fear this man, on or off the track.

As the starter pistol popped to initiate the 200-meter race, Damian left the starting blocks in a burst of energy resembling that of a category five hurricane. He won without contention and looked as if he had applied no significant effort.

Maya whispered, "Can you imagine what a horrible life he must have? No way he was welcomed in the elite class. I'm sure they keep the poor guy locked up at the training facility like some animal in the zoo, without any real human contact."

Ben sighed, torn between which life would be better, that of a slave in the slums, with the freedom of family, or a slave in the world of elites, alone. No worries of financial ruin or starvation, but nobody to share his life and dreams with. He concluded that they both sucked, and he wished neither on anyone.

An hour later, and after a series of commercials attempting to sell products that neither Ben nor Maya could have afforded at any time in their lives, came the event they were most excited about.

The 3000-meter race was going to be a head-to-head competition between Cyrus Cray and Archer Sinclair. Cyrus was a wild child, frequently partying and enjoying the high life that came with celebrity, whereas Archer, by contrast, could only be described as a machine. Ben thought that if Archer didn't have a race today, and if he lived on the east side of Cleveland, he, too, would have been out there in that blizzard.

This was the first race Ben would watch since he'd decided to compete in St. Malachi, and he was enthused to be the student of the masters. He watched from a different perspective.

Just as the runners prepared for the line, Maya's dad turned in his chair and snorted loudly.

Ben found the situation rather funny and gave Maya an expression like that of a five-year-old who'd just got caught stealing a cookie from the cooling rack.

Maya shook her head in disapproval. This was much more serious for her, and she had no tolerance of anyone making fun of her father.

The only thing she ever did that really got under Ben's skin was be loyal to this foul man passed out in a chair on a Sunday afternoon—or any day, for that matter.

Another grunt came from her dad, but this time, his eyes opened. He sneered at the two of them cuddled up together beneath the blanket. Eyes red and glossy, burning with rage.

"What you doin' here, you little scat?" He stumbled to his feet, almost knocking the chair over in the process. "You invite this scrawny shit over to my house?"

Maya stood as well. "Yeah, Dad. He's watching the races with me."

He looked at the TV, then threw an empty can at the screen. His eyes spat fire. Glaring at Maya, then switching toward Ben, who was now also standing.

"What the hell you want with my daughter, boy?"

"Sir, I love your daughter."

He grabbed another can—this one was not empty—and chucked it at Ben's head. It grazed off his cheek and smashed in a fury of mist against the wall. In a wild yell, he screamed, "Get outta here!"

Ben's hand shot to his cheek, and he snapped his eyes back toward Maya. "Come on, we gotta go."

She shook her head. "No, I'll talk to you later."

Ben was speechless. Frozen.

"Go," she persisted.

Ben had to pass him to leave the house, and as he tried to run by, Maya's dad raised his hand as if he were going to strike. The threatened blow never came.

He grabbed his shoes and sweatshirt and ran into the snow in his socks. The door slammed behind him, rattling the frame.

While desperately pulling his shoes on, he heard muffled yelling. Maya shrieked.

Hot rage rushed within him, and he ran back inside prepared to start a war. To destroy the man who had been breaking his girlfriend since she was a child. To destroy evil.

Her hand covered her left eye, tears streaming from the right.

Ben had earned the full attention of her dad, whose chest heaved from the physical exertion.

Maya waved him away. "Go away, Ben." Then she screamed in a shrill voice, "Now."

He did.

Chapter Seven

Her black eye faded to a grotesque yellowish-green, then slowly dissolved to nothing. A small scar near her right eyebrow still hinted at the event, but an uninformed bystander wouldn't have noticed. Months after the incident, Ben still had nightmares and probably would for some time to come. The scar was a stark reminder of that cold, bitter day. He, too, was scarred for life. Not of being attacked, but by the image of her willingness to stand by that monster. Ben's fear was of his own inability to protect her. He felt helpless . . . He *was* helpless.

The morning after the abuse, she had defended her father as if he were misunderstood for the way he acted. She said that he was just surprised by having an unexpected guest and he apologized later that same evening. An apology she accepted without hesitation.

Ben couldn't comprehend how she could shrug it off. At the time, he was angry with her. As the situation rolled through his mind a million times as he covered as many miles on his long runs, his anger shifted toward sadness for her. Her interpretation of the event had been shaped by years of abuse. It was her own father, her only family, ever since her mother had abandoned the two of them. Maya said that she felt responsible for him.

When she was born, her dad had had the burden of finding an income that could support the new child, the house, and her mom, whose new job was as a mother. His job at the steel plant wasn't enough. When the cupboards ran empty, as a last resort, he turned toward gambling, which had covered them for nearly a year. One night, his luck had run out, and he didn't know when to pull back on the reins. He lost everything.

Maya's mom knew of the gambling and turned a blind eye as long as it went well. However, the night when the bottom fell out, she disappeared. Ben knew that there was much more to the story, which there always was, but Maya never explained the rest. It was then that her father approached the darker side of the ghetto. He reached out for high-interest loans, and with some luck and a few overextended promises, he was able to manage and retained the house. He had also turned to alcohol to dampen the emotional toll of his new single-father lifestyle. Maya had once explained to Ben that everything her father did was for her. He was only a victim of the ghetto, and it was because of her that he'd lost everything.

The worst of winter was over as March brought on new hope. Ben and Maya ran across the expanse of Center Street Bridge on their way to the St. Malachi road race. Neither of them had ever seen a live race before, let alone had a chance to participate in one. Maya had also registered to compete.

The newspaper, which was revved up with the politics of including slummers, made it the front-page article that morning. "Despite Free Entrance, Slummers Expected to Be No-Shows," it read. The media had a clear intention to emphasize the fallacy of allowing the slummers to join—minimalize those who attempted to break down the barrier.

The picture beneath the headline was of a protest group from yesterday who'd stood in front of the St. Malachi's Church with picket signs. *PAY YOUR OWN WAY*, *GO HOME SLUMMERS*, and *NO FREE RIDES*, they read. Other signs not depicted on the front page were mentioned as being far worse.

Ben just wanted to run a five-mile race. He had no need to get involved with some stupid politics, but he also knew that it was inevitable.

"Wow," Maya said as they neared the race scene, her eyes wide and mouth agape.

Thousands of people meandered around, decked out in high-end running gear. A stage, including lights and a podium, stood at the end of an open square. A banner stretched across the street that read, *104th annual St. Malachi Church Run*. Upbeat music blasted into the fresh, cool air, jiving with the audience.

"I've never seen anything like this," Ben replied.

Their arrival was not unnoticed. As exhilarating as it was seeing all the Clevelanders out there for a running event, those same people noticed a couple slummers joining the party. Little poops floating in the punch bowl, they must have thought.

A lady was dressed in an all-pink outfit, head to toe, including a hat with sequins, gloves, a jogging suit, and shoes. She looked like she had never run a day in her life. Her outfit most likely cost more than the Brandt family's entire annual income. She stepped toward them as her face went from bubbly and enthusiastic to "Who pissed in my rosé?" Pink was just a cover; her true colors emerged in a much darker hue.

"Go back to your tents," she shouted. Others heard the battle cry and gathered behind her as if *she* were the victim needing protection.

A man who also looked like he hadn't been training for the event added, "This isn't some charity event giving free handouts."

By this time, across from the open area in front of the stage, a man charged toward them wearing a shirt that read, *Event Staff.* He pushed through the crowd.

"Hey, hey," he announced ahead of his arrival. "This is indeed a charity event, and it was the good people of St. Malachi who decided to accept these young guests to our race this year." He turned toward Ben and Maya. "Please come with me. Let's get you all checked in. I apologize for the ignorant greeting you received. Change is hard for some people."

His kind eyes hardened as he shot a glare back to Mrs. Rosé before departing.

Ben had almost turned around to leave the event all together. His dad's voice echoed through his mind. He knew he shouldn't be here; he just hadn't seen it until now. However, his brave Maya marched forward without hesitation.

"Come on, Ben," she said in a stern whisper.

Ben sucked air through his teeth and followed the event organizer and Maya to the registration table. Pink Panther began to follow, but without the interest of her supporters, she gave up and circled back to the festivities. Apparently, her laziness trumped her hatred.

The ladies working the table seemed genuinely pleased to have Ben and Maya join the event. They were both issued race bibs featuring a number, with built-in transponders, a set of four pins to fasten it to their race shirt, a free long-sleeve shirt with St. Malachi written across the top with a leprechaun running in the middle, and a small bag of odds 'n ends including deodorant, samples of shampoo, and a few other small treasures.

Ben looked into the bag and whispered, from the side of his mouth, toward Maya, "Score. This is my new nicest shirt."

The lady's face behind the table crumpled, seeming to fight off tears. It was most likely her closest encounter with true poverty. Her heart bled.

Maya leaned into him with wild enthusiasm and wrapped an arm around his waist and squeezed. "Me too."

There was a large clock above the starting line counting down to the race, which apparently would begin in twenty-five minutes. After twenty minutes, while they had been cowering in a corner, away from the agitated crowd of joggers, they made their way to the starting line.

"There are thousands of people here. Should we just join in at the back?" Maya asked.

"Don't know, but these people don't even look like they can *walk* five miles, let alone run . . . I'm gonna squeeze up a little. Those guys look more like runners." He pointed to a cluster of people in the middle.

They both waded into the mob. Dozens of angry faces emerged on cue as they passed. Several people even landed elbows.

Ben and Maya looked at each other, then he said, "Don't really care if they like me." He pushed deeper into the enemy camp toward the front.

Before Ben reached the front line, when he was still twenty rows back, a man with a megaphone climbed up a ladder. "Welcome to the St. Malachi Run, the longest-continuing running competition in Cleveland history."

The runners applauded in a thunderous response. Even Ben's angry neighbors had turned their attention to the excitement.

"Thank you for joining our charity event. This is a five-mile race, and I wish all of you health, safety, and a wonderful run."

Ben didn't feel like the mob of people were there for charity.

The man lifted a starter pistol. "Get set."

BANG.

Ben had officially started his first race. He had at least a hundred runners in front of him with no chance of getting around them, but his enthusiasm outweighed the frustration. The first steps of his first race were taken walking.

As the race proceeded, he was able to move forward, whittling the crowd down to size. As early as the half-mile mark, he had exited the congestion and was free to roll, and did so.

It took a few minutes to regain the leaders, who obviously had the starting advantage, but as he approached, he was surprised to see their pace was rather pedestrian.

Ahead of the lead pack was an SUV. It was used primarily as a pace car for the purpose of guiding the leaders on the right course. The cameraman filmed the leaders through the lifted rear window. It dawned on Ben that he might even have a chance to be on television. His dad would be furious that Ben had attended the event, but the chance of him seeing it was quite remote. *Hopefully the neighbors don't say anything,* he thought.

The excitement of the event began to settle. Ben was in his element, running. He focused on conserving his energy as usual and enjoyed the freedom. The two-mile mark had a large timer, which read out 9:55, as he glided by with a dozen other runners.

A small smirk crossed his face as he thought, *This feels good.*

The third mile was rather uneventful for both him and the other runners in the pack. Ben thought maybe one or two had fallen off, but the remainder were looking good as they came through at 14:55.

Ben figured it would be fun to play a little in the fourth mile. Each time he came across a turn, he punched it and accelerated into the new straight. This fourth mile was their fastest so far, which also broke the lead group down to just three remaining runners. The clock ticked over to 19:45 as the young volunteers offered small cups of water from a table beside the street. A luxury he had never had before, and a luxury he surely didn't need now.

His two remaining competitors looked like road warriors. Both of them wore legitimate racing shorts split high to their hips and high-tech shirts designed for maximum breathability, warmth, and moisture reduction. A far cry from Ben's oversize white cotton long-sleeve shirt, which was more of a grayish-brown now, and his baggy general-purpose sports shorts, which he had found at the secondhand store for a dollar and a half.

What Ben found most peculiar was that one of the guys had knee-high socks and a headband. He thought it was a misplaced fashion statement.

While contemplating the modern athletic fashion of his fellow runners, something more vital dawned on him. Only about three-quarters of a mile remained, and although he knew he was running at a good clip, he felt fresh and powerful. He dialed it up a notch. Still comfortable. Again.

He found great pleasure in watching his competition become weary. Half a mile to go. Ben decided that it was time. He knew at this point that he could crush these moderately talented runners. So he did.

The last half mile was blazing. He even made a hard surge in a playful attempt to catch up to the pace car, which caused the cameraman to shout "Faster" to the driver. No longer concerned about his competition, he earned almost one hundred yards on second place, coming into the finish line at 24:08. Ben didn't realize it until later in the afternoon, but his final mile was a blistering 4:23.

Ben didn't expect to win the race and certainly didn't expect to be booed across the finish line. He saw a raw and unbridled hatred in the eyes of the spectators, which his father had cautioned him about. His life was more sheltered from the other half than he previously realized. Mr. Peterson at the factory was hard, but he spent his life dealing with slummers and had built a sort of *relationship*. What Ben was witnessing today was something altogether different. He was deep in enemy territory and he wore no camouflage. Exposed, naked, and vulnerable. Each angry face lacerated his heart ever so slightly.

He found free orange slices chopped in quadrants with the skin on. The next table had a bright-yellow sugary liquid to drink. Both were quite luxurious. Water was available, too, but he had had that before. He grabbed himself a few slices and a cup like a thief, then swept around the back of the crowd with his head down. He found a safe-ish place to wait to cheer his girlfriend into the finish.

From the bottom of the hill charging upward was his Maya. She looked fantastic. Fluid, strong, and glowing. There must have been just a few women who had come through already.

He screamed as she approached, "Go, Maya—destroy them."

He was astonished that she began to laugh as she kicked into the finish line. She shielded off the boos and allowed Ben's voice to penetrate. He wished he could do that.

Ben quickly met her with extra orange slices and another cup of that strange yellow drink.

"How did you do?" she asked through pulsing breaths.

Ben's face lit up uncontrollably.

"You won?" she shouted, then hesitated to read his radiant face again and smacked him on the chest. "Get outta here."

He rolled his head back and forth, giddy as a child.

They stuck close together and moved around to a safe place, avoiding the onslaught of heckling. Two people went so far as to issue violent threats, but it was clear they were hollow. Brave in the shadows, cowardly in the light.

Somewhere beyond the crowd was the event organizer on his megaphone once again. "I would like everyone to join me at the stage for the awards ceremony."

Immediately Ben felt as if a boulder was hurled into his stomach. He was the overall winner and was surely going to be called upon. The last thing he wanted was more attention. A spotlight on him was a terrifying prospect.

After some general comments, the announcer said. "Okay, we will begin with the overall winners." He looked down at his paper. "Third Place is Andrew Whittaker from Rocky River."

The crowd cheered as the man with the funny socks hopped up onto the stage to receive his attractive trophy.

"Second place is Joseph Adams from Independence."

The other competitor hopped up beside the first and obtained his equally nice yet slightly larger trophy. His expression was not one of excitement, though.

The announcer cleared his throat. "And to everyone's astonishment, I offer a grand welcome and round of applause for our 2084 overall champion of the five-mile run, who has set a new course record of 24:08, Benjamin Brandt from . . ."

The announcer looked at the registration form where it asked for the city, looked at Ben for confirmation, then read to the audience, "Benjamin Brandt from the slums of Cleveland."

The crowd came to life in a thunder of mixed boos and shouting. Some shouted truly terrible things. Slicing through the hatred were a few words of encouragement, cheering on his unexpected accomplishment.

Ben climbed onto the stage to collect his hardware. His competition stood beside him for a moment, but quickly the second-place runner jumped down as the cameras approached. Awkward. Dethroned by a slummer. The man with the long socks and headband remained beside Ben. A nod of the head and a soft smile. A subtle appreciation for Ben's final mile, perhaps.

"Slummers don't count," one of the onlookers shouted. "He didn't pay to be here."

The race organizer ignored the comment and shook Ben's hand and said, "You're a diamond in the rough, my young friend. You have uplifted me today. You may not see it, but you have opened a few eyes."

Ben shook the man's hand in return, unsure of how long to maintain his grip, and what to say in response. An elite had never shaken his hand before. Never. All he could come up with was, "Thank you, I had a lot of fun."

The guy with high socks snorted and gave the slightest nod toward Ben. "I bet you did."

As Ben turned to leave the stage, the local news channel stood there with their huge camera pressed into his face.

"Benjamin Brandt," the reporter shouted over the rabbling of the crowd, "is this your first race?"

Ben looked toward Maya for some kind of advice, but all she offered in return was a dramatic shrug.

He was alone on this one.

Ben finally climbed down from the stage. He had no idea what questions were asked of him or, even more strangely, what his answers had been.

At a distance of thirty feet was an old tree, gray and dormant in the winter months, looming over an older black man, who was noticeably one of the few nonwhite people at the event. He was around sixty or perhaps seventy years old. Clothes were heavy, woolen, and slightly worn. It was the man's curiosity that struck Ben. Their eyes locked, and it surprised him when the man did not veer away. Something about him was familiar, but Ben couldn't place it.

Just then, from the side, Maya approached the man beneath the tree. She broke their eye contact. He was startled by her approach but bounced back to offer a warm welcome. His eyes lit up with recognition.

Ben's interest was piqued. He pulled his head back, trying to put the pieces together, and then joined the two in a desperate attempt to solve the mystery.

"Hey, Ben. This is Mr. Sands," she said. "He lives on the street behind me, you know, in the Towers complex."

The man extended his hand to greet Ben. "What a performance today, Ben. I've seen you running a few times from my little balcony perched over the street below."

"Nice to meet you as well." Reciprocating the handshake. "What brings you to the race today?"

His voice was grisly, and he sounded like he had many hard years under his belt. "Well, I'm here every year . . . nowadays to watch. Oh, it's been a lifetime now, but I used to run Malachi. I knew the organizer, who passed some years ago. Used to sneak me in under a false name so I could race. Even back then, they didn't let slummers run. But it was a new thing, and people didn't really prod into people's background like they do today."

"Really?" Ben was enthralled. He never knew another slummer to be a real runner, besides him and Maya. "It's a pleasure to meet you, sir."

"You really caused quite a stir today, Ben," he said as his eyes panned around the crowd. More distracted than he was a moment before. His voice softened to a near whisper. "Haven't seen a talent like yours in a *very* long time. Slummer or not."

"Oh . . . well, thank you. I absolutely love running."

Maya added. "He is nuts about it, and truly brilliant, right?"

Ben blushed at the praise. Running had always been a way to purge the pent-up frustrations of his life. His girlfriend frequently complimented him, but to have a stranger saying kind words to him about running sent him to his heels.

Mr. Sands's gaze was penetrating. "So, have you thought about where you wanna go with this?"

"This?"

"Running, Ben. Where do you think running can take you?"

"Oh, sir, I'm a slummer. I don't even think I will be allowed back here next year, you know, after they realize how everyone reacted . . . Did you see these people? They hated us."

"Well, change isn't easy for people. Something happened today, which was quite a thing to watch. Sometimes it takes just a spark, Ben."

Ben hadn't recognized any change; from personal experience, it was much worse than he expected. "I don't understand."

"The camera, Ben. Although they wear cloaks in these times to protect their secrets from the malicious majority, there are plenty of supporters among the elites who would love to see a slummer face off with these genetically manufactured athletes. It is in the spirit of humans to cheer for the underdog."

"Oh ... no, I don't think I'm that guy. I hated the interview; I don't even know what I said."

Mr. Sands pulled his lips in as if he were about to share some regretful news. "Well, nobody in Cleveland is going to forget what they see on the news tonight. They built this event up so high that it had nowhere to go but come crashing down on them. You were the dynamite."

Ben swallowed hard, just now grasping the potential consequences of his interview. He wasn't a spark; he was just a runner. Regret for running the race absorbed him. The only thought that consoled him was that he knew these people would never set foot in his neighborhood. As long as he stayed out of sight, this whole thing would just blow right over.

"I'm not sure if you realize this, but races like this today, you can win a very nice trophy." Mr. Sands looked around him to ensure nobody was eavesdropping. "But there are other races throughout the year. Overall winners win money."

Ben's eyes widened. "How much?"

"Well, it varies, but easily a few thousand."

"Dollars?" he asked, already knowing that the man wasn't talking about continental currency.

"Look, Ben, I am getting old. The greatest thrill of my last ten-odd years was watching you run today. I mentioned that I was runner many, many years ago. Far less talented, mind you. But I was also a lunatic for running. Every morning before the sun rose, I was out pounding pavement. Every day after work, I was doing the same."

"Oh, I had no idea." Ben couldn't believe he had found someone who truly understood the most unanswerable question of "why do I run?" The reality was that there were no words to explain it. You were either a runner or the person asking why somebody would run. There was nothing in between. This guy was one of the few on his side of that dividing line.

"My wife has passed on, and my only son . . . Well, we aren't in touch anymore. Wasn't really there for him when he needed me most." His face saddened with a dreary reflection. "Kinda botched that one up. But anyway, it would be an honor to help you along the way."

"Help me, you mean, get into races?"

He nodded. "Yeah, I got some old contacts that can open a few doors, but also—I don't know if you would be interested—I'd love an opportunity to coach you."

Ben dropped his head. He looked at his tired and taped-over shoes. "I'm sorry, Mr. Sands, I can't accept. I really don't have any money."

He chuckled. "Ben, *none* of us have money . . . Free of charge, entirely. The reward of working with you and seeing you run more frequently would be enough payment. Sincerely, it would mean a lot to me."

When Ben woke this morning, he had no idea what the day would bring. He had been restlessly considering today's event for several months now. Not in his wildest dreams had he considered finding a potential coach. A fellow slummer.

"Mr. Sands, I really appreciate your offer, but I need to think about it, okay?"

He extended his hand to thank the man for the offer. A smile swept across both of their faces, both knowing that this chance meeting could be the beginning of something. An adventure into uncharted waters.

***

That night, at 7:00 p.m., Ben hurried over to Maya's house. He had been informed that the race would be included in the evening news and couldn't wait to see what he had actually said to the reporter. Maya's dad was gone for the evening, for his second consecutive shift at the steel plant down the road.

As he entered, Maya already had the news on. Over the past months, there were substantial protests in New York City regarding a law passed about the slummers. They were forbidden to enter areas designated by the city as tourist locations. Fines and even jail time were possible, even for first offenses.

The screen showed a video of picketers from both sides. Slummers, with the help of a few softhearted liberals, against the high-society elites. The latter of the two would have preferred for the slummers to be shipped off to faraway lands. The slummers surely thought the same of the elites. Both sides had already abandoned hope for solidarity. Tear gas and rubber bullets rained down upon the slummers. A tragedy to the equality of the American way.

Following a commercial for a moisturizing face cream, the TV belched out, "And today, at the annual St. Malachi Run, an unexpected change of events stirred the crowd. For the first time in forty years, the race organizers successfully fought against the city council, allowing the unfortunate souls of Tent City to join the race."

"Hey, we don't live in Tent City," Ben shouted.

Maya looked at him flatly. "From their perspective, there is no difference between you and the tents ... Anyway, they always try to make stuff more dramatic than it is."

The television showed several interviews of participants sharing their varied and almost entirely negative opinions about this new effort to include the slummers. The clip bounced to a midrace stretch of a few seconds with Ben sitting with the pack of three, then finally transitioned to him charging to the finish line alone. In the distance, and partially out of focus, one could see his competition huffing up the hill behind him. Ben had never seen himself run before, besides his reflection in glass storefronts, which he frequently relished.

"And today, Benjamin Brandt from the Cleveland slums took the victory. Single-handedly, he turned what was once a staple of Cleveland's annual events calendar into the political flashpoint of the decade. So, who is Benjamin Brandt?" she asked.

The video phased over to Ben on the stage.

"I am a runner . . . ," he declared on the TV, and then was cut off for the next segment.

He struggled to understand why everything was so politicized. Nothing could be taken at face value any longer.

"I am a runner? What the heck is that? Of course I'm a runner. Maybe I should have said that I am human . . . That would really twist their panties, wouldn't it?"

Maya laughed. "Could have been worse, Ben." She swung around and sat on him, planting a kiss on his lips. "My little celebrity."

"Really, that's what I am now?" Ben said. His anger began to melt.

"To me you are." She planted a deeper kiss, pressing his cheeks with her palms like a vise, intentionally not allowing him to respond.

He didn't fight against it.

Chapter Eight

Before he finished the secret knock, Maya had already swung open the door, as if she had been waiting on the other side. He was still sweaty from an easy fifteen miler—over an hour and a half of thinking about running, life, and the people of Cleveland. He had new puzzle pieces to play with, and the jigsawed picture was slowly revealing itself. His muscles ached in the best of ways; just twenty-four hours after winning Malachi, it felt as if he was on the edge of a new world. Ready to embark on a rocket ship to Mars.

"Hey, stud," she said, as she stepped aside, inviting him to come in.

"Sorry, not now. Tonight, meet me at the tree." He nodded back toward the path, but there was no question which tree he was referring to. "I got a surprise . . . Let's say midnight?"

She looked over her shoulder to ensure her dad wasn't lurking around the corner with some twisted agenda. She squinted at him. "What are you up to, Benjamin Brandt?"

"Midnight, yeah?"

She scoffed at his clear dismissal of her question. "Yeah, I'll be there."

He wagged his eyebrows and then turned and bounded down the steps. He started to jog back toward his house without another word.

"Bye," she shouted after him, with a tone of surprise that he had left so quickly.

He punched his hand into the air to reciprocate her good-bye wordlessly, without turning back.

She walked to the sidewalk and watched him run toward the path, then disappear between the houses.

***

It was three minutes till midnight when Ben arrived at the ironwood tree. The evening had chilled quickly once the sun escaped over the horizon, and by now, the air had turned cold and still. The moon snuck small glimmers of hope between the scattered clouds. It was dark and secluded, and he couldn't wait to see Maya. He'd spent the entire day thinking about this evening.

Ben looked for his watch and found nothing but bare skin. Habits were hard to break. He heard a small rustle from the bushes. Too small for a person. *Perhaps a raccoon,* he thought. His eyes focused on the area, deep in the shadows, and no matter how dilated they became, he still strained to see anything.

Abruptly, she leaped out from behind the bush at the very moment he turned to look away.

"Boo."

Ben jumped backward. His heart jumped even further, perhaps permanently. Their neighborhood wasn't the worst area in the slums. Minimal gang activity on their immediate streets, but it was certainly not a place you should be hanging around after dark. There were always creatures of the night lurking. Some of whom thought scaring their friends was funny.

He grabbed her in a bear hug to exact his revenge. Heart still pounding. Adrenaline pumping into his veins.

She seemed to enjoy the bear hug, or probably, even more, the expression of fright that flooded his face in that uncertain moment.

"What the heck are you up to, anyway?" she said, cross-examining him.

His smile gleamed. "Come with me."

"Really, you're still not gonna tell me?"

Ben grabbed her hand, and what started out as a speed walk shifted into an intermittent jog toward the building across the street from Ben's. His eyes darted up and down the street to ensure the coast was clear. They proceeded to the side door, which was propped open with a broken cinderblock.

"Where are we going, Ben?" Her tone started to become irritable.

He placed his finger to his lips, indicating that she should be silent. Always a risky move, but this time she followed the instructions.

They climbed the five stories up the concrete staircase entombed in dingy gray peeling paint, flickering lights, and a smell that could only be human piss. One flight had no lighting at all, which caused them to slow down and ascend step by step, holding their hands out in front of them.

The top door was also propped open. He paused before pushing through, then turned and kissed Maya's warm lips. "I love you."

Her eyes narrowed and face warmed, she repeated, "What are you up to, Ben?"

Leaning backward into the door, he pushed it open. They arrived on the rooftop of the building. A single lit candle sat on a small, rusty table in the middle of the space.

"I made dinner."

She grabbed him by the cheeks so that he looked like a sideways duck. "You are in trouble, Mr. Brandt . . . trouble."

His squeezed cheeks burned from her grip. It felt good.

He hurried her over to the table and pulled out the chair. His attempt to mimic the classic gentleman felt awkward, but he wanted this to be a special evening. A night to remember. Tonight was a turning point, and he didn't want to slide through life without appreciating these moments of significance.

The table had a small square white plastic sheet that was just a bit too small to cover the surface. The candle danced in the off-and-on breeze, casting swaying shadows into the night. The moon had momentarily been engulfed by cloud cover, and the radius of the orange glow extended to the edges of the rooftop and then evaporated into the void of the infinite night. A dome of blackness without walls. Two chairs and place settings were already prepared. Ben's trusty cooking pot on the side.

"Oh, Ben, you shouldn't have. What were you thinking?"

He smiled at her and lifted the lid off the pot. Macaroni and cheese with hot dogs. Steam billowed into the night. He grabbed the big spoon and slopped a couple scoops of the cheesy noodles onto each ice-cold plate. His specialty meal, and this time, he'd made it extra cheesy.

She smiled as she looked at him. "Well, thank you . . . this is a very nice idea. Maybe better on a summer evening?"

He squirmed into his chair across from her. "But what I want to say can't wait till summer."

He could tell she was going to say something sarcastic, but she held herself back. She had a good eye for reading people but was also quick to throw down a joke to break her own anxiety.

"Go ahead, let's eat." Ben took his first bite. The noodles had turned cold, and the cheese had coagulated. It was forty-five degrees outside, and he hadn't considered how fast the food would cool. He curled his lip in slight disgust of his inadequate meal. He looked up at her, realizing he had botched the plan.

Maya snorted once, then put her fork back on the table. Her eyes glistened in the candlelight. "Let's reheat it tomorrow."

"Yeah, I think that's best."

Her smile grew toward a breaking point. Despite her best effort, laughter won the battle. Ben joined her. Embarrassed, but in love. People laughed at Ben for his running, laughed at him for being a slummer, both of which cut deeper than anyone would ever know. He was fragile and predominantly self-conscious; it was his best-kept secret. A secret that tormented him through long, restless nights. However, when Maya laughed at him, it was something altogether different. She was his soul's protector and had absolute power over him. He never doubted that her intentions were always in his best interest. He never doubted that her love for him far exceeded his shortcomings. He felt the same about her. Ben also knew that she was irreplaceable, and despite everything else, he was the luckiest man on the planet.

"So, what is it, Ben? I know we're not here for a new frozen noodle recipe."

"I didn't . . . couldn't sleep last night. I was thinking about the race . . . about Mr. Sands."

She moved the plate a few inches forward so she could place both elbows on the table and rest her chin in her hands. Silent and listening. Warm flickers of candlelight danced upon her face, silhouetted by the darkness of the night. An angel, he thought. His angel.

"And on my run this morning, too . . . Well, I think I made my decision. I wanted to hear what you think. You know, I am not gonna do anything if you think it's a bad idea, or if you aren't by my side. It would be worthless without you . . . seriously."

Her eyes twinkled and she whispered, "I love you, Ben."

"I love you, too," he blurted back without much attention. "I don't want to run anymore, Maya."

She pulled back. A gasp escaped her open lips.

"I want to be a racer, not just a runner." He inhaled deeply. "I can't even explain how I felt in that last mile yesterday. For those minutes . . . I wasn't some nameless slummer. I was Benjamin Brandt, a talented human who could blast those two well-trained runners out of the water."

"Yes," she said casually.

"What? What do you mean, yes?"

"Yes, you should talk to Mr. Sands . . . Yes, you should be coached by him, and yes, you should not waver from your dream. I do not know a single person who has as much talent as you . . . at anything. It pains me deeply that you are trapped in this cage with the rest of us. Sometimes I cry at night, wishing I could do something for you, but I am powerless. You were never meant to be here in the ghetto. A mistake on a cosmic scale. Another time, one hundred years ago when a talent like yours could flourish, you would have been a national treasure."

Some people were born ahead of their time. A genius whose ideas were so out there that they could not be appreciated until people had a better understanding, years or even centuries later. But their time, dead or alive, would come. Ben was the opposite. Born after his time, with little chance of ever being remembered. His time would never come.

Ben's emotions overcame his attempt at manliness. His guard, which he was only capable of lowering with Maya, was down. "I can't do this alone . . . I don't mean Mr. Sands. What I am trying to say is that I am terrified about this. You're the only one who can see into my soul. You fix the breaking pieces before I even see a crack. I would fail without you."

For a long minute, not a word was spoken. Their eyes locked, reflecting the dancing candle in the gentle breeze. Ben could stand strong, infallible, now that he had his angel watching over him.

In the distance, east of where they were, two gunshots cracked into the night. Not everyone had an angel watching over them. Not in the ghetto.

***

Work was a nightmare. The minutes ticked by as if they were hours. He had zero patience for his boss, Mr. Peterson, his brother, or that weird scrawny guy who always tried to slander him.

Today was a turning point, though. Ben had decided to stop by Mr. Sands's apartment after his shift was over. He would change the trajectory of his entire life in a single discussion with Mr. Sands. A milestone in Ben's running career. He couldn't let these people ruin it. He wouldn't allow it.

Ben went directly toward the building that Maya described as being Mr. Sands's. She didn't know the room number or even floor, but somebody was sure to know. He hated speaking to people he didn't know, but today he was on a mission.

A young boy, perhaps seven or eight and covered in dirt, was digging for lost treasure in the barren tundra in front of the building.

Ben cleared his throat to obtain the boy's attention.

"Hello, young man."

The boy's head popped up like a woodchuck. His eyes filled with curiosity, not fear.

"Do you know Mr. Sands? He lives here." Ben nodded up toward the building.

The boy studied Ben, then also looked up at the building. "There." He pointed high overhead, toward the top floors.

Ben squatted to gain his perspective. "Top floor?"

He sighed in frustration from the misunderstanding. "No, the one below that . . . farthest to the left."

"Thanks, buddy."

As Ben approached the building, he noticed a woman on a nearby balcony, much cleaner than the junior informant. *His mom*, Ben thought. She glared at him from her perch with an eye of mistrust. Ben raised his hand to her. "Sorry, just looking for someone."

The lady nodded to him but maintained her watchful eye. Trust was hard-earned in the slums.

Ben entered the dreary building, which was primarily a faded green. Large sections had been spackled over but were unpainted. He climbed the steps to the seventh floor, second from the top, and couldn't imagine an old man making this climb every day. It was an older building, which meant that there had once been working elevators back when the city spent more money on housing projects. Recently, they'd gutted them for parts to be repurposed and the doors to the elevator shafts were boarded over. Newer buildings in the slums didn't have elevators to begin with, independent of the standard practices for the privileged people on the west side of Cleveland.

Ben hesitated at the door. His breathing was labored from the stairs, despite his peak fitness, but he knew it wasn't the effort. His mouth ran dry and was flooded by nervous tension. On the other side of this door was a man he didn't know. A man who could promise him a future in running. He inhaled deeply to compose himself, then knocked. Through the door, he could hear the muffled sound of a TV, which was quickly either turned off or muted. The anticipation rattled him.

The door cracked open with a chain across. Mr. Sands peeked through the opening cautiously. Despite the obstructed view, Ben could see the man's face immediately transform into a radiant smile. Warmth washed over him.

"Benjamin, please come in." He slammed the door closed, unclasped the chain, and reopened it to its full potential. "I don't get many visitors, and now the star of the town has arrived. I am feeling rather special right now."

Ben shifted his weight from one foot to the other. "Hi, Mr. Sands."

"It's Martin," he interrupted. "Just Martin."

"Sorry, Mr. Sands . . . er, Martin. I haven't slept since we saw each other at Malachi."

Martin gestured for Ben to enter and guided him to the sofa. "I have been doing a lot of thinking myself. It is nice to see you."

Ben's eyes darted around the dark room. The apartment was lined with bookshelves that were packed with more books than Ben had ever seen. Thousands surrounded the living room, adding texture and an atmosphere of intellect. Ben had never read a full book before. A couple magazine articles and some training manuals at the foundry, but never a real book.

As he sat on the well-worn, lime-green sofa, he squirmed to find a comfortable position. "I want to be a racer ... If you're still willing, I could really use your help."

Although Martin clearly assumed that was the intention of the visit, a tear came to his wrinkled eye. He brushed it away as quickly as it had come.

"I will give you everything I know. Open every door I can, Benjamin." He lightly bobbed his head. "You may never know how much this means to me. These books are my only passage outside these walls anymore, and I feel like I am slowly slipping. You know—away."

Ben didn't know exactly what he meant by slipping away but could see how appreciative the man was. He'd entered this man's apartment asking for the most significant favor he had ever asked for from anyone, but he didn't know he'd be a savior for this lonely soul, too. A perfect match.

"Wait right here, Ben," he said as he turned and headed into the kitchen.

Out of sight around the corner, Ben could hear the rustling of papers and odd items moving around a drawer. Ben studied the shelves of books with wonder.

"You read all of these?"

The rustling paused. "Yeah, mostly ... the good ones I have read a dozen times." The search commenced.

"Aha," he said under his breath before returning to the living room, an old magazine in hand, which he raised into the air. "Got it."

Ben could see that the magazine, which was folded over longways, had been read many times. The cover had lost its shine from repeated readings, but the picture of a man and woman jogging in expensive high-tech running gear and wearing manufactured smiles was still sharp. Neither of them looked like serious runners, though.

As he walked toward Ben, he unfolded the magazine and handed it to him. "It's a few odd years old, but I think it would be a good starting point."

"*Runners Journal*," Ben read aloud from the cover. "Special Issue: 2079 race schedule."

"Flip over to that little paper sticking out there ... That's got all the big races in the country. The dollar symbol is next to the ones with a purse."

He flipped to the marked page, and in small print, two columns per page, was a list of events with places, dates, and a short description. "What's a purse?"

"Ah, so here." He pointed to a specific race on the open page. "Cash rewards for the winners."

His eyes widened. "That's in Youngstown."

"Yup, the top winner could win five hundred dollars."

He looked up at his new coach. "That's almost four months' pay at the factory."

Mr. Sands offered a sly wink. "Now, this issue is kinda old, so I'll need to make some phone calls to ensure they haven't canceled it over the years. I know an ol' chap over there who can get you registered under a false name, false identity. Maybe you could be an out-of-town visitor from Oklahoma."

"What's this?" Ben turned the magazine around to show him. "Thirty-five dollars entrance? I could never spend that much to get in. I can't even afford shoes."

"Ben, listen. I am confident you can win this. It's simply an investment in your future."

"I don't know. Investment or not, I don't have that kind of money."

The man grunted as he sat beside Ben on the couch. "I figured that might be the case. So, here is the deal. I would like to invest in you."

Ben looked up from the magazine. "What?"

"I'm gonna cover the first registration fee and the car to get you there. However, you gotta save the winnings so you can fund your next races. Deal?"

"Oh, I couldn't ever take your money. You don't even know me."

"Ben, I believe in you. I insist." He patted Ben on the shoulder. "This is as much for me as it is for you. And besides, everyone needs to get a start somewhere. When I was young, somebody helped me out, so in some way, this is my chance after all these years to pay it forward."

Ben felt an enormous weight. He needed to race, and this was the only option. He also didn't want to let this man down if he were to take the money, then screw up the race. Although Ben didn't say it, he would pay him back under any circumstance, and if he lost, that would pave a hard road ahead. However, five hundred dollars was a lot of money. He thought of Maya, who would not allow him to walk away from this opportunity.

"Okay, Coach. I'll do it. You are way too kind. I'll do everything you ask. I'll work twice as hard as I do now."

Mr. Sands smiled and rose to his feet. "I know you will, Ben. I'm looking forward to it."

Ben nodded as he stood as well.

Mr. Sands walked over to the bookshelf and ran his finger along the spines. "Hmm, I think it is right along here . . . Ah yes, here it is."

Ben craned his neck, attempting to see what the man had found.

He turned toward Ben, a small book in hand with a green cover and no title. "Here you go. This is for you."

Ben received the book and flipped it open to the blank pages. "What is it? It's blank."

"Well, then you should probably start from the first page. This is your new running journal. I want you to fill in every workout, how you felt, your resting heart rate—everything. When you are done with this, it will no longer be blank, it will be an extension of you."

Ben smiled as he pondered the potential. "Thank you. This is great."

He laughed. "Not yet, Ben. But it will be."

Chapter Nine

"Talked to Mr. Peterson this morning. He needs you to come in tomorrow for an extra shift," Ben's dad said to him as they scrubbed laundry together in the kitchen sink.

"I um . . . I can't. I got plans tomorrow."

His dad stopped scrubbing and looked at Ben in silence. Ben didn't look up from his chore but could feel his father's eyes study him as if he didn't know when or where he had failed at raising him. A disappointment on the most fundamental level of life's priorities.

"What? I can have plans, too." Normally going to work on the weekend to earn a few extra dollars was a guaranteed yes. But this weekend was different.

"Ben, please explain to me what is possibly more important than earning extra money for the family and, more importantly, keeping your position at work in good standing?"

Winning five hundred dollars in a race tomorrow, he thought. "I can't tell you. Get Daniel to do it. He's got nothing in his miserable life to do."

"He is also going to be there; so am I. They got a huge order yesterday, and they're bringing almost everyone in . . . Mr. Peterson is certainly going to notice if you aren't there when he needs you most."

"Sorry, Dad, it's not possible." Ben would have canceled almost any plans he had ever made, but not this time. Not tomorrow.

"I already promised Mr. Peterson that you would be there. Why are you being like this?"

Ben sucked in a deep breath. "Dad, there will be a day when I can tell you everything. On that day, you will absolutely understand why I cannot help tomorrow. But I can't tell you now. You have to trust me."

His dad eyed him. Benjamin was often late, or said the wrong things occasionally, but in the deepest sense of the word, he was reliable. He would always be there, and his priorities were always formed with the best intentions. His dad knew that.

"Come on, trust me on this one, Dad."

He huffed out a burst of air, then nodded. "Okay, Ben, I will try to cover for you. But when you are able to tell me, I want to know that story . . . It better be good."

"Thank you, Dad. I'll explain everything to you." *If it is successful. If not, then you'll get a slightly different version.* Ben realized that he would need to create a plan-B story just in case plan A backfired and he had no money to show for it.

They continued working through the laundry. He hated this duty, and for some reason, his brother always found a way out of it. Hours of scrubbing, wringing, and hanging everything on a string stretched across the balcony. The hanging part was tricky, since the balcony floor was too risky to step on, so Ben had to lean out, holding onto the doorjamb, while hanging the clothing to dry. *Death-defying laundry day,* he thought.

Later that evening, Ben had the place to himself. His brother was out with Amy, and Dad was out with some friends for a game of poker. Maya was tending to her father, as she often did.

Ben sat in his bed with his duct-tape-covered running shoes in hand. He needed to pass himself off as a member of at least the lowest end of the elite class, as opposed to a slummer. He peeled off the layers of duct tape, working back through the years, then scrubbed and picked away the adhesive residue, which had long since hardened from the tape. With a needle, string, and a wooden stick in place of a thimble, Ben stitched the shoes back into a single piece. He still had some glue from the factory and bonded the split sole of his right shoe back together. The flapping had grown overwhelmingly annoying.

Ben thought about the race tomorrow. Going solo without his protector, Maya, was frightening. He wanted to run more than anything but didn't want any of the angry-crowd stuff. He could always say he had to go to the factory instead. He could tell Coach that he didn't have an option. What he realized, though, is that he did have an option. There was a risk of losing his job, but if the race worked out, that wouldn't be such a big issue. It was more risk than he was comfortable with. It hung heavy on him.

After nearly two hours of intensive work on both shoes, he lifted his right shoe up for inspection. He rotated it under the yellow light cast from the nightstand lamp.

"Not bad," he said to himself. He propped up the nightstand, then placed the shoe beneath the leg to compress the glue while it dried.

He turned out the light and lay awake for hours, contemplating his decision and every possible outcome. Every problem came to mind. The lowest risk was to ignore the race and running altogether and go back to work with his head down. Just like his dad, brother, and every other coworker from his neighborhood. Everyone would be happy ... except Ben. The worst scenarios he had tossed around were all about the race. . The varied outcomes were bleak. His final thought as he faded off into the night was of Maya's words of encouragement.

***

It was Ben's first trip in a car. The coordinates had already been entered into the board computer. His destination was Youngstown, Ohio. Just seventy-five miles away, however Ben had never been there. He hadn't been anywhere that he couldn't run to. All he had to do was climb into the car and confirm that he was ready to begin the journey.

"Would you like to hear some music, Mr. Brandt?" the computer voice asked as the car started to roll down the street.

"No thanks, ma'am," Ben replied. He also had never spoken to a car.

"The trip will take exactly one hour and twenty-two minutes," she added. "Please let me know if you would like me to adjust the temperature."

Ben wasn't sure if he should reply but assumed the typical human-to-human courtesies were unnecessary with a car. Then again, she was nicer than most humans.

He looked out the window and saw the slums zoom by from his highway perspective. He had that time to consider every possible outcome of his attempt to win the purse. Coach had told him to not get wrapped up in all of the potential problems that may or may not occur.

"Don't even think about it. You just gotta go out there and do your thing," he had said just yesterday, asking the impossible.

Upon arriving, he had to check in. This time Ben was alone. No Maya, no Coach, just him. He signed in under the fake name that coach had given him, a visitor from Oklahoma, where Ohioans might just assume that his meager appearance was common where he came from. He received his bag of goodies, which was not too dissimilar than Malachi's loot. He actually wore his Malachi shirt, as it was the only one he owned that didn't look like it was from the slums. His remodeled shoes would at least not draw attention. Not as much as the duct tape, anyway. Despite everything, he still encountered the slandering comments. His brown skin tone was something he couldn't hide. The elites did have a fair amount of people with different skin tones. However, if a person wasn't white, there would always be a watchful eye. Trust was for the majority.

Without fail, Ben secured the victory. He asked for the check to be made out to his real name. The sum far exceeded any cash he had ever had at a single moment in his life. Despite his registration under a false name, the other runners caught on that he was a slummer. He wasn't sure how exactly, but he guessed that someone had seen his little TV interview in Cleveland. Perhaps some of the runners were also at Malachi and got to watch the spectacle firsthand. A brown-skinned runner who won the race wouldn't go unnoticed. This time, money was involved, and he received some of the nastiest comments he had ever heard. *Racism is alive and thriving.*

Ben was aware of the social divide between the slummers and the elites primarily because of people like his boss—the handlers of the world. His dad had also shared plenty of stories while the boys were growing up. However, he had no idea what hatred could do to one's facial expression. It could contort an attractive and kind-looking person into a monster—as if they were the spawn of something wicked.

He already had the check in hand, so he made a run for it. Literally, he jogged to his car and headed back to the east side of Cleveland. The ride was long, but after taking a few minutes to calm down, pride washed over him. His mission was successful, and he had just robbed the prized jewels from deep in enemy territory. A race organized by elites and for elites.

Ben, like everyone else in his neighborhood, didn't have a bank account. He needed to take a heavy loss while cashing the check, but every cent he received was a cent he didn't have yesterday.

***

April, May, and June rolled through like a thunderstorm. Ben met with his new coach outside his apartment every day at the same bench. Many days, the boy with the smudged face was playing nearby in the dirt. At one point the boy began to wave at him as a friend, and Ben learned that his name was Logan. Mom always stood watch from her balcony. Ben noticed that she'd rehang clothes just to appear busy on her watch duty. She was a good mom, Ben thought. Most kids were on the sink-or-swim parenting program in this neighborhood.

The bench was mostly business. They discussed the planned workout, how he felt regarding aches and pains, increased tiredness, and the like. Then he would be off on his run.

Most runs he did by himself. Coach would head back up to his apartment to do who knows what. But sometimes, during interval or hill workouts, Coach would ride his rickety bike over to supervise the event. To bask in the energy of training. It was then that Coach appeared to be in his prime. Ten years younger and inspired like a poet. For him, Ben's workouts were the best show in town, and he had front-row tickets.

Mornings before work, Ben would go out on his own to put some miles in the bag. Nearly every weekend, Coach Sands had found another race and had another contact to get him registered. Somehow, he was well connected. Ben often wondered how he had gotten so involved in the road racing community, but whenever he asked, he received a waving hand and "Oh, it's a long story." They both had the time, but it seemed there was never enough to hear the tale.

Besides paying for his own entrance fees and travel arrangements, and reimbursing Coach against his wishes, Ben saved every cent in a large yellow envelope. Within that envelope, he also saved his race bibs. He discarded his trophies, as he had no place to hide them. Telling his dad was still not an option. Ben shrunk away from the thought of that conversation. He wasn't going to tell anyone besides Coach and Maya about his trips, and certainly not about the money. The risk was too great.

***

It was already June, and one race in particular was a 10,000-meter event in Columbus, Ohio. The race started along the Olentangy River and offered a sizeable purse of $2,500 for the top position. Ben had already achieved a winning streak, and it was no surprise when he handled this field, too. With the higher purse, more talented runners showed up, and the best of them were better than the other races. However, Ben was rapidly improving, too.

There was still a large quantity of angry faces shouting slurs in his direction. But something was changing. It seemed that the road racers in Ohio were a community. He recognized more and more competitors of all skill levels from previous races. Some of those who had shown raw hatred at Malachi had started warming up to him. A seed of respect had begun to germinate. The change was minute, but noticeable. The hateful insults still cut deep, but the hope of progress helped him heal. He no longer dwelled on it, which made all the difference.

After the event, he headed to the nearest bank to cash his check. He had saved enough and promised himself that if he were to win today, he would go on a shopping spree. He was going to buy a pair of running shoes. A pair that didn't require duct tape or stitching to hold them together. No more glue-hardened soles.

He walked into the store, which was just around the corner from the big event, and the clerk recognized him from the race. The young boy looked uncertain, and mostly remained silent. However, he offered Ben assistance with finding the best shoes at an affordable price. After trying on a pair he liked, Ben left them on his feet as he purchased them. The store clerk looked at him as if a third eyeball had appeared in Ben's forehead. It wouldn't have been surprising to see a six-year-old do this, but it was probably the first time he had seen an adult wear his new shoes out of the store.

The boy wished him luck as Ben pushed the door open and headed back out to the streets. Around the corner, heading to his next destination, Ben left his old tired trainers in a nearby trash can.

He had learned to not throw away anything that could be used or repurposed, but this was a symbolic moment for Ben. A new chapter in his life was unfolding, and his feet felt fantastic.

Today, he had one more item on his shopping list. Another new chapter in his life.

Chapter Ten

"Welcome to the 2084 National Track and Field Championship at Hayward Field," Samantha Bell announced through the television. "This year's five thousand is shaping up to be one of the most anticipated championship races at any distance we have seen in a decade."

Ben leaned toward Maya and said, "Didn't she say the exact same thing last year?"

"I think the year before as well," she added as she repositioned herself on the couch, snuggling in closer to Ben. "But you know what?"

"What?"

"Next year is going to be even better."

Ben laughed.

Samantha continued, "Cyrus Cray has split the series wins with Archer Sinclair, while Eric Richardson has been struggling to keep the pace. That is, until two weeks ago, when Archer launched himself back onto the scene with a huge and dominating victory. The season's fastest time, in Tennessee. This year's title is up for grabs."

"I've been looking forward to this all week," Maya said as she leaned forward. "I think it's going to be a fast one."

I've been looking forward to it for fifty-two weeks. "Me too. These guys are on fire this year," Ben said. In the back of his mind, he was also excited to watch the battle with his newfound eye for racing details. Over the past three months, he had also become a legitimate competitor.

Samantha Bell, looking as graceful as ever, said, "And for this year's feature video, we have a very special and talented man from the 1960s. A man who raced with heart. A bold front-runner who took the lead even before he stepped onto the track. An artist who used his stride as a paintbrush and the oval as his canvas. He was the namesake for this very event. Here he is, the legend who sparked a national boom of running and jogging across America, Steve Prefontaine."

The screen flashed over to a documentary about a legendary runner from more than a century earlier.

Ben had only heard of him because his name was the same as that of the championship.

"Oh, I read about this guy," Maya said at the edge of the couch. "You're gonna love him."

Within the first five minutes of the show, she was right—Ben had a new idol. A runner who was not genetically designed. A runner who was not from a rich upbringing. A runner whose greatest talent was his ability to fight with his guts to the brutal end. Steve Prefontaine lived in a very different world, long before genetic engineering, but Ben could identify with him. He was inspired to a depth previously untapped. He had always followed the elite runners, but now he had an inspiration of his own kind.

The documentary lasted forty-five minutes, and Ben wished he could watch it again. *Ten times wouldn't be enough,* he thought.

"Wow, that was awesome," he said. He hadn't breathed since it started.

"A new crush?"

"Absolutely." Ben was giddy. He almost wanted to go running instead of watching the race. Almost.

There was something special about Pre, which is what the people called him back in the day. In Ben's mind, the DNA designer babies competing for the title today with Mommy and Daddy's money lost a little something. Their pedestal wasn't quite so high in comparison to a runner who raced with courage as his leading quality. Today was the first day Ben could see that the elites' secret weapon, gene editing at conception, was nothing more than a performance-enhancing drug. He also knew that today's race was going to be intense, and their pace was not comparable to that of his new hero from the olden days. These guys didn't need the same level of guts to compete at far faster speeds.

The 5000 meters was set to begin. The best runners were named, along with their statistics, the records they'd set or their fastest times of the season. Ben watched as a student.

"On your marks." The runners jogged two steps forward to the waterfall start, and almost immediately, the infield cannon blasted the runners into motion.

"Eh, Eric got the shaft," Maya said, pointing at the screen. "Boxed in against the rail."

"Cyrus looks like he got shot out of the cannon himself," Ben added. His guy got a great start.

The race was as exciting as predicted. The top three guys jostled for position, frequently overtaking each other, or attempting to.

Once the athletes took the bell lap, it was already clear. Cyrus was not going to win his first championship this year, either. The young star, with his wild approach to life, in some ways reminded Ben of the late Prefontaine. But today, he failed to close the deal once again with a third-place finish. He got smoked by the veterans who unashamedly never looked back.

***

After watching the competition, Ben and Maya were fueled up. Adrenaline chased through their veins, and they needed to open the release valves.

They left Maya's house and made their way, nestled against the edge of Lake Erie, toward Edgewater Park for a sunset run together. A perfect location to watch the sun slowly descend into the vast and endless body of water.

Ben spoke of the elite distance runners in a different way. His comments about their strengths and weakness were not made as a fan, but as a fellow racer. He spoke of them from experience. Road races were a far cry from the national championship, but he now knew what it was like to truly compete against another well-trained athlete. He himself had tasted the blood of victory. He'd also suffered an unexpected defeat at the hands of a young runner in Sandusky a month earlier. Ben played his cards wrong and suffered the consequences. Everyone needed to fail.

Today, the day of the national championship, was always the most special day for the two of them all year.

They sat in the sand. Toes pushed and pulled against the grains, which sifted through them like hourglasses. The sun was preparing for the final drop. It shifted from yellow to richer tones of orange and grew larger, as if it was preparing for the collision. Today was no longer going to be their special day just because of the race.

Ben pushed himself from the sand. He took a knee in front of Maya, with the sun silhouetting him from behind.

"Maya, you are the most unique and inspirational person who has ever existed." Ben could see her eyes grow as the sun had. Also preparing for collision. She took a deep, uneven breath.

He pulled the ring from his pocket, which he'd spent a small fortune of his prize money on while in Columbus. This was no drugstore aluminum band. He could hardly keep his own breath, but he managed through a highly abbreviated version of what he had recited for weeks: "Will you be my wife, Maya?"

"No," she said rather loudly.

Ben sucked in a gulp of air. His mind raced in an attempt to comprehend what he had misread. As many times as he had covered the proposal, he'd never considered this scenario.

"I'm just kidding, you fool," she said, losing herself in a hyena-like laugh. She fell back into the sand and looked directly overhead, into the reddening sky. "Of course I'll marry you."

His heart pounded like thunder, still reeling from her joke. His trickster got the best of him once again.

She pulled herself forward, wrapped an arm around his neck, and drew him in for a long, deep kiss, which lasted until the sun submerged into the depths of Lake Erie.

As the enduring embrace ended, she said, "I was waiting all day . . . You've been looking at me so funny ever since this morning. I didn't know I had to wait until the flipping sunset."

"Yeah, but that was romantic, right?"

"Sure, I guess, if you're into that kinda thing."

Ben knew she wasn't some mushy girl, which is one of the million-odd reasons he loved her. "Hey, but you will remember my attempt forever."

"I will indeed." She kissed him again, then pulled him next to her on the beach as the sunlight faded. "When we are old and gray with twelve small runner kids, I will remember tonight. I promise."

"Twelve?"

"Sure," she said with a wink.

"Well, we better get started then."

They talked for hours. That mid-June evening was warm with a gentle breeze kicking up scents of the lake. Waves lapped at the coarse sand in the darkness, slowly grinding them into smaller and smaller grains.

Ben wasn't sure how best to broach the subject. After watching the races all day, especially the clip about Steve Prefontaine, and experiencing the high of being in love, he had made his final decision. An impossible dream. However, with his stubbornness, he was going to go down in flames trying to achieve it. He couldn't do it alone.

"Maya . . ." He paused, collecting his thoughts, realizing how foolish he was about to sound. Further realizing that she would remember this as part of their engagement evening, too. He didn't care.

"Yes, Ben?" she asked with a tone of sarcasm. "Are you pregnant, *already*?"

He scoffed at the interruption. "Well, um . . . I want to race at Hayward Field next year . . . at the championships."

Maya eyed him for a long moment. She studied his face, only partially surprised by the comment. "Ben, you already know what lies before you. You know what the qualifying times are, and where you are at now. You know about the social class restrictions. And you know about your work responsibilities. This is the wildest dream anyone has ever conceived, except for a few of those guys in the nuthouse. But I believe in you. I believe that you will accomplish great things on the way. I believe that you may even have a chance to go all the way. I will be with you, by your side, every step. Just remember one thing."

It was almost as if it was a preprepared speech. "Yeah?"

"Don't ever leave me behind while you chase your dreams."

He realized that he'd just gotten engaged to the best person ever. With her beside him, he knew that he was going to fight to the very end. Without her, somewhere along the line, he would quit on his dream—he would quit on himself. "I could never leave you behind. I promise you a life of joy. Long into our twilight years, with an enduring love. But after we are old and gray, I want to die first . . . I couldn't ever live without you."

"Sounds like a deal. I am just glad you're not pregnant," she added with a sarcastic wince.

Chapter Eleven

Mr. Peterson thought it would be an excellent idea to assign Ben a trainee. A new employee who would shadow him for a few days and learn what he could, as quickly as he could, before the boss would assess if the rookie had what it took. Most didn't. Mr. Peterson surely thought that this was an excellent idea. Ben felt quite the contrary. This guy wasn't just a slummer, he was either a member of the St. Clair Mafia, or wished to be. The tattoo of a skull with a machete inked into his forearm was a dead giveaway. Judging by the fact that he was working in the factory, he was very low level or still in the recruiting phase and needed some buy-in cash.

Ben's rule was to stay out of harm's way. Spending the day with this guy wasn't his idea of keeping his head down. He kept his mouth shut, was polite, and never allowed long-lasting eye contact.

Prior to lunch, Ben's brother walked by. He glared at Ben, as if to taunt him for who-knows-what reason. His new ill-fated trainee picked up on the exchange. He nodded in Daniel's direction with a snarled lip, then whispered into Ben's ear, "Want me to take care of that?"

Ben's eyes jolted wide open. "No, no, no . . . that's my brother. Um, we always joke around like that."

The gangbanger's eyes never left Daniel's back as he strolled through the factory. He wasn't Ben's new pal, nor was he his new guardian angel. This guy was looking for any reason to break somebody, anybody. The justification was a mere checkbox on an inconsequential form. Ben hoped that his answer was enough to persuade him to look another way. He thought his brother could use a smackdown every once in a while but would never want him to become a maggot farm.

During the lunch break, Ben secluded himself beneath his reliable maple tree off in the corner of the property. Over the long, uncut field of weeds, he saw the gangbanger approach his brother for just a moment, share a few words of wisdom, then depart as quickly as he had arrived. Later, Ben heard from his brother that he was offered a suggestion that brothers should have a great respect for each other. Daniel's skin had turned grayish when he told Ben the story. He also turned a degree warmer toward Ben.

Once he broke free from AluMag for the day, Ben bounced through his apartment to grab his fresh new running shoes from his Columbus trip and changed into his running gear. He headed over to the bench outside Coach Sands's building, where Coach was already patiently waiting. Ben figured that he must have been late again.

He waved to the lady on the balcony, who offered the slightest nod in return. Her son must have been inside, as the dirt field in front of the apartment building was empty.

"Sorry, Coach, am I late?" He winced apologetically.

He smirked. "Ben. I got more time than I know what to do with. As long as you don't leave me hanging, I have no problem if you're running a little behind. Lord knows that you're not slackin' off."

"That's for sure," he said as he tossed his right foot up on the back of the bench to stretch his hamstring.

Coach studied Ben. His eyes glistened when he asked, "Ready for some hills today?"

Hill workouts were brutal, and because of this, they were also Ben's favorite. He winked, then said, "Let's rock 'n' roll."

His coach grabbed his antique bike, which was leaning against the bench. It looked to be older than he was—certainly in worse condition. The bike had been damaged all over with dents and scratches. Not to mention that the front wheel was lacking the ever so vital and defining characteristic of roundness. Ben thought, *If a wheel isn't round, is it still a wheel?*

Ben jogged back over to Edgewater Park with Coach pedaling by his side. Just two days ago, Ben had slept beneath the stars with his new fiancée over on the beach. His dream of racing against the elites covered him like a warm blanket, which forbid him from sleeping at first, then allowed him to fall into a deep and fulfilling rest. His life was finally in order. He had purpose, which, in the slums, was a rare aptitude.

Ben pulled in a deep breath of fresh lakeside air. The Cleveland skyline loomed in the distance over his coach's shoulder.

"I'm going to go after it. I wanna race at the championship next year."

Coach glanced over at Ben. "Well, I guess we're going to need the right training program, huh?"

Ben was astonished by Coach's lack of surprise. His confidence grew, thanks to the people closest to him, who saw more potential in him than Ben did of himself. His ferocious commitment to training was unquestionable, but stepping into the spotlight was something else. Without Maya and Coach, he would be condemned to run alone along the beach or the Metroparks. He would get quicker as his body matured, then slower again as it aged. Nobody would notice, either. He'd be doomed to live in the shadow of his own fear.

He stretched out on a grassy patch beside the beach. The ground was dry, and the browning grass prickled his bare legs. He readied himself to push the limits of his physical boundaries. Ben hopped up and down a few times to get the springs ready and blood pumping. Physically ready to push the limits. Mentally electrified by his supporters.

Edgewater made a perfect place for hills. The route started in the sand, transitioned into a paved road for the ascent, then finished at the top of the hill, into a long grassy stretch. The route circled back to the bottom as the recovery, then repeated. Again, and again.

"Okay, Ben. I'm heading to the top of the hill. Wait for me to get there. When I wave, go for it."

Ben watched as Coach abandoned his bike and climbed the hill on foot. He continued to stretch out his muscles, which were hard and powerful.

Coach waved his hand as he covered the final yards. An indication to begin whenever Ben was ready.

Ben nodded, even though Coach hadn't turned yet. He stretched to touch the ground one last time. Right foot toed the line, then he pushed off from the thick and energy-absorbing sand.

The sand took everything Ben gave it and returned little back. A terrible place to accelerate, but as he reached the path on the hill, he ratcheted up the gears. High knees as required. Coach stood at the crest; Ben pushed up over the top directly by him.

"Keep going," his coach shouted, despite Ben already clearing the top. "Twenty more yards. Push to the tree."

A good hill workout included the transition from the slow uphill segment into an acceleration back to race pace at the top. At Edgewater, this top section was in the grass, and the finish line was a large oak tree shading the area, as it had for a century or more. On paper, it sounded great, but in practice, this final gear shift hurt something fierce. This was the beauty of it.

Ben touched the tree with his hand, then coasted back to a jog while swinging around in a tight U-turn. He passed his coach on the way back down; he said nothing as Ben went by. From the top of the hill, Coach gazed out over the waters of Lake Erie in the direction of Canada. Nothing but endless water was in view.

Ben turned again in the sand at the bottom without stopping.

"Ready for number two?" Coach yelled from the top of the hill. "Run into it."

Without pause, he ramped up in the sand, which was much easier than a cold start. Back to the pavement, he could already feel the added strain caused by his high knee lift.

Each time he passed Coach, he shouted clever, encouraging things like, "Push hard, Ben," or, "Dig in." He accelerated for another twenty yards to the tree. It wasn't the words; it was the fact that he was there that made the difference.

One after another, Ben had now pulled through twelve circuits. Each of them tougher than the last. Slowly sucking the life from his legs, like a leech consuming his blood until he was empty—eventually killing the host.

The workout plan was fifteen circuits. As he crested the hill on the final round while accelerating to the tree, he shouted through heaving breaths, "Another one, Coach."

Ben circled around again for number sixteen.

Again, he shouted "One more, Coach."

As he cleared his seventeenth hill, he no longer said anything to Coach. His madness was already assumed by this point. Ben was going to go until his legs were bloody stumps. His pace slowed considerably, but he didn't want to stop. He couldn't. Coach had resorted to sitting in the grass beneath the shady tree, occasionally spouting out, "Nice one," or, "Lookin' strong," even when his attention was diverted by pulling the leaves off a clover.

Each hill bore down on him. It took everything he had to fight through each circuit; however, the recovery got him just enough. His legs felt like lead ingots. Visions of the final lap at Hayward Field. Visions of Cyrus, Eric, and Archer leading the field as he tucked in right behind them for the final kick.

That Monday afternoon, Ben cleared thirty circuits at the lakeside hill. Fifteen more than his prescribed workout plan. His jog home, with his coach cautiously riding beside him, was quiet. Slow and achy. He could feel the burn of blisters on his feet and the wetness beneath his left big toe. Most likely blood squishing with each push-off through his saturated sock. He nearly tripped while transitioning up a curb from the street to the sidewalk. He could no longer pull his knees high enough and stumbled over small cracks. Utterly depleted.

Once back at Coach's apartment building, they sat on the bench, enjoying the fresh summer evening air. Logan had returned to his excavation project and greeted him cheerfully.

Coach grabbed Ben's shoulder. "Some workout, huh?"

Ben inhaled deeply, heartbeat still thumping rapidly. Neither the hill, nor the sand, nor the grass was his foe. He was victorious in his battle against his worst enemy: himself.

"Yeah, another great one in the bag." His coach looked at him. Paused as if he wanted to say something, but nothing came out.

"Coach?"

He maintained his gaze.

"You think I have a chance to qualify for the championships next year?"

He inhaled deeply. "Only one way to know, right?"

Ben looked into his eyes for sincerity, which he found. He nodded to acknowledge their enhanced agreement as he stood from the bench. His muscles cried in agony.

"See you tomorrow, Coach."

"Get some sleep, kid. You're gonna need it."

Ben smiled. After a long day in the factory with his newfound thug friend and the hill workout, sleeping wasn't going to be the issue; as long as he could stay awake long enough to make it home. He momentarily considered sleeping below the ironwood tree, but then this thought was displaced by the vision of his pillow calling him.

Ben trudged home with bowed legs, as a cowboy might after a long ride. Every muscle ached. It felt amazing.

***

Several days later, Ben knocked on Coach's door.

"It's open," came a muffled voice from the other side.

Coach lounged on his sofa, surrounded by stacks of books and magazines on the cushion next to him, as well as on the coffee table.

"Come on in. I'm glad you're here." He grabbed the stack beside him and shuffled it over to the coffee table.

Coach had requested a special visit to talk about their training plan. Ben couldn't wait to strategize with him. Learn from him. Ben had read up about running in the past. However, reading old magazine articles and having a mentor who had actually lived it and knew how to apply the knowledge were two significantly different things.

He patted the cushion beside him, which Ben swiftly occupied.

"How you feeling? Your legs recover from those hills yet?"

Ben nodded, contrary to the latent ache for the third day since the workout. He wasn't going to let a little discomfort soften his training plan though. "Ready to go."

"That was a tough one. You really put yourself out there, which is great here and there. But you need to get the proper recovery to ensure you don't get injured." He intentionally made eye contact to emphasize his point.

"Yeah, I feel good." Ben knew that he wasn't going to get hurt and knew even more so that he didn't have time to lose another day before his next hard workout. The elites didn't need as much time to recover because of their genetic coding for minimal lactic acid production as well as their readily available ice baths, massages, and dietary regime.

Coach slid a notebook paper over to him on the coffee table. Ben leaned forward to study it.

"These are the three phases of your training program. We have nearly a full year to get you ready, so we will schedule the phases based on your final race at the championships."

Ben felt a sudden recognition that his dream just got real.

"We also need to stay flexible to ensure the recovery is suitable. Running a 120-mile week just because it is on the schedule doesn't consider the quality. Running tired reduces the value of those workouts, and I need you to listen to me when I tell you to back off."

Ben nodded again.

"We need to build your base, strength, and speed. We will always work on all three, but the priority will shift as we get closer to the big event."

He liked what he was hearing. He knew that Coach had some experience but was impressed by his overall competence on the subject.

Coach went on to explain the details between each of the training phases, types of workouts, and exactly what each of them developed and why they were crucial for a fast 5000 meters. He was perplexed that running slower long runs could allow him to run faster by teaching his body to improve its ability to move oxygen to the muscles.

Ben studied the paper, front and back. The workout plan was sketched out for fifty consecutive weeks. Each week detailed two hard workouts, the long run duration, and his total mileage target. The volume of mileage was staggering, but Ben looked at it as a badge of honor. A fate that he had self-prescribed. "Wow, where did you learn all this?"

He shrugged. "I don't know, just picked up a few things here and there."

"No, seriously. I can't get over the fact that you have so many contacts at the road races and you are a master with training programs."

Coach inhaled deeply and studied Ben's curiosity. He then looked across the room to the bookshelf. "One moment."

Ben felt that the mysteries of his coach were about to be revealed and held his breath to ensure he didn't accidentally derail the progress.

He stood and walked to the shelf, grabbed a large brown book from the top, then returned. He handed it to Ben. "Here, my scrapbook. Nobody has ever seen this."

Ben opened it up, and the pages were made of cardstock covered with pictures and glued-in newspaper clippings. The photos were of a younger man who had the faintest resemblance to his coach. Clearly a well-trained runner. Thin, lean, and with a look of determination.

"I've never shown this to anyone," he repeated. His voice was faint—on the fringe of regret.

As he flipped through the pages, he could see it was Coach, but his name wasn't Martin Sands. Ben looked back toward his mentor. "Michael Sandvik?"

He shrugged. His expression was flat. "Best I could come up with, anyway. It was in the early days when they started segregating slummers. It is a tragedy how fast and how far this whole thing has gotten. My fake name was hardly required, but it did help me out from time to time when I ran up against the wrong guy. In some ways I thought it was kind of fun, back then, anyway."

"It must have been horrible to watch the world turn. I mean, for me, it was always this way."

"I remember my first race. Just a kid, maybe ten or eleven, and it was before the resegregation started." He laughed. "They never did like a little brown boy beating the adults, though. I tried to use this lotion that made me look more white, but the sweat just washed it off . . . Didn't fool anyone."

Ben smirked uncomfortably. "I thought you said you didn't win any races ... You won tons of stuff ... everywhere. Even Malachi."

"I didn't win, Ben. My alter ego, Michael, did."

Ben raised his eyebrows. "What do you mean?"

"When you live as somebody else for so long, you begin to believe you are someone else. That guy you see winning races had forgotten himself. Forgotten who he was and where he came from. He also forgot his own family as it slowly dissolved into nothing. Worse than nothing. Michael Sandvik had everything he dreamed of, but Martin Sands became a hollow shell."

"Is that why you don't talk to your son anymore?"

"Better said, that's why he won't talk to me anymore. I would invite him over in a heartbeat if he would take my call."

"I'm sorry, that's horrible."

"Well, I had a lot of good memories along the way, but the hole that was left in my life has tarnished even the best of them. Don't ever lose sight of who you are, Ben. You're a good kid, and Maya is absolutely a keeper. It would break my heart if you fell into the same trap I did. I will always keep a watchful eye on you, though. I regret every single thing I have ever done in my life. Everything except helping you. You are the chance I need to prove that I learned my life lesson. The day I met you was the first day I didn't need a drink to go to sleep without the fear of guilt-riddled nightmares."

Ben looked at him in adoration. His mentor, not in running but in life. Who led by the example of what not to do. He thought of Maya and couldn't imagine living without her. He could never fall into the trap Coach had, but then again, he was walking into the abyss. Everything in front of him was unfamiliar territory. And he's wasn't just walking toward it, he was running into it at breakneck speeds.

Chapter Twelve

Ben's fingertips were pressed deep into his hamstring muscles to loosen them up for today's workout. He flexed the muscle, which had grown considerably larger over the past eight weeks. He enjoyed the noticeable change in hardness, toughness.

The light shadowed across his thigh, highlighting the triangular muscle. The ancient Greeks built statues to celebrate the Olympians. They were made of marble; Ben was cut from granite. Beautiful in a gritty and unpolished sort of way.

Eight weeks of calculated intensity. Ben had broken through a barrier that he previously thought would be impenetrable. He could only look at his former self as a child—an infant to the sport.

He hadn't run a race since he started legitimately training, to maximize the effects of his workouts. Coach had him on a crash course toward perfection.

Two intense workouts per week, on Tuesday and Thursday, with a Sunday long run that ranged between twenty and twenty-five miles. Every day, with exception to his long-run day, was a morning five-miler to get the machine warmed up. Each workout—hills, intervals, tempo runs, and ladders—focused on his speed, strength, endurance, or mental confidence. They were an orchestra. Individually impressive but collectively a masterpiece.

His body, powerful beyond recognition, grew weary. Each morning he measured his resting heart rate directly after waking. Forty-six beats per minute was noted as a steady increase over four consecutive days from its more typical thirty-eight.

A distance runner measures life by time. Seconds that edge down the personal records. Hours in a day to squeeze in a workout, stretching, massage, and rest. Days in a week to oscillate hard and recovery workouts, to maximize the potency of applied effort. Months to prepare for a momentous event—the championship. And a year to start the building phase from the beginning, but one significant step ahead of the previous year.

Right now, Ben's magic number was forty-three. Forty-three weeks until he could smell the scents produced by the Oregon pine forests, wafting across Hayward Field at the championship. A scent that seduced him toward his ultimate achievement.

Before that, he would need to qualify with a specific time at a sanctioned event. A race legitimized by the national track and field association. The thought of it made him shudder. The required qualification time was faster than anything he had gotten so far, but all things considered, within range.

Overtraining, which is what his increasing heart rate insinuated, couldn't be overcome by toughness or determination. It required rest, and rest alone.

Coach Sands rode along with Ben toward the towpath as Ben prepared for his ten-mile tempo run. Even at the casual warm-up pace, his legs felt like his muscles had turned to lead.

"How ya feeling, Ben?"

Ben analyzed the situation. *I feel like I got run over by an eighteen-wheeler, how 'bout you?*

"Great, Coach, ready to rock this one."

"Now is the time to listen to your body, Ben. You good?"

"Yup." Ben knew that his coach had seen through his mask, but he didn't have the time to play that game. He needed another hard workout in the bag.

As Ben lined up for the start, he hoped that he would bounce back once his legs got into a rhythm. After two hundred yards, he could hardly maintain pace. He made sure he rounded the bend, out of Coach's sight, before he showed signs of his struggle.

His speed bounced all over the place, and no steady rhythm was to be found. Through two miles, his time was slow, but not terrible. However, it wasn't sustainable. By the tail end of mile three, gravity sucked him to the ground. His tempo pace slid back toward something more representative of an easy run, without the pleasantness of being easy.

Just short of the three-mile mark, he stopped.

An involuntary frown tormented the muscles of his face. He moved to the grassy side of the trail and picked up a stick, nearly a log at two inches thick and three feet long. With both hands, he hurled it into the river—a battle cry sprung from deep within scaring off birds in the distance.

He watched the ripples dissipate. Turned back in the direction he had come from and lured himself into a jog of shame. A tear streaked over his cheek.

From a distance, he could see Coach sitting in the grass, drenched in the warmth of the August sun.

Once Coach spotted him slogging back, he stood.

Ben stopped in front of him. Jammed both hands across his face, then into his hair, where he gripped hard. Hard enough for the pain to flirt between pleasure and agony.

"I'm done, Coach. This entire thing is stupid. I can never compete against those hybrid human-machines with their microchips and shit. Machines optimized for maximum performance. Schedules allowing them to rest as much as necessary."

"You done?"

"Yeah, I'm done. I hate running."

"No, Ben. Are you done whining like a three-year-old?"

Ben stopped, looked at Coach with a fit of fury. "Three-year-old?"

Coach laughed. "You just need a little rest. Come on, man, you will pop back from this in a week. You will be faster and stronger once you reset your system. Rest is the way to break through the plateau. You've been burning the candle at both ends, and your body is feeling it. We need to be careful, but everything is going to be okay. It's all normal."

"Coach, I don't have the time to rest."

"You just said you want to quit. Sounds like you got lots of time now."

"Ugh, come on."

Coach smiled. "Gotta be crazy if you want to be a great runner."

Ben cautiously returned the smile. "Okay. I'll run one less hard workout a week. Okay?"

"Better to do an entire week of easy runs. Really reset the system."

"It will be fine. Don't worry. I will let you know if I need more rest. Today was just a bad day. I'll be good tomorrow."

He placed his hand on Ben's shoulder. "The reason you will become a world-class runner is the same reason that you are going to burn up in the stratosphere: you are one stubborn mule."

"Thanks Coach. See you tomorrow, same time."

***

He cast out his worm and bobber through the still, mist-laden morning air. It plunged into the water, returning a sound of kerplunk, and rings circled out from its epicenter. The lake rose and retreated gently, sloshing upon the concrete block jetty where Ben sat.

Only three feet to the right, another bobber and worm splashed into the unsuspecting water.

"Oh, sorry," Maya whispered. "Not where I wanted to throw it."

Ben's feet dangled off the side of the stone block, hanging a foot above the water. He glared at her sarcastically. She could do no wrong by him.

"You don't suppose the fish ever wonder what that white and red thing is, hovering over the worm?" Maya asked.

"A guardian angel for the slowly drowning worm, perhaps."

Her smile, warmed by the new sun, filled Ben with a comfort. "Or an alien spaceship that's finally found intelligent life on earth."

Ben dropped the tip of his pole into the water as he laughed. "Did the alien bobber-ship travel through a wormhole?"

Both of them cracked up. All fishing rules broken, loud laughing, splashing the water with the pole, Maya's bobber plunged into the murky depth.

Her reel zipped as the line zigzagged out into deeper water.

She snapped back the rod to set the hook. The fight was on.

"That looks huge," Ben said as he noticed how much the rod was bending.

Maya didn't answer. She focused on landing this bad boy. She worked the rod against the fish's intentions and relentlessly brought it closer to her.

Ben reeled in his own line and placed his rod behind him so he could help pull the creature from the murky water.

Outstretched over the stone block, he lay on his stomach.

The fish smashed into the surface directly under Ben, spraying him across the face. He made a run for it back into the water, but Maya gradually wore him down.

Back to Ben, this time the fish was lethargic, indicating its survival skills had been conquered by fatigue. He thrashed until he could no longer.

Ben grabbed the fish behind the head and under the belly. The ferocious teeth looked menacing. He, too, felt like a predator who'd lost his fight to a higher power, who had succumbed to exhaustion.

"Yes," shouted Maya as she punched a hand into the air. "How big is that thing?"

Ben hoisted him up as he clattered to his knees then rose to his feet. "Over eight?" he guessed.

"Eight pounds?" Maya said. "That's gotta be my biggest one ever."

Ben was doused in her enthusiasm. The numbness of his own exhausted defeat melted away. In his last two months of training, he had had no time for anyone: he worked, he trained, and he slept. Today, he understood what he had been missing.

"Want a picture?" Ben asked.

"Of course," she said as she rolled her eyes. She grabbed the fish in the same way as Ben had and held it up.

Ben used his hands to appear as if he was holding an invisible camera and said, "Click, click, click."

They always made fun of the elites taking pictures of themselves with their future fish dinner. *Kind of cruel,* Ben thought. *Then again, doing the same thing without a camera is probably worse.*

He grabbed the large burlap sack, and Maya placed the fish inside.

Back with their bobbers bobbing, Ben asked, "So, what do you think? Am I a fool for trying to run at the championship? Maybe I just focus on road races instead and make some money."

She studied his face. "Ben, do you want me to tell you it is okay to give up on your dream?"

He raised his eyebrows. "Um, no . . . I just mean that we could use the extra cash, right? Doesn't it make more sense to take care of our future? You know, thirteen kids."

"Twelve, Ben. Twelve kids." She exhaled, then looked out over the water. "Ben, it is *your* dream to run at the national championships. Nobody else's. You have one chance to go after this. I know regret, Ben. It's not something you want sleeping beside you every time you close your eyes. Sure, maybe you fail to achieve your dream. But at least you will know you gave it everything. If you quit because you have convinced yourself that you can't do it, that is when you have failed. Every day there are reasons to quit."

She was a year younger than Ben, but he looked at her as if she were the embodiment of wisdom. She grounded him when he needed it, and he was never worried that she would misguide him.

"I'm afraid."

She nodded. "Anybody would be."

"Yeah, I guess so."

"Could be worse," she said as a smile brightened her cheeks.

He raised his eyebrows. "How?"

"You could be that fish, pulled through the wormhole."

Ben smiled, too. "Or the worm from the planet Xorog."

They fished for the next few hours. Ben was at peace. He decided to rest as Coach prescribed, and when he was ready, he would continue his quest for glory.

Chapter Thirteen

His heart rate descended to near-normal levels after a week of easier runs. Ben caved to Coach's insisted rest period.

Same training plan as two weeks prior; however, Coach cut the workout in half. Five-mile tempo at the towpath.

Ben felt much stronger in the warm-up. Muscles rejuvenated. Mind refocused. Fresh.

His foot ached, but nothing he concerned himself with too much. At the mileage he was running, he thought, what *wasn't* a little sore.

"Okay, Ben. Remember, we just gotta get the wheels turning at tempo pace today. Nothing over-the-top. When we have a good one today, we will ramp up into your full routine. Got it?"

"Yeah, Coach. Ready to blow the doors off."

Coach glared at him.

"Just kidding, come on. Yeah, in control. Check."

Ben lined up, then returned to the battlefield that had conquered his body and spirit just one week prior. Risen from the dead.

The top of his right foot throbbed. *Just need to get the machine moving again, then everything will be good,* he thought.

His pace was solid through three miles, profoundly better than his previous attempt. Controlled, quick, and effortless.

The burn approached in the fourth mile as it should. He concentrated on the pace. Thumbs tapping his hips. Tap tap tap.

In the final mile, Ben turned the throttle up. He dug deep to overcome nature's intention to burden him. He was on the verge of a solid negative-split five-miler, a triumphant return to training. His mind rattled through the quick progress he would make in the coming weeks, further spurring the adrenaline through his veins. He was confident that his training plateau was going to be shattered.

With a half mile to go, his throbbing foot rapidly got worse. At one precise moment, it became unbearable. Sharp pain shot up his leg with every impact. Despite the excruciating fire coursing through his foot, his pace slowed but he still finished the workout.

Coach Sands looked at his watch as Ben came through the finish. "Hey, looks pretty good. How did you feel?"

Ben didn't answer. A wave of emotion struck him harder than the pain. His face was hot, his eyes burned.

"Hey, you okay? Looks like you're hobbling a bit."

Ben looked back to his loyal coach. A burning tear raced across his cheek, intermixing with the dripping sweat. He buried his face in his hands, and in a muffled voice said, "I'm a freaking idiot, Coach."

"Oh no. Ben, sit down and let me look. Take off the shoe." He hurried to Ben's side and kneeled in the path. "Where's the pain?"

Unlacing the shoe was fine; however, removing it was horrific. Ben lifted his leg and simultaneously felt along the top of his foot until the sharp pain returned. A wince contorted his face. With his index finger, he pointed precisely to the spot. "Here."

"Okay, relax, let's take a look." Coach Sands took the foot and placed the heel on his own thigh. He slid his fingers over the bones in the vicinity of where Ben had pointed. He paused on the precise spot and gently squeezed. Thumb on the hotspot and fingers wrapped under the arch.

Ben twisted instantly and sucked air through his teeth. "Why did you do that?"

His coach placed the foot back to the ground, lowered his head, then sat up to look him in the eyes. "You got a stress fracture, son ... a small crack in your third metatarsal."

Ben already knew it. However, the confirmation sent a rock into his stomach.

Coach returned to his feet and grabbed his bike from where it had been leaning against a tree just off the trail. He extended his hand to Ben, offering additional support to keep the weight off the injury.

"Come, sit on the bike. Let's get you outta here."

Ben pulled himself up with Coach's help, then climbed onto the bike, resting his injured foot on the pedal while his left foot pushed off the ground. Coach steadied the bike. It was slow going to get the three and a half miles back home. Enough time to shape and mold the type of regret he would be prescribing himself tonight.

"It's over, isn't it?" Ben asked as they pulled up in front of his apartment.

"Just because you can't run, doesn't mean you can't train, Ben." His eyes were dead serious. "It's not going to be the same, it's not going to be easy, but we can get you back in three months while maintaining your fitness. We have the time."

Ben didn't respond. No words could capture his wild and contradictory thoughts. Hope, fear, and shame.

"In the water. You can run in the water while your bone heals. It's not going to be fun, though. You will be hardened by the experience. I promise you that much."

"I am not doing this for fun," he said. He thought of Maya's words: *Every day there are reasons to quit.*

"Here. Take my bike as a loan. Give yourself a couple days to let the pain ease, then bike down to Lake Erie, maybe Edgewater Park, and wade out until you can't touch. Run back and forth along the shore without touching the bottom. Do this a few days in a row, then we will start designing some water workouts. Okay?"

Ben nodded. "Yeah, I'll give it a shot ... I'm ... I'm gonna find my way through this."

Coach reached out and squeezed Ben's shoulder. "Yes, you are. That is something I am certain of."

***

The following day, Ben woke up for his morning run as he would any other day. He swung his legs out of his bed to the cool tile floor. As he put weight in his foot, he crashed to the ground. The pain shot up through his leg and directly into his soul.

For fifteen minutes, he lay on the ground sobbing. Not from the pain, but from the realization that his nightmare last night was not fictional. It was real, and it was just beginning.

Chapter Fourteen

Using a crutch gifted to him by Mrs. Withers down the hall, Ben made his way to the dilapidated bike, which had been gifted to him by Coach Sands. It took several days to grasp the reality of his situation. He hadn't left the house, and besides using the restroom, he hardly left his bed. He called into the foundry to take a few days off work at some risk that he would be replaced. However, with his experience and job training, it was unlikely. Today was different. Something inside of him called on him to breach the barrier of the front door and go into the autumn air. He was ready to move past his grief. He was ready to test the waters of Lake Erie, and to test the depths from which he would have to swim back.

The front wheel was worse than it looked. Every rotation, the flat section would come around, producing a rhythmic thumping. Not to mention its desire to pull to the right, which made it seem like the bike was possessed to meet its maker.

At long last, he arrived at Edgewater Park. He pulled onto the sand and let the mangy war-torn bike drop with a dull thump. His crutch, which he tied to the side while riding, was unbound, and he hobbled over the coarse grit until he came upon the water's edge. This morning, the lake was glass. That was quite something for a lake spanning nearly ten thousand square miles. A light fog billowed over the surface, and seagulls cracked their morning voices.

Stripping to just his running shorts, he could only imagine how cold that water truly was. In just months, it would be frozen over. He'd known how to swim since his childhood. He and his brother used to come to this very spot in their youth and splash around, which ultimately became competitive. Ben always won their swim races—always.

He dropped the crutch next to his shirt and hobbled into the water. Ripples ran off in all directions as the cool water surged a sense of refreshment through him, tickling his nerves. The temperature was too cold to lounge, but it would be perfect for a workout.

The chill felt good on his injured foot, too. Once he was knee-deep, he twisted to sit. This was the shock he needed to get past. As he adapted to the temperature, he rolled to his belly and swam into the depths, to where he could no longer touch. The water was even colder there. He scissored his legs forward and back, and his arms made large arcs to the front, then back, with hands cupped like oars. The water was pushed downward with each movement.

Coach had told him to get used to it before he would prescribe workouts, so today was only about getting some time in. Feeling it out. *Can't be so difficult,* he thought.

He paddled out more, then turned parallel to the beach. He simply had to run upright, which in theory should keep him afloat, like treading water. Trace the arching shoreline back and forth . . . in theory.

While transitioning from treading water into a running motion, two things occurred. First, he began to slowly move forward. Second, he lost altitude quickly. With his head tilted up to keep his nose above the surface, he broke back into the treading water motion to reassess the situation. *No problem, Coach said. Hah.*

The average American male's body fat percent, which correlated to a person's ability to float, was upward of 25 percent. Ben had just 8 percent body fat. Buoyant as a rock.

He prepared for another attempt. He studied the water's resistance and now intended to move his hands in an oar like motion to help lift him. Although he acknowledged that sinking to the bottom of the lake would not be so terrible, he wasn't exactly ready to end it all . . . not yet, anyway.

His new strategy improved his level control, and although lower in the water than he'd been while treading, he securely kept his mouth and nose high enough without needing to look straight up into the sky.

Ben couldn't imagine a worse workout. He was moving at a sloth's pace. The blasting wind, painting trails with his eddies—that was what he longed for.

He momentarily closed his eyes, captured an image of the last national championship, where the elite athletes stepped forward to the starting line, then reran all 5000 meters through his mind. Teleporting himself far away from the cool lake water. An exact replica of the race with one miniscule modification. Ben was in the ranks, and he was a contender.

The water sloshed all around him as his effort increased, pace quickened, and heart pumped the much-needed blood to his muscles. With only a slight dull ache in his foot, he knew that he was going to get through this. A glimmer of hope shone through the gloom.

Ben ran through the water as the waves picked up from a northwest breeze encouraged by the sun's warmth embracing the region. Lost within his fantasies, he had covered two hours worth of water back and forth along that arching beach. New and previously undiscovered muscles in his abdomen and arms were wearing down. Ben had found himself struggling to maintain the pace required for buoyancy. He decided to wrap up and head back to the beach beneath the late-morning sun.

Since he'd started, several people had arrived to enjoy the park. All of them had a curiosity bestowed upon them as they watched Ben perform his circuits. Their interest was piqued, and he witnessed friendly smiles of inquisitiveness. He had never seen such approachable faces at the park before today.

As Ben dried off and pulled his clothes on, he could see them begin to realize that they had just been gawking at a slummer. Ashamed of themselves, they restrained from shouting their usual, "Get off the beach," and just turned away in disgust. Embarrassed from revealing a chink in the armor designed to protect them from such a cruel invasion of their privilege.

A young boy, perhaps four or five, who had been playing in the sand, attempting to create the ugliest sandcastle known to mankind, turned to Ben and asked, "What ya doing out there?"

Ten yards away, his squawking seagull-like mother shouted, "Thomas! Don't talk to him."

Her eyes burned into Ben as if she were attempting to ignite him into a fireball.

The child looked, confused. Despite obeying his mother, he shared an exaggerated grimace with Ben, comically, as if he had just been caught stealing a second ice cream out of the freezer on a hot summer day.

Ben reciprocated the grimace, then winked at the boy, who marched back toward his mother. He thought to himself, *Don't worry boy, she will teach you how to hate me soon enough.*

Ben returned to his home in the same method as he had arrived. Thumping and squeaking in a symphony of poverty. He decided he was going to buy Coach a functional bike someday, but not until after he no longer needed to borrow it, so it didn't appear as if he had purchased it for himself.

A new box in his running career was checked. Although it was a far cry from running, he had accomplished a training method that left him utterly exhausted. He closed his eyes and nestled his head deep into the threadbare pillow on his couch. The apartment was empty, and he found himself amid an unscheduled nap.

***

Ben raced along the edge of a wooden pier that stretched high above the water below. A man with the face of a cheetah closed in on him, his claws protracted and ready to pounce. Blood smeared across the white tuft of fur beneath his mouth.

The pier turned ninety degrees to the left, and as Ben attempted to make the turn at full speed, each step crept closer to the edge. Each stride, the cheetah gained on him. With all his might, he was unable to accomplish the turn, and with his final step Ben teetered on the edge before slipping into the depths below.

Midair, Ben jumped into a sitting position on his couch. Sweat beaded over his forehead. His heart pounded thunderously.

"What cha' doin' over there, speed racer?" Daniel said. "Chasing squirrels?"

Ben looked toward the kitchen, where his brother had his head buried in the refrigerator.

"Nothing in there but an empty ketchup bottle," Ben said. Prior to his nap, he had also scoured the fridge for scraps.

"Arg." Daniel slammed the door shut. "You eat everything in this house."

"Everything? What *everything*? We never have anything here to begin with."

"What about your noodles you're always eating?"

Ben's pulse increased in annoyance and his voice raised. "They're on the shelf . . . Just gotta cook it for yourself."

While distracted by his intellectual dietary discussion, he stood from the couch. Pain shot through his foot into his leg, sending him back to the seat. His wince was audible.

"Little boy hurt his foot?" Daniel said, like he was mocking a crying baby.

Ben grabbed the pillow and squeezed until his knuckles were barren of blood. With a mighty blast of breath, he screamed into the room with his eyes clamped shut, "Go away."

Daniel froze. Speechless. A smile emerged, as if he had found what he was looking for. A button to push his brother over the edge.

Ben thought of his new thug friend from work and wished that he had a phone number to arrange an appointment. Nobody could get under his skin like his brother could.

The door popped open, and their dad stepped in abruptly. "What the heck is going on in here?"

Ben grabbed his crutch and hobbled back to their shared bedroom.

"Stay out," he said as he shut the door behind him.

There were no locks on the interior doors of the apartment, and he had no way of barricading himself inside. He was trapped in his life. Nowhere to hide. Nowhere to be alone.

Despite the good water workout in the morning, he knew that he was using a tin can to fill an Olympic-size swimming pool. His effort was futile.

He could hear the muffled voices of his brother and dad talking in the family room, but they were not decipherable enough for Ben to understand the conversation.

Ben reached over to the nightstand and grabbed an outdated copy of a running magazine Coach had lent him. He pawed through it for the tenth time, looking at pictures and the advertisements for running products he could never afford. Tech socks cost as much as a month at the foundry.

Two rapid knocks echoed from the hollow bedroom door.

Ben sighed and let the magazine drop to his lap. "What?"

His dad emerged and pulled the door closed behind him. His face was long.

Ben folded the magazine and placed it back on the nightstand. He looked at his dad with an eye of suspicion. Something was cooking.

"Can I sit here?" he asked as he sat toward the foot of the bed without approval. "How you doing?"

"Ugh, Dad, everything is fine. Daniel's just a jerk, that's all."

"Yup, can't deny that, but that's not what I am asking about." His eyes were soft, and he appeared ready to listen.

Ben skootched into a more upright position and pulled his knees toward his chest. "I'm good . . . life's dandy in the slums of Cleveland."

"You know, Ben, your mom was quite a special person. She had a way about her. She was beautiful in every way imaginable. At first, it was her smile that sucked me in. But it didn't take long for me to see who she really was."

Ben was surprised by the direction this conversation had turned.

"You know, for people in the slums, it's best to just keep our heads down. Work when we are told to, and to do a good job without making a fuss." He shook his head. "That was never enough for your mom, though. Wow, she was a passionate dreamer."

"What's wrong with that?" Ben replied harshly, on instinct. He sensed his father was trying to draw a negative connection between him and his mom.

Unphased by Ben's attitude, his Dad said, "It was the thing I loved most about her."

"Oh." He pulled back in surprise.

"The only problem, Ben, is that hope is the worst thing you can carry through the slums with you. Zero chance that the cards will be reshuffled. We have only one place here, and that is to work our butts off to earn enough food and shelter to stay alive. It is a game of survival, not luxury."

"But Dad, it doesn't mean that I can't do something, a hobby that I enjoy, and also do my job."

He nodded. "Yeah, but what you're doing Ben isn't a hobby. It's an obsession."

He had no counterargument for that. There was no question that his running, wet or dry, was all consuming—everything else fell victim to its wake. He had never even met someone who was so fixated on anything, let alone a hobby.

"You know, I don't care if you're out running here and there. But what you're doing, Ben, is going to destroy you. Sooner or later it will all crash down around you. You will be your own victim. A cautionary tale of flying too high."

The defensive tension in his heart returned. "Good talk, Dad. Thanks."

His dad looked him in the eye. Ben could see a glimpse of pity as well as defeat as he had lost the point he had set out to make. His dad patted the bed, then stood.

"Love ya, kid," he said as he headed to the door. With one last look, he left the room quietly, closing the door behind himself.

Chapter Fifteen

The sun cast down on Ben's face. The warmth contradicted the chilled water to come, making the anticipation even worse.

"You ready?" Coach asked, nestled into a nice place on the beach, pushing his toes around, mixing the dry sand on top with the wet sand an inch below.

Ben looked at him, then snorted. "You're enjoying this, aren't you?"

"Well . . ." He paused, then nodded. "Well, I can't say I'm *not* enjoying this."

He pulled his shirt over his head, then threw it in the direction of his basking coach. It fell mere inches short.

"Good thing you don't play baseball." He smirked.

Ben recognized that Coach was in an unusually good mood today. It was more than just the pleasure of watching a young man suffer. He also found out that Coach had a much nicer bike locked away in the basement of the apartment building. He explained on their ride over that he was afraid of someone stealing it, so it rarely saw the light of day. What he didn't explain was the casual comment he made regarding his former wife and how biking into the Metroparks was one of their favorite pastimes.

"Okay ... So, we're gonna do ladders today. One minute, two minutes, four minutes hard, then back down. Recovery will be two minutes between and ten minutes between sets. Four sets in total. I'll yell out the times as we go. Got it?"

"We?" Ben asked, squinting with one eye, challenging the comment.

Coach laughed. "Yeah, Ben, you know I got an important job here, too. Who else is going to sift the sand on the beach with their toes? I mean, look at this place. There is a ton of sand."

Ben grunted, then turned to the lake. He hobbled over the few yards to the water's edge where white frothy foam had collected and now buzzed from the attracted flies. With the warm sun, it felt refreshing as the water rushed between his toes, but cold enough to wish for a wet suit.

After a ten-minute warm-up, Coach yelled from his place on the beach, "Go."

Twice a day, every day, Ben found himself plunged into the cold waters off the shoreline of Cleveland. Coach had designed workouts that were very similar to the ones he would have done while running. Repeats, endurance, and tempo workouts, all of which were scribbled into his running log, including the detailed accounts of his foot's gradual progress. Coach attended many of the hard workouts, but mostly, Ben was fighting the currents alone.

One evening, weeks later, he looked at his expensive running shoes he had purchased in Columbus. Haphazardly tossed beside his bedroom door, they still looked as fresh as they had when he purchased them, and they hadn't moved from that very spot. Frozen in time since the day he broke his foot, memorializing the dreadful day.

One thing Ben recognized was that his effort from water running, no matter how intense it was or how drained he felt in the afternoon, allowed him to recover much faster than when he was running. He could turn up the heat much more often than he was able to while running. It wasn't the same, but maybe this small fact would prove to be an unexpected bonus. His running legs were not progressing, but his cardiovascular system would be a powerhouse.

Ben had become a water runner. No more issues with keeping afloat. His arms strengthened, his core hardened, and if there was a competition for open-water running, he would be a ferocious competitor. He fantasized about being the world's most elite water runner in history. Ben knew that a runner must always fantasize about everything they apply effort toward. It is the fantasy that shapes their reality. The secret is that if you know you will become something, you will have a chance. If you doubt yourself, you will most certainly not.

***

An hour before the normal start of his shift, Ben grabbed the next pack of paperwork. He sat at the small wooden desk off to the side of the manufacturing floor. Production routers were shoved between different-colored transparent sleeves and stacked high. Each order required a sequence of manufacturing steps, and these documents guided the order where it needed to go and captured stamps for each quality inspection step. It was better than his usual mopping of the floors every second day.

He took the next one off the stack to the left, then pulled the paperwork out. He verified that all the manufacturing stamps were there, then signed off on the order to be invoiced. Once he was done, he lobbed the pack over to the completed pile on his right, which was far shorter than his to-do tower.

"Come with me, Ben. We need to talk," said a grizzled voice from behind him.

It was the boss man, Mr. Peterson. Ben knew where this was going. His stomach turned over the emptiness inside. Long before the start of the shift, they were the only two in the factory besides security at the entrance.

For weeks he had been doing odd jobs and coming in early to compensate for his disability. Lifting the fiery magnesium crucible was no longer possible with his bum foot.

Ben grabbed his crutch and followed his boss across the factory floor from the small wooden desk where he had been pushing paperwork. They headed to a closet-sized conference room with a scratched-up plexiglass window.

Dozens of people waited outside the factory every day, hoping for work. Trying to fill in for a sick employee, or more permanently for someone who had been kicked out the back door. The latter sequence was often initiated from within this room.

Once inside, his boss pulled the vertical blinds closed to conceal their discussion from potential onlookers, despite the two missing segments. This morning, it was symbolic, as there were no other workers in the factory yet. This room was reserved for private discussions, which mostly resulted in the issuance of probationary measures—or termination. "The room of doom," the employees called it.

"Close the door," he said.

Ben did as he was instructed and stood before him humbly. "How may I help you, sir?"

He sighed. "Look, kid, a few months ago I was looking for a reason to kick you out to the street."

Ben's brow raised in realization of how close he had come to termination. Thoughts rushed through of how he would explain to his father that he had lost his job because of running. He also realized how badly his boss stank of smoked sausage and whiskey, especially at this early hour.

"I'm not unhappy with your extra efforts now. You, know . . ." He pointed at Ben's leg, incidentally the wrong one. "With that problem. You got some kinda friends here picking up for you."

Ben knew that his dad was proud of all the extra work he had been putting in as well. He often commented to other supervisors to ensure that the hard work didn't go unnoticed. Both his dad and brother were the ones doing double duty on Ben's behalf. He nodded.

"Thank you, sir."

"Don't thank me yet . . ." He sucked in a deep breath. "I heard that you got hurt from running, which was the same excuse for you being frequently late in the past months."

Ben didn't want to be in this conversation. A dance that he had been in all too many times. A dance where he would end up flat on his butt.

"Management has informed me that because of your training and experience we should try to keep you." He puffed up his chest, as if he were mighty, and wielded his authority like a double-sided battle-ax. "But it is under one condition."

Ben saw the opportunity to keep his job, whatever the condition was—working nights, extra hours, or weekends, cleaning the toilets, making smoked sausage—anything would be better than telling his dad that he'd lost his job.

"Well, we need you to move to sixty-hour weeks to make up for your reduced efficiency because of that thing." He pointed again, and again to the wrong foot. "Once you recover, we will discuss if you can move back down to fifty. No extra pay since this is your fault, of course."

"Yes, sir. I will get the extra hours in. Thank you for the opportunity to make it up to you." Ben could almost puke. He knew his place in the world and knew that the only way to keep his job was to shovel the manure. Every day, Ben was on the edge of mouthing off to his boss, but there was no backup plan. Getting labeled as a "rebel" would follow him to every job application.

"Good," he said as he nodded.

Ben turned to leave.

"And one more thing . . ."

He stopped.

"You must stop running."

"Sir?" Ben needed absolute clarification on this. He was hoping to hear that he should stop running the refrigerator at night, or anything that was contrary to what he thought he had heard.

"Your running caused this injury. It caused you being late all the time. To be honest, it's just a huge distraction for us here at AluMag. You will be required to stop running altogether and be a company man. Isn't that what you want to be? Like your dad, a company man."

Ben didn't know what his expression must have looked like. He had been blasted in the gut by a cannonball. There was no way around it; he had to keep the money coming in. He couldn't compete in paid running events any longer, even if he wanted to—unless they started opening water running events, that is. His family could hardly keep food on the table and the electricity on at the same time, especially with the cold Cleveland winter brewing.

"Sir, I will do anything you ask, but please, running makes me a better worker."

His boss scoffed. "I've heard it all before, Ben. It's already been decided. I need your answer now. Don't be stupid."

Ben was falling from a high cliff, gravity pulling him to the ground at breakneck speeds. The boundaries of terminal velocity seemed to no longer apply. An impossible question lay before him, and he had to decide his fate this very moment.

He could lie, he considered. Independent of his situation, his integrity was too robust. His father taught him that. His father also taught him that life was about putting food on the table and that the only thing you needed beside work was to spend time with your family. No time for hobbies. No time for dreams. No hope of anything better.

Mr. Peterson crossed his arms and looked up at the clock. "Come on, what's your decision, boy?"

Ben stood tall, pulled his shoulders back, and lifted his head. His filter had finally and catastrophically failed. "Sorry sir, you got the wrong man to be your slave. Wash your own fucking floors, sausage boy."

***

"You said what?" Daniel howled.

Ben's pride at standing up for himself diminished rapidly upon seeing his father's expression. What was funny to his brother was appalling to his dad.

His brother egged on the conversation. "Come on, tell me what he looked like after you said that."

"Nah, Daniel, don't worry about it . . . It's done." Ben looked at his dinner plate. Untouched noodles and beans. He could feel his dad's heavy eyes, which weighed him down in shame. Eyes he couldn't look into tonight and perhaps not for uncountable nights.

His dad huffed a breath, then stood from the table. "I need some fresh air."

Ben had never seen his father truly disappointed in him. Uncharted and turbulent waters.

***

The next morning, Ben rode his borrowed wobbly bike into downtown Cleveland. He hadn't spoken to Maya since his abrupt termination and needed to explain it to her before she heard a contorted version of it from his brother or dad. He crossed Public Square, which was a large open space in a park-like setting. An enormous Civil War monument rose high between the surrounding skyscrapers. The fountain danced as the elites meandered through the crisscrossing pathways.

Maya worked for the City. She primarily cleaned up the trash, which was strewn about by those too excellent to bother with finding a trash receptacle. She had one of the premium jobs a slummer could obtain. It didn't pay more, but it was relatively stress free. They could work at their own pace so long as they weren't caught sitting on a bench all day. The only other job requirement was that they had to be attractive. The workforce was comprised almost entirely of youthful women who didn't cause as much of a stir with the businessmen strutting through the city during the workweek.

Ben spotted one of her coworkers dressed in the evergreen-colored vest with the City logo printed on the back. They recognized each other but hadn't actually met before. "Hey, I was looking for Maya. Do you know where she is?"

She pointed her chin across the park. "Check over by the statue of that guy sitting in a chair . . . The green one."

"Okay, thanks." Ben knew of the statue but had no idea who he was. It was frowned upon for a slummer to be in the city center, let alone peruse the historical plaques. There was no need for slummers to get inspired by the Civil War monuments. Everything was exactly the way the elites wanted it—segregated.

As he hobbled across the expansive space, using his bike as a crutch, he spotted another green vest that looked like it could be Maya. The figure began walking, which removed any doubt. It was her, and the way she strolled was unmistakable—adorable.

He whistled two tones, which she didn't notice. He continued getting closer and did so again. This time, she snapped her head in his direction, and at fifty feet away, her smile radiated a warmth comparable only to the sun. She looked around quickly, then headed toward him and gave him a bear hug.

"What the heck are you doing here?" she asked. Ben had only been here a few times, as she worked during the same hours as he. "Shouldn't you be at work?"

He shrugged. "Um, yeah, well there's an interesting story about that."

She looked at him in a way that he already knew he would have to dig himself out of a hole.

He explained the entire conversation with Mr. Peterson. He also shared his regretful dinner conversation with his dad.

"You know you're never gonna work in this city again . . . Why did you say that?"

"I don't know . . . it just kinda slipped out."

She shook her head. "Slipped out? You know, Ben, I understand your decision, but you can't be burning bridges like that."

She was right, and he knew it. But he also thought back to that moment, and at no point did he feel like he made a conscious decision to say those words. It felt good to blow out the release valve, but there was never a chance to weigh the consequence. "I know. It was foolish, but I can't take it back now. They don't want me at the factory. He told me that he was considering canning me before anyway."

"Come here." She reached out and hugged him again. "I love you . . . just don't be stupid."

An elite walked by at that moment and shouted obscenities about their public display of hugging.

"Love you, too. We're gonna to be okay. I promise."

She looked over her shoulder. "I gotta get back to work . . . We will talk more later."

They parted ways and Ben headed home. The conversation had gone better than he expected.

Chapter Sixteen

Ben felt as if he were the first fish who had evolved to walk on land. It was already late October, and Lake Erie had become increasingly frigid.

His foot hadn't ached for some time now, and Ben had finally been given the green light by Coach Sands to go for his first jog.

"Jog. Do you understand the premise?" Coach asked. He looked as enthusiastic as Ben for this symbolic milestone.

"Coach, I hear you speaking, but I am a runner and do not understand what you are saying. What is this word, *jog*?" Ben said, looking up into the crisp blue sky. He laughed from deep within. As he looked back at his loyal coach, he got the evil eye. "Okay, okay, I got it. Jog."

They were at one of the last remaining cinder tracks in Cleveland. Smokestacks from a shut-down steel plant loomed overhead, casting an ominous long, dark shadow across the second turn. The grassy infield was overgrown and filled with broken bottles and plastic bags, and Ben had even seen a used diaper along the backstretch. The inner two lanes, although unmarked, remained relatively clear of weeds despite the decades-long abandonment.

"One mile, Ben. Okay . . . and *slow*."

Ben offered a grin, testing his face's elasticity. However embroiled in his enthusiasm, something else was lurking. An unidentified fear itching at his psyche. Just because Coach thought his body was ready for a return to the track didn't mean that his body was in agreement. Ben's opinion seemingly didn't matter in this equation.

What he did know was that if he rounded the second lap and his foot started to hurt again, especially after he gave up his job for this, it would all be over. He would decide to run into the lake, perpendicular to the shore, until he escaped into Canada or, more likely than not, sank to the darkest and coldest depths reserved for long-lost shipwrecks and the fabled serpent of Lake Erie, South Bay Bessie herself. He would become her chum.

He scuffed his feet on the track, kicking up a small cloud of dust. Memories flooded in of his racing days. His own speed generating eddies in his wake. Jogging was foreign to him. It had been nearly three months of water work, and it all culminated in this singular moment.

He inhaled deeply and leaned forward into a perpetual motion that carried him down the track, his once-fractured foot beneath him. "It will grow back stronger than before," Coach had once said.

There was nothing more satisfying than running again. The one thing that he loved so very dearly had been snatched away from him without warning or consent. It was held captive for months, then finally released, allowing him to taste it once more. Anything more than a single lick was strictly forbidden. Not even enough to draw a sweat, but it would have to satisfy his craving, his addiction.

"Slow down," Coach yelled across the track.

Ben couldn't believe how good his legs felt. The rotation was goofy, perhaps rubbery, but he felt strong. His lungs and heart had evolved from his lake running into something nearly unrecognizable.

As he rounded out the final lap and headed over to his coach, he wanted to do more. The workout had not quenched his thirst. It left him more parched than when he had begun the short run. His addiction raged—a forest fire creating its own vortex of self-feeding wind.

"Can I do another half mile?" he asked as he walked over to his coach, who had been sitting on the partially caved-in metal bleachers.

"Nope," he said nonnegotiably and without hesitation, as if he was prepared for the question. "How do you feel?"

"Great. I want to do more."

"Nope. Any aches and pains?"

"Foot doesn't hurt at all. One more lap?"

"Nope. Anything else sore?"

"My Achilles is a little weird, that's all."

Coach Sands's face twisted, looked at the eager young man. "Get some ice on it tonight, stay off your feet, and see you again tomorrow—another test run."

Ben nodded while rubbing his Achilles, hopeful that it was nothing more than working his way back into things. He hated the lake.

***

Ben walked on the track toward Coach as the cinders crushed beneath his feet. His mind played games with him, as everything started to ache, hurt, or pull. It had been twenty-four hours since his first run, and every minute in between, Ben could think of nothing else.

"You ready to try again?" Coach asked. He looked worried.

"Yeah, but I don't know *how* I should be right now. What's normal?"

"Just slow it down a bit from yesterday. If it's worse than yesterday, we pull the plug. Got it?"

"Slow down? I couldn't slow down if I wanted to. You mean . . . walk?"

He nodded casually. "If that's what it takes, then yes."

"How am I going to train if I am walking?" He knew the answer, but the question needed to be asked. "You mean I stay swimming with the fishes?"

Another nod. Coach stood from the bleachers and called him closer. "Okay, listen. If you are only running right now with this slow ramp-up, you're gonna lose your hard-earned conditioning. We gotta mix it up, but it will take some weeks, Ben." He sighed. "Something we need to be conscious of is if we don't play our cards right, and you get reinjured with something new, the lake is going to get too cold for workouts. I don't think you want to wade through the ice blocks for a workout, right?"

Ben inhaled deeply, closed his eyes, and shouted a profanity into the cool air.

"You okay?" Coach asked. He was asking about something more fragile than his foot.

Ben returned from his distant gaze to Coach. "Yeah, I'm okay."

"Good. Get a half mile of walking and jogging, then head back out to the lake for a tempo workout."

He inhaled deeply at the disappointing news. "Yeah, okay, Coach."

"Oh, and Ben, when you're out there in the lake . . . Use this frustration and hammer the crap out of it."

A light laugh escaped him. "I don't think that's gonna be a problem."

Chapter Seventeen

"Water is getting cold," Ben said to his coach. They looked out over the ghetto together from the window in Coach's seventh-floor apartment. A November storm was rumbling outside, stacked high with dark clouds and ferocious gusts of wind. The clouds moved rapidly and powerfully across the turbulent sky. Sheets of rain hammered on the glass, relentless in its effort to clean the dirt-filled slums of its impurities. It was mesmerizing, and they were both captured by its rawness.

Coach's arms were crossed, with one hand half covering his mouth. "Yeah, I think our window of getting you back on the roads is closing. You need to run in the lake every day when it's possible while you still can. Nobody knows when the season will shift, but it could be soon, and it's going to change overnight without warning. How's the ramp-up with your running going?"

"Oh, not bad, but slow. The aches are going away. Each day I'm getting a little more distance while running and have phased out the walking." He bit his lip, still unsatisfied that he wasn't back in the full swing of things yet.

"What is it, two weeks now?" He looked at Ben. "I think you're ready to pick up the pace a bit. Need to get you road worthy as soon as possible." He tapped lightly on the glass with his knuckle. "I really don't like the look of this."

"I'm feeling good. This morning before the storm came in, I ran a mile. I tested a couple faster stretches, and everything seems to be going well. Followed up with two hours in the lake."

"You have already proven yourself as a wholehearted warrior. I wouldn't ever want to compete against such a determined athlete as you."

"Yeah, well, I am sure bone density is included in the base athlete package of the elites. Those guys would never know what I am going through. Poor man's injury."

"You're right. They haven't ever had to deal with this. But remember one thing, which is different than many events. The 5000-meter race requires much more than just endurance training, speed training, and a boosted DNA bill. It requires strategy, a learnable skill. Instincts, which can't be coded. And as much as anything else, it requires mental toughness and guts. Not many events are as intense and grueling as the 5000. An event where you can *think* yourself into failure. And nobody you will ever compete against has been hardened like you have over the past months. A man with nothing to lose and everything to gain is a dangerous opponent."

His depth of appreciation for Ben's passion could only come from having lived it as well. He knew that Ben was on the verge of a breakthrough, and also knew the relentless fight required climbing to the top.

Ben looked through the glass, through the storm, and into the eyes of the competition. Nobody was going to be better prepared than he was. That would be impossible.

"When you race against these elites, remember one thing: They may be designed to run an amazing 5000 meters, and they have been trained by the best to do so. However, when it comes right down to it . . . When you are gliding along side by side with them, who is willing to dig a little deeper? Who is willing to dig down so deep, that one could never imagine the hurt that lies in front of them? Do they have that motivation? Will they dig a little deeper to please their well-funded daddies who chose that life for them? For the family name or maybe to pick up girls? What I mean is this: What in their entire existence is going to motivate them to dig down as deep as you? I want you to think about that during your next workouts. Day in and day out."

A lump grew in his throat. He teetered on the edge of confidence and fear. "I will, Coach. I will also think about it in Oregon during the final mile."

He smiled and patted Ben on the back.

"And Ben, one more thing." He looked toward his bookshelf to avert his eyes before returning to him. His lips curled, with emotions tugging at him. "I am so proud of you. Not just because of your running, but because you refuse to allow this . . . this system to swallow you. Your fight against their attempt to conform you to these low standards. You have inspired me as well . . . to take a more proactive approach like I once did so many years ago. Things in my life, which you have helped me get past. Dark things that only I will ever know."

Ben didn't know what he was referring to, but he understood all too well. He couldn't find words to express his gratefulness. All he could muster was a tear in the eye. "Thank you . . . for everything."

Ben looked out the window once more as the heavens grew darker and borderline demonic. The rain hammered into the building as waves of wind accelerated the drops like shrapnel exploding from a landmine.

"Coach?"

He turned to look at Ben. "Yeah?"

Ben nodded as his confidence grew. "I gotta go. I need to get in another water run workout now."

Coach looked out the window and raised his eyebrows. "Now?"

"Yeah, you know. I'm gonna get wet anyway, right?"

Chapter Eighteen

Ben woke to a shiver, turning to find only more cold sheets. It must have been in the middle of the night because his room was pitch-black and dead silent. He was restless. The cold bit at his toes, and now it had crept through the worn blanket. He was losing his battle to maintain body temperature, so he pulled the blanket over his shoulders, wrapped it tight with his chin above the fabric shield, and headed to the living room. His bare feet were greeted by ice-cold laminate.

Ben's breath pushed out in a cloud, leading the way. They always let the thermostat run low to save on electricity, but tonight there was a much more severe edge. A bite that Tent City endured every night through the harsh winter months. Year after year, slowly ebbing away the elderly and children alike.

This winter was being reported as one of the coldest on record. In December already, a low-pressure cell dropped down from the north like it had taken a superhighway for arctic temperatures.

Usually the apartment was brighter, even in the deepest hour of the night. Ben peered out of the ice-frosted window and recognized that the streetlights were dark. *Must be a power outage*, he thought. He turned to the kitchen, and the digital clock display was also blank, confirming his suspicion. The power went out frequently in the winter, and with their all-electric heating, that meant they were in for a cold night.

Ben pulled out an extra blanket that was neatly folded below a small end table beside the couch. He wrapped that one around him as well. This one went up over the top of his head and just below his nose. He breathed into the blanket, attempting to warm it, as it, too, was ice-cold.

It was December 10, a Sunday, which Ben wouldn't soon forget. Temperatures dropped to minus eighteen, a record for December, and a severe wind chill ripping off the lake added an unnecessary extra might.

As he went back to his bedroom, he suddenly appreciated that his return to running had been successful. The window for running in the lake had not just been shut, but rather frozen over.

"What's going on?" Daniel asked, still mostly asleep, lying in his own bed a mere foot away from Ben's.

"Power's out," Ben said as he climbed back into bed with his double-stacked blankets, looking like a microwavable frozen burrito. "Go back to sleep."

"It's freezing."

Ben snorted. "Yeah, I envy the slummers living in Miami, Florida, huh."

His brother didn't respond. He'd probably fallen back to sleep or froze to death. Ben was no longer in a condition to sleep. He had gotten enough rest that there was no chance of fading back into his pillow, but not enough to get him through the day. His eyes were wide open, staring into the vastness of his dark room. Only edges of objects could be identified as his vision adjusted.

Images of a summer track race in Oregon crept into his mind's eye. Sunshine beamed down on the athletes, creating a vivid scene of colors in contrast to the grays of the Cleveland winter. Sweat dripped from his brow while rounding into the backstretch. The surroundings filled with intense forest greens and wildflowers offering their pollen to bobbing bees.

The cold had been chased away, at least a little. Ben spent more time fantasizing about his hopes and dreams than he did thinking about the current moment. Covering the weekly mileage that he did, it would be impossible without this competence.

***

As dawn emerged, the apartment glowed in a silvery overcast. Ben waited for hours for a touch of light to justify exiting his self-made cocoon. He pulled on three different shirts, sweatpants over his long underwear, and three pairs of hole riddled socks. He had utilized almost 50 percent of his wardrobe and added 20 percent to his total mass.

The three Brandt men sat shoulder to shoulder with one another on the couch, sharing a communal duvet. Mouths hidden beneath the edge to capture the warm breath before it escaped forever into the bitter coldness. Dad was in the middle surrounded by his grown boys, all crammed together.

Breaking a long moment of silence, Ben's dad began to laugh.

"I wish your mother could see this," he said, muffled through the blanket.

Ben turned his head toward him. His dad rarely spoke of her.

"I remember, oh gosh, I guess it was just after Daniel was born ... we lost power like this. She always kept candles around." He snorted. "She loved those stupid things. We all tucked into the bathroom, lit probably two dozen candles, and placed towels at the bottom of the door to seal off the gap to keep the cold air from rushing in."

Small lines appeared around his eyes as his cheeks lifted, revealing that he was smiling beneath the blanket.

"Oh, that room got so smoky. It was hard to breathe. I don't know, I guess after an hour or so, we had to rush back into the freezing living room just to get some fresh air.

"Oh, I miss her so much." The lines disappeared as his eyes gazed into the open room. "Ben, you have no idea how much you remind me of her. She was *so* stubborn ... She hated living here in the slums, just like you. Not even for a single moment did she accept that we would live our lives out in this shithole."

It was now Ben who was smiling. Something about feeling connected to his mom brought a wave of hope. He'd grown up without his mother, which in his case also meant that he'd grown up as the family's black sheep. He was the apple of her tree, a connection he had never actually met.

"She would have been so proud of you with your running . . ." He paused, perhaps to carefully not overcommit. "I know I am hard on you guys. This life we live is so . . . so brutal. I don't know what the heck I am doing sometimes. All I know is that we need food on the table to survive, and we need each other. The only way I know how to do both is by working hard at the foundry. It's our only chance. We have no money to invest in the future, and I know that means you are going to hand down these miserable lives to your future children. But together, the Brandt boys, we have each other to hold one another up. Your children will hold you up as you hold me. That is exactly what family is. We must cherish our time together."

"Yeah, just wish Ben didn't lose his stupid job. Now we gotta cover him, too." Daniel added in disdain.

There was an idea that Ben had toyed with, but only now did he know for certain. He had saved for his next races, but he knew where it really belonged. Most of it anyway.

He slid out from beneath the blanket and headed to his dresser in the bedroom. In the back of the top drawer, behind his socks, he pulled out the envelope.

He reached in and pulled out a stack of bills, quickly counted through them, and returned just a few alongside his accumulated race bibs.

Once back at the couch, he tucked under the cover again. "Here."

"What's that? Where did you get that, Ben?" his dad asked.

"It's not just a hobby, Dad. This is for the family account."

The family account was nothing more than a small wooden box that his dad kept hidden in his bedroom. It was their life savings. A life savings that trickled down to as little as five dollars most months and occasionally contained nothing more than dust. Banks wouldn't touch a slummer, but the Brandts never had enough to make a bank account worthwhile even if they had.

"How much is there, you hoarder?" his brother shouted into the blanket.

"About twelve."

"It's a lot more than twelve dollars," Daniel replied.

Ben smiled and leaned over his dad to obtain eye contact with his brother. "Twelve hundred, you moron. It's my race money."

Their dad grabbed the stack. "Ben, I will keep this in the box. But we will not use it unless we absolutely must, and even then, we will repay you every cent. Your mom would have my hide if I took your race money. Especially after I called you a fool for chasing your dreams."

Ben was speechless. His heart warmed. His body was still freezing.

Chapter Nineteen

Ben's dad raised his plastic cup of low-end wine. "This has been another great year. I look at my boys and their wonderful ladies, and this old man couldn't be prouder."

Ben looked at Maya. She was astonishing. He was amazed that this perfect jewel of the slums had not just chosen him but adored him. He raised his cup to join the others.

The mismatched plastic cups clicked together.

"To another great year, Dad." Daniel said.

"Hear, hear," Ben added.

New Year's Eve was a day of hope, even in the slums. Hope was about another year of survival opposed to gaining wealth or fame. Hope of staying healthy, keeping a miserable job, and maintaining their dismal residence. There was never hope of moving upward; it was merely the prevention of the downward spiral pulling at them relentlessly. Hope to not succumb to its gravity.

Ben looked out the window, which was glazed with ice crystals around the perimeter. Despite the cold night, the streets were enchanted with activity. Mobs of neighbors huddled around trash cans with fires burning within. Smells of burnt plastic wafted through the air and even drifted through the closed window of their apartment. The tradition of celebrating New Year's under the stars was in full effect. Part of him wanted to join the big party just once, even though it wasn't his scene, just for the experience of it. But it was forbidden by his dad because it always ended up being drunken and disorderly.

"I love New Year's," Maya whispered in his ear. She stood beside him at the window, looking out into the night. One arm wrapped around him tightly. She raised her cup to just him as the others were now in the kitchen discussing the foundry. "Here's to us."

Ben smiled. "We gonna get married this year?"

Her eyes twinkled. She exaggerated her nod to ensure there were no mixed signals in her confirmation. "Yup."

"I guess you already got the event all figured out, huh?"

She smiled wildly like a child would when asked to say cheese for a photo. "My parents got married at Edgewater Park on August 23."

Ben was surprised. It sounded like she had a plan already, and even a date in mind. Furthermore, that it was one in the same as her parents' unsuccessful union. "Let me see that ring?"

Her face glowed in the bluish light cast through the window, and her hair was highlighted in yellow from the family room light behind her. "I love it, Ben. It's gorgeous."

He absorbed how beautiful her thin fingers were. She improved the ring, not the other way around, he thought.

Her smile was contagious. He already knew the answer but asked anyway. "Do you wanna get married at Edgewater, then?"

She nodded, with her tongue sticking out the side of her mouth.

"On August 23?"

Her smile amplified, causing her eyes to squint. Another nod, but a small tear reflected the bluish light.

Ben leaned over, then held a long kiss before saying, "I love you, my sweet Maya."

She embraced him with a bear hug. "You, too, my scrawny little runner boy."

"Knock it off over there," Daniel shouted from the kitchen. "Want more wine?"

Ben snorted. "We're gonna get our own place one day, too. That way we can hug as much as we wish."

Daniel rolled his eyes.

They moved into the kitchen and joined the group. Maya drew Amy's attention and started chatting about their jobs. Maya picked up trash in downtown, and Amy worked at a corner store a few streets away.

Ben watched as the girls bonded with each other. They had become better friends by the day and had already become more compatible than he and his brother had ever been. This paved the way for the boys to grow as well. Ben's sense of family was maturing. It was an uncertain time for the slums, and considering the trend, it was only going to get worse.

Work was drying up, and their foundry was on the rocks. As unemployment rose, the line between those with the apartments and those in Tent City changed as well. The line had once been crudely drawn around social dysfunctions, alcoholism, psychological disorders, and physical disabilities. As the economy collapsed and the population in the slums grew, more tents were erected. The line moved upward, and even the people who were willing and able to work fell victim. Some to the tents, others to the gangs. Not everyone who was deserving had made the cut, and those that did lived in a daily fear of slipping down the food chain. The difference between one family and the next was marginal and unjust. Unemployment across the country was at historic highs, and the extended Brandt family was teetering on that edge. The Brandts, as well as the majority of Clevelanders in the slums, had no security. For the moment, they remained the fortunate ones.

Daniel asked Ben, "Hey, did you ever hear back from Mr. Peterson? I can't believe he would even let you close to the building after what you said to him."

Ben smirked. "I think I earned a little respect with him. He also now had this to hold over me. He kinda likes the power of it, I guess. Yeah, last week I stopped in . . . for the third time. They're still not hiring anyone. He actually told me that they might be making *more* cuts and that I should look elsewhere as he doesn't think things are going to improve anytime soon. He kinda opened up to me and complained about how he already doesn't have enough people to get the job done, but he has to now cut even deeper. 'Fat was gone, now they are carving out muscle,' he told me."

Their dad shook his head. "Yeah, the guys are all talking. Two guys from my team were let go recently. They're going to lose their apartments, too. One of them has a couple young kids at home. I think two boys, just like you guys were. I can't imagine what they are going through."

"That's terrible. Do you think it's going to pick up again in the spring?" Ben asked.

Dad's shoulders slumped as he leaned up against the refrigerator. "Actually, I'm kind of worried that they will shut down the foundry. The war in Europe is easing, so the demand may dry up completely. It's hard to tell, since they never share anything with us."

Daniel quickly looked over. "Really, you think?"

"I don't know, but they sure keep us in the dark," he said, shaking his head. "The other day, some executives in suits came through with their clipboards. Asked a bunch of questions of Mr. Peterson. He was sweating and looked like he was heading to the guillotine."

"Well, that explains why he was acting funny when I was—"

BANG BANG BANG.

Three gunshots rang out from the street below. They looked at each other, then all five of them rushed to the small window, squeezing together. Daniel turned off the light to cut down the glare and to avoid being noticed if it happened to be gang activity. Witnesses didn't live long. Usually their street wasn't a hotbed of gang activity. However, it was still gang territory, and everything was under their cruel thumb.

Two guys were shouting at each other, one of whom wore the brown camouflaged clothes reserved for the St.

Clair Mafia. Both of them had small groups behind them, but the Mafia were the only ones wielding weapons. Handguns and knives.

Ben couldn't make out what they said, but most likely it was about drugs, girls, money, or wrong place, wrong time.

The man confronting the gang members was in his midtwenties and lived in Ben's building. He always talked trash with his neighborhood buddies. Ben didn't like him much and usually went the other way when he saw them hanging around. They always acted like they were something special, but in the end, nobody in this neighborhood was special. He raised his hands in the air, unarmed. Friends hovered behind him in anxious anticipation.

Two more shots blasted directly into his chest. His body fell backward as his raised arms and head collapsed forward until he crashed to the street in a heap.

Half the group standing behind the now-deceased neighbor hit the dirt. The other half charged forward toward the gang members.

Many more shots marred that New Year's Eve. A day of hope was as fragile as anything else around this neighborhood. Destroyed without notice.

Six bodies lay strewn across the street as the blood froze them to the ground overnight. Just one of them was camouflaged.

Cops didn't show up until the next afternoon. Same old thing in the ghetto.

Chapter Twenty

"Quarters till death." Coach wrung his hands as an evil smile gleamed. Ben noticed that the more grueling the workout, the more playful his coach became. *Something sadistic about him*, he thought.

The air was crisp. However, the low morning sun warmed his skin as it warmed the colors across the old cinder track. Golden halos sparkled on the frost-covered weeds.

Ben scuffed his feet into the grass, which was still icy in the shadows. He knew the workout well. Even though he had only performed it a few times, workouts like these achieved a legendary status. It would be felt in his legs for days, and his heart would never forget. Quarters till death was Ben's favorite workout for these very qualities. It was the one that would hold him together in the final laps of the championship, and the one that would shove him to his knees by the end of today.

A well-trained runner had never officially died during the workout, but the toughest of them wished they had. Ben figured that everyone had a breaking point. Quarters till death would not only find that point but would place it on center stage. It had become a part of who he was, for better or for worse. He thought that fate would find you anywhere you hid. The only way to finish the workout was to die.

The frigid Cleveland winter was beginning to loosen its grip, and it had been months since Ben slithered out of Lake Erie onto dry land.

Despite the coldest winter days and the knee-high snow, the past eight weeks had been the most intense training in Ben's life to date. His legs caught up to his cardiovascular system, and from then on, he was truly breaking new ground. Two weeks before, he set his own 10,000-meter record on a training run through the towpath that had started as a moderate run and evolved unintentionally into a blood-curdling scream through the forest. He then followed it with repeat hills directly after, offering himself no mercy.

Nobody knew of Ben's training level except Coach and Maya. Ben was the secret lurking in the shadows of the giants. They had no chance to see him coming, and he was not just ready to race, he was a hurricane brewing off the coast.

The track was mostly clear from snow, which had melted into puddles that pooled in the low spots. A small drift remained in the shadowy sections of the outer lanes on the south side, where the bleachers stood.

Coach stood beside the starting line with his stopwatch. Ben joined him, stripped off his sweatpants, baring his legs to the forty-degree temperature. He grinned at Coach.

"I've been thinking about this workout all week."

Coach snorted. "Yup, I have been looking forward to it, too. Looking forward to your *death*."

Ben looked at him and shook his head. "Really?"

He laughed. "Keep it together, Ben. Focus."

Ben sneered as he toed the starting line. He felt the cinders grind against each other beneath his feet. It became clear to him why Coach wanted to be a coach. *You like to watch people suffer, don't you?*

"Ready . . . Go!" he shouted. Steam billowed from his mouth, as if he were a human starting pistol.

Ben heeded the call and sprang into motion. The grit slipped on take-off. His goal was sixty second quarters until failure. A single lap at race pace, followed by a half lap easy. Over and over again.

His pace was quick, too quick. He had a long day in front of him, and the early stages were entirely about conservation and finding the target pace. Ben hadn't done either. He came around the 200-meter mark, and Coach yelled across the field, "Twenty-six. Calm down."

Definitely too hot. He eased back, then cruised through the line at fifty-eight.

"Good, good. Nice 'n easy."

Ben's pumping heart quickly stabilized. His breathing was controlled. After the first turn of the recovery, his vitals were fully back to normal. The starting line on the backstretch came quickly. It always came quickly. Ben knew that every repeat, that same standardized 200-meter distance would somehow become shorter and shorter.

"Go," shouted Coach from across the field, exactly when Ben crossed the mark.

He rallied up into pace again and glided through the line at fifty-nine.

The second interval's rest section was indeed shorter. Ben figured that runners had somehow found a way to override the laws of physics. Relationships between distance, time, and speeds. Perhaps the laws applied differently, he thought. Perhaps it isn't when an object approaches the speed of light, but rather when a runner approaches race pace that their mass becomes infinite. A normal runner is not capable of running faster than their own race pace. Ben knew that he wasn't a normal runner. He knew that he must break the laws to progress.

"Go."

Ben had drifted off into thought until the announcement snapped him back. He punched forward on instinct to his exact race pace. His mind wasn't involved; it was his muscle memory.

Another one in the bag. *Check,* he thought to himself.

As he neared the next start, directly in front of Coach, he asked, "Having fun with the watch?"

The sadistic grin returned. "Go."

The first eight were easy, but number nine began to test his conservation effort. As Ben made his way through the midway mark in front of Coach, he looked forward, opposed to making eye contact. He had to focus.

"Thirty-two. Gotta pick it up."

Ben knew the wicked game all too well. If he missed the mark once, it was okay, but if he missed it twice in a row, the game was over . . . death. It was too early to miss the target.

Ben ratcheted up his pace and glided through right at sixty. His muscles burned as the lactic acid coursed through.

The next one came long before he could get his breath under control.

"Go."

Ben heaved forward. He had to fight his way back to pace.

"Sixty-two. Gotta get under."

He thought he had it, his first miss, and was now on probation. Two strikes equaled death, and it was too early to die.

"Fifty-six. Find your pace, Ben."

The pendulum started to swing. Overcompensation when the pace is no longer natural. Each swing became less stable, which meant that the end was near.

"Sixty-three. You're losing it. Focus, Ben."

You're losing it, Coach. Your stupid watch is broken. He knew that wasn't true, but it was the only way to shift the suffering elsewhere.

Ben blasted the next one with everything he had.

"Sixty."

The reservoir was empty. Fumes weren't enough to maintain race pace.

"Sixty-five. Ben, dig, dig, dig."

"Sixty."

He was surprised he got his pace on that one. He earned himself more suffering as a reward.

Ben contemplated lying on the track before his next lap started. He considered that death was inevitable and he might as well cave to the natural and organic process of decomposition. There was never a winner in this workout. *Just like life,* he thought. *Everyone dies. Everyone must hang up their shoes at the end of the day. When life is over, there is only one question. Am I proud of what I accomplished?*

"Sixty-four. Come on, Ben, hang in there."

His legs were numb. Saturated in lactic acid. Lungs burned as if the raging fire had coated them with ash. His heart pounded in heavy, rapid pulses. An image crossed his mind of Cyrus, Archer, and Eric, jogging up to the starting line with him. *You guys are going down. I will bury you.*

"Go. Make this one count, Ben. Dig, dig, dig." Spit flew from Coach's mouth.

Ben laid it all out, racing side by side with the DNA laboratory experiments. He could hardly lift his knees any longer. Every stride was a monumental effort. His pace was choppy, requiring constant surges.

"Sixty-one. Okay, you're done." Coach clapped at his funeral.

Ben fell to his knees, elbows and forearms planted on the cinders. He panted like a panda in labor. The cold air burned.

Coach walked over. "Good workout, Ben—seventeen, a new record."

Ben knew his race was twelve and a half laps, twelve and a half quarters nonstop. He couldn't imagine maintaining his target speed for the full 5000 meters.

Between breaths as he stood again, he said, "That was freaking brutal."

"Always is," Coach added. "Okay, ten miles easy, see you tomorrow."

Ben bent over his knees, still panting. "Right on, Coach. See you tomorrow. Get some rest tonight, okay?"

Coach laughed as he walked toward his bike without turning. "You did good today."

The ten-miler was a walk in the park after that workout. He took it easy as intended and allowed it to be a fantasy run. A run where the mind was encouraged to daydream to its fullest extent. To lounge in the fantasies of greatness. Ben let the visions of the championships run wild. His fantasy excluded the pain and suffering that was required to truly achieve greatness, but after quarters till death, he had enough misery for one day. A runner's fantasies could only be explained as arrogant and conceited if anyone could watch the reel. It was a necessity of the sport but could never be shared with anyone else. The secret dreams of a dreamer, too extreme to be understood.

Despite the feeling of defeat, which quarters till death always promised, there was also the other side. While being tortured, everyone caved. It was only a matter of time. Today, Ben had forged himself in the fiery pits of the foundry and had been crafted into a gleaming steel weapon of destruction. He was hardened, both physically and mentally. Ben had never run at levels like this before, and Coach Sands was responsible for it. He imagined that he was a fire-breathing dragon flying down upon the stadium to scorch his competition. Sear the hatred from the stands. He would perch on the scoreboard, overseeing the chaos and destruction he had created. Watching the faces look upon him in fear and in wonder. His fantasy was vivid, albeit slightly unrealistic. He would need to do it without fire and wings. However, he would see their fear and wonder nonetheless.

***

His muscles burned each time he stood or even moved for that matter. He climbed down the steps from his apartment on his way to meet Coach for his long run. Each step resulted in a groan, a grunt, or a moan.

Sitting on the bench was his sadist. But today, as Ben approached, he could tell that he wasn't enjoying the role.

"How you feeling?" he asked. His voice was hollow and eyes puffy.

Ben smiled and attempted to brighten the gloom. "I feel fantastic, Coach."

It was only partially true, as he did feel like crap. However, his confidence was flying high from yesterday's workout. He already knew, but he asked anyway. "What have we got today?"

"Just a long run . . . as you feel. Shoot for twenty, but don't overdo it."

Ben nodded. He already knew the planned workout and had already decided he was going to journey over to the west side of Cleveland along the lake into Rocky River or maybe even to Bay Village.

"Hey. Come up to the apartment when you're done. Okay?"

He knew something was wrong and that his coach was waiting to tell him something terrible. Something that needed to be put off because it was most likely unbearable. He could see it in his eyes. "All right, Coach, see you soon."

The run was slow and easy. His heart rate thumped in a gentle rhythm. He enjoyed the views of Lake Erie peeking between the mega-wealthy homes of Cleveland as he transitioned to Lake Road. The palaces could support ten families but didn't. He knew that the residents of Tent City, who had taken over much of Industrial Valley, would be forever grateful to sleep on the floor of a garage during the worst winter days. However, these garages were off-limits and reserved for the extravagant toys of the four-wheeled type.

Initially he intended to run through the parks in Rocky River, but he couldn't shake the feeling about Coach and the expected discussion. Ben turned at the ten-mile mark. He had to know what was going on.

Upon his return, he knocked on the door, which was left partially open.

"Come in, Ben."

He entered. Across the room, by the window, Coach sat at his table with several papers and envelopes chaotically laid out. He approached and could feel the gloom permeating. *Is Coach sick?* he thought.

"Come, sit down." He pointed to the chair.

Ben sat as he was instructed.

"So . . ." He paused, apparently looking for the right words. "For you to compete in the championships, you need to run a sanctioned race this season."

Ben's stomach dropped. He knew exactly what was happening. For months, Ben knew the risk and chose to push it aside. No sense worrying about something that he couldn't control, he thought. *You can't live in fear of a risk, but that doesn't mean the risk won't become reality.* He needed to post a time that qualified him to race at the championships. But that time had to be achieved at an official event to ensure there were no falsified results.

"So, I applied at every sanctioned event I could think of. Well, I got a bunch of responses in the past few days." He sighed as he pushed the mass of papers toward Ben.

He looked at the pile of papers. His dreams hung in the hands of the elite event organizers.

"None of them will accept a slummer. Some accuse slummers of not having the medical history to disprove performance-enhancing drug use. Others state that it is mandatory to have an official sponsor or be a member of an elite track and field club. One of them had the audacity to simply say that slummers aren't welcome."

"That's bullshit, Coach. I don't take drugs. I haven't ever taken anything. And how can *I* get into an elite track club when they also forbid slummers?"

"I know. Even if we could prove that you haven't, you know what's really happening, right?"

Ben knew exactly what was happening. A slummer racing in the championship was bad for business. The organizers would risk losing the viewership that Harvey Woodard had built over his lifetime.

"Has everyone answered?"

"Almost. There's a couple still out there. But I guess they won't even respond."

Ben's face crumpled. His hands shot over his eyes, then he slammed them on the table in white-knuckled fists. "Every freaking step . . . they . . . they just try to crush me. I freaking hate this place . . . this world is never going to give me a chance at anything."

Coach inhaled deeply. "No, Ben, it's not going to *give* you anything. You gotta take it."

"I'm trying to." His eyes blurred as he fought back tears of rage.

"I know, I know . . . Well, I don't want to get our hopes up because it's a long shot, but I have one more idea. I know a guy. I really don't think it would be his decision in the end, but I have to try."

"Yeah?"

Coach reached across the table and placed his hand on Ben's clenched fists. "Don't get too excited. Keep training like the machine you are, and I'll worry about getting you into a sanctioned event. Okay?"

Ben sucked in a deep breath. "Thank you, Coach. No matter what happens. We know that we belong there. This has been the best time of my life."

"Me too. Me too, Ben."

Chapter Twenty-One

"Hey buddy," Ben said to Logan outside Coach's apartment. He was wrapped up in multiple layers as he splashed through the half-mud, half-slush puddles.

"Hi," he said softly. Eyes captivated by Maya, who smiled at him.

His mom was sitting on the bench, and for the first time, she spoke to Ben. "You have a good soul."

Ben pulled his head back. "Um. Thank you."

"I mean, nobody even looks at my boy, and somehow you are the only one he talks about. He loves that you are outside every day, too. He wants to be a runner someday."

"Oh, well, he is a very nice boy, and he looks like he could be a fast runner." He looked at him and winked. Logan winked in return, then giggled.

"Anyway, I don't think he is home. That guy you always meet here. Haven't seen him in a few days actually, but I guess he could have come home when I wasn't looking."

"Okay, thanks."

"Thank you," Maya added. She turned to Ben and asked, "Should we try anyway?"

Ben nodded, then pulled open the old creaky door to Coach's apartment building.

"You think he is back?" asked Maya.

"Hey guys, where are you going?" said a familiar voice from over their shoulders outside the building.

"Coach," Ben said. "We were just checking in. Didn't know if you got back yet or not. Where have you been?"

"He was worried about you," Maya said.

Ben shot a glare at her.

He waved for them to follow him to his apartment. Ben grabbed Coach's duffle bag for him and threw the strap over his shoulder. As they ascended the seven flights of stairs, Coach asked, "How is the running going?"

Ben was more interested in what Coach had been up to but played the game anyway. "Great. I mean really great. I've followed our workout plan exactly, and I couldn't feel stronger. Not even exhausted."

They went back and forth, discussing aches, pains, sleep, and resting heart rate statistics to ensure nothing was getting out of hand. Everything checked out.

"Come on, you gotta tell us where you were. We stopped by every single day for the past week checking in on you."

"Ah. Yes, I have been busy." While rounding out the last flight of stairs, he perked up, noticeably proud.

Ben knew that he carried good news, but what exactly was killing him.

"You know how those letters I sent out to get you into the sanctioned races didn't pan out? So, I started making some phone calls. I mean, I called everybody I have ever met in the running community. Anything to get a window to open or even see through a crack for an opportunity. Nothing. Zip. I figured these guys hid behind the phone, and after they hung up, I would be sooner out of sight, out of mind—a simple brush-off."

"Wow, you're persistent. Just like Ben," Maya said, then chuckled to herself.

Ben sarcastically glared at her.

"Come, let's sit down first." He unlocked the door to his apartment. "Take a seat on the couch. I'll be right back."

"Really, at this part of the story, you leave us hanging?" Ben said. He dropped the bag by the door.

"Can an old guy take a leak? Sheesh." He turned and headed down the short hall toward the restroom."

Maya smacked Ben on the shoulder.

"What, I can't wait to hear . . ."

She glared back at him to clamp his lips shut, which he did.

Ben looked around the apartment from his position on the couch. Nothing had changed since last time, but the place smelled musty, as if it hadn't been opened up in a year.

Coach returned down the hall. "Anybody else gotta go?" he asked, then laughed at Ben's noticeable impatience.

"Okay. So, where was I?"

Ben scowled at him, which Coach apparently thought was hilarious. Maya was also finding the scenario entertaining.

He pulled over a chair toward them and sat facing the couch. "Anyway, I decided I needed to get right in their faces, so it was harder for them to shove me out the door. Maybe I could get in a few more words of convincing, you know. So, I rented a car and hit the road all week. Picked out the closest ones first and thought maybe I could get lucky somewhere."

Both Ben and Maya hung on the edge of the couch. Captivated by Coach's positive attitude. Ben knew something worked out. He *must* have gotten something worked out.

"I was shoved off at a few. I'll never tell you all the details, but one of them went really bad . . . Got taken to the police station in cuffs for trespassing, which I clearly wasn't. But you know, black man on campus is sure to raise some eyebrows." He shook his head to push the memory away. "But finally, the head track coach at Kent State University was willing to listen to your story. He was at Malachi and was curious how you have been doing. What kinda training you do, that sort of stuff."

"Kent?" Ben said softly. He felt the whisper of potential becoming a turning point in his life. He hadn't heard what Coach was about to say yet but had already started fantasizing about racing there.

"Well, he was extremely impressed by your progress. I told him the type of workouts you're doing, weekly mileage, intensity, that sort of stuff. He is a Cleveland guy, too. Not the same way we are—he's not a slummer—but he showed a spark of pride for his native city. I got a sense that he considers you a hope . . . He bought me lunch, actually, and we talked for hours."

"So, can I race?"

"Well, that isn't as easy as it sounds. You're gonna need to take several drug tests, get some immunization shots, fill in a bunch of forms . . . But he said that if you can get this stuff submitted in time, he would get you a position at the race."

"Yes." Ben jumped to his feet. Fist pumped into the air high overhead.

He turned to Maya, who quickly added a smile upon making eye contact with him. She didn't seem as enthusiastic.

"One thing, Ben: this stuff is gonna be expensive."

Ben sat again, deflated. "How much?"

"Could be nearly two thousand dollars. The biggest problem is the immunization shots. Since the elites already have an upgraded DNA structure, they don't need the shots. That means they are primarily for slummers who work in close proximity to the elites . . . So, naturally they push the prices up. But Ben, some of it I already paid for. And the rest, maybe we can split between us. I will help you out as much as I can. I don't have much, but I couldn't have a better way of spending it."

"Oh, I can't let you do this." Ben thought about his road race money, still saved in his dad's bedroom. He didn't have enough.

He nodded assuredly. "Ben, don't worry about it."

"I guess there isn't prize money, huh?"

He shook his head. "Everything from here on out costs money, it doesn't pay money."

"Everything?"

"Yup. Entrance fees, travel arrangements, the paperwork."

He hadn't predicted that he might find his way, and then not be able to afford to race.

Coach leaned in close, as Ben's face began to hang. "Ben, if I die broke, and you had the chance to see this dream all the way through, I would die a happy man ... Understand?"

Ben nodded but still felt like the good news walloped him on the head with the sting of reality.

"So, we doing this?"

Ben nodded, building with more enthusiasm. "When is the race?"

"April 1."

Ben pushed back. "You're joking with me?"

Coach Sands laughed. "No, Ben, it's real. The race is on April 1. But it's 100 percent real. Remember, if you can't qualify for the national championship at Kent with your time, you could still qualify for Penn Relays, or Sea Ray to give it another shot."

Ben inhaled deeply, pumped both fists into the air, and screamed at the top of his lungs, "Yeah."

"You got four weeks, Ben."

As they left the apartment, Ben gave Coach a hefty hug. "I can't believe how much you have done for me. I'll never forget this."

"Let's not end the good memories here, got it?" He smiled with a fatherly pride.

Ben and Maya headed down the stairs, and as soon as they broke into the fresh outdoors, they began their long slow run together into the Metroparks.

"I can't believe I've got a chance to qualify. Can you imagine?"

Maya matched him stride for stride. "You're gonna be amazing."

"You don't sound so enthusiastic?" He turned to examine her expression.

"Ben, I'm extremely happy for you."

"Well, why do you look like your cat just got run over?"

"Sorry, Ben. I'm just tired or something. I couldn't be happier for you, for us. I know you're going to do a great job."

Ben wasn't convinced. Her tone was off, as if something was eating at her. Something that started during the discussion with Coach. Maybe the money was bothering her, he thought. Maybe she saw it all as a waste . . . for nothing.

"Come on Maya, what's up?" he prodded.

Maya stopped dead in her tracks beneath a large maple tree hanging over the path. "You're an idiot, Ben. Just drop it."

Ben was certainly not known for dropping things. "You mad that I am going to run at Kent? Is it the money?"

She scoffed. "The money? Come on, Ben. Just let it go. Everything is fine. I am really proud of you."

She wasn't fine. He could see her long face shadowed by the tree. She looked tired indeed, but not from a lack of sleep. She worried about something. "Maya, you can tell me anything."

She sighed, then looked up into the tree for apparent answers. "I know you're going to do great, and that you deserve everything coming your way, but . . ."

Ben dropped his head but maintained eye contact, anticipating her next point.

"I am terrified of how they are going to treat you. The fans, the media, the other athletes."

"You don't want me to run?"

"Absolutely not. I demand that you run that race, which is why I didn't say anything ... But you forced me to. Aren't I allowed to worry for you without you dissecting me like some frog in a school class?"

Ben felt foolish. He clearly forced it out but was glad to know what was eating at her. That doubt would have been more devastating than the truth. "Come on, let's keep running ... It's *those* guys who gotta be worried ... I'm gonna be the one teasing them. Tell them they can't run without having DNA boosters." He started to laugh. Maya reciprocated until both of them were almost rolling on the ground.

"You good?" he asked.

She tightened her lips and nodded.

"Good."

She rolled her eyes. "You're going to show them who's boss, that's for sure."

Still standing beneath the tree, Ben nodded in the direction of the trail. "Let's go."

So, they began running again. However, Ben's enthusiasm was dampened. *Should I be worried? How bad is this going to get?* For the next hour and a half, he couldn't get it out of his mind. The unknown could be much worse than he expected. Maya had a sense for things, and he needed to prepare for the worst.

His silence was noted.

"Ben, don't worry about it. I am sure I am overreacting. Just let your legs do the talking. You won't even need to open your mouth."

Legs do the talking, he thought to himself. He wasn't going to let his legs talk . . . he was going to let them scream. Belittle them with surges, insult them with a ferocious pace, and offend them with a finishing kick that would blow barn doors off their hinges. He would melt them into puddles of goo. This was Ben's voice.

Chapter Twenty-Two

Ben picked at the decaying wood of the bench seat as small pieces crumbled beneath his fingernails. He decided to stop, however the satisfaction of the chunks breaking free was too great to resist. Something primal lured him into the destruction.

Three weeks feels like an eternity when you are a five-year-old looking forward to Christmas. Ben's last three weeks leading up to the Kent race were longer. Much longer.

"How are you feeling?" Coach asked, sitting on the bench beside Ben.

He nodded. "Yeah, I feel good. Kinda want to get it over with, though."

Maya squeezed his leg. "Don't forget to enjoy it."

Ben raised his eyebrows, then smiled. "What, you don't think I am having fun?"

"As much fun as an old dog going to the vet for the last time," she said.

Coach interrupted. "All right, Ben, no worries. I know the time to qualify for the national championship is a lofty goal today. But remember, if you at least qualify for Penn Relays, which is much easier, then you will get to race against the very big boys head-to-head. They will help carry you through to a faster time. It will also give you the chance to face them before the *big* show."

"I feel good, just not sure how early I need to take the lead if the pace feels slow."

"You'll know. You've got a good instinct and an excellent sense of pace."

As optimistic as that sounded to Ben, he still needed to run his fastest 5000 meters to date to qualify for Penn. If he didn't, it was the end of the road. The chances of being invited back to Kent next year were slim if he didn't demonstrate that he was worth it for the meet organizers. After all, they'd stuck their neck out for a slummer to join, and the last thing they needed was for Ben to blow up in their faces.

Ben, Coach, and Maya all waited at the bench for the car to arrive. The driverless vehicle arrived exactly at 8:30 a.m. with the gentle whirl of its electric motors. His race was at 3:00 p.m. at Kent State University, which was a touch less than an hour's drive away.

Maya climbed in first, then Ben sat beside her, facing forward. Coach took the left front seat facing to the rear. Ben glided his hand along the seam of the soft synthetic leather bucket seat, which was one of the most comfortable things he had ever sat in. Much nicer than the cheap one he had used during the road racing days.

The car darted forward along the potholed road.

Coach pulled out a piece of paper and handed it to Ben. He and Maya studied the list.

"This is the lineup for your race today," Coach said. "I don't really see anyone who is a threat to you, but a couple guys are decent. My biggest concern is that nobody in the field runs a qualifying time, which means you *must* win the race."

Ben had won many road races, but something about an organized track event felt much more significant. More official. "The time is the time—nothing else matters, right?"

"Today, that's exactly right. You're not racing, you're running efficient and fast. Save the racing for Oregon."

Ben blankly stared out the window as they accelerated up onto the highway. He turned toward his coach and nodded, then glanced at Maya. She snapped to a smile. He knew that she was still worried about the protestors. So was he. Humans were conditioned toward routine, and everything about today was anything but routine.

"Hey, I almost forgot," Coach said as he opened his small black backpack. After a moment of rummaging. "Just got them last night."

Ben leaned forward to look as he pulled out a pair of broken-down racing flats.

"You're going to need these," he said as he tossed them toward Ben, who caught them in his lap.

"Hey, Coach, these are great. I thought you didn't find any."

He scratched his chin. "Well, I actually wanted to get racing spikes, but this is the only thing I could find in your size."

They had once been white, but were now an aged yellow. Ben lifted one up in the air. "They are so light. Gotta be half the weight of my trainers."

"Almost," he said.

He handed one to Maya, who studied the shoe. "Cool. Try them on."

Ben looked to Coach, who agreed with a nod. He smiled, then slipped off his training shoes and laced up the flats. "Wow, these are awesome. It's like I am only wearing socks."

"Not far off. Guess how many steps you take in the 5000?" Coach asked.

Ben smiled. "No idea . . . maybe a thousand."

Coach looked toward Maya, who shrugged, then answered, "I would guess more . . . maybe two thousand."

He winked toward Maya as if she were on the right track. "Ben, your pace is about 180 steps per minute, so I would say you are somewhere around 2250 steps in a race. Those shoes are in the neighborhood of four ounces lighter than your trainers." He squeezed his eyes shut, doing the math. "That means you will be carrying 550 pounds less during your race. What do you think . . . Ready to race your fastest time?"

Ben's smile sharpened. "Absolutely."

"Okay, once we arrive, we're gonna find a place for you two to sit quietly, out of the way. I'll go check you into the event. I want you to arrive at the race not a minute early to avoid any unnecessary drama. Got it?"

Ben and Maya nodded simultaneously.

"Ben, you need to be prepared. They are going to make a really big deal about you today. I heard that it leaked out that you will be racing. You gotta brush it off. Stare off into the distance like a lion at a zoo imagining a hunt in the Savanna. Got it?"

Ben nodded.

"When the time is right, we are going to open the cage doors and let you loose. Wreak terror on the spectators."

Ben nodded again. He stared off into the distance, but imagined he was a caged lion, as opposed to the vision of freedom that Coach had imagined.

As the car pulled up outside the track and field facility, thousands of people swarmed around the area. The athletes wore team jackets. Spectators were all done up in the highest and most colorful fashions. Ben scrunched in his chair, peering through the tinted glass at the mob of people. They looked happy. Enthusiastic to be at the races. Oblivious that a slummer was sneaking in through the gates to ruin their party—a Trojan horse.

Parked just to the side of the main gate was the news van from the station that had interviewed Ben at Malachi. However, beside it was what piqued his interest. A white van with thick red and blue lines stretching from the headlights toward the back. CSUS, the national news that covered the biggest sporting events. The same channel that Samantha Bell represented.

Ben tapped on the glass with the nail of his index finger so he could point it out to Maya.

"You think she is here?" she asked.

Ben shrugged. "A little below her ranking, isn't it?"

They both looked around frantically. Overwhelmed by the scale of everything.

"Come on, let's find you somewhere to hide," Coach said.

What set Ben apart from the spectators and competition was his DNA coding. A construct invisible to the naked eye that defined how he looked and breathed. His bone structure and his ability to pump blood through his cardiovascular system. None of this could be seen.

It was their appearance, including their clothes, hair, and simply the dullness of their skin, that told everybody what they needed to know. He was darker skinned than most, and Coach even more so. Some elites did have darker skin by choice, a golden color, but it was rather uncommon. Everything the elites needed to inspire hatred toward them was in plain sight. Natural birth equaled poverty equaled hatred. As simple as that. Ben couldn't believe how fast they would be able to identify him, as if he were the donkey showing up to the thoroughbred race.

The car doors flipped up at the main entrance, and the three of them stepped out into the cool air.

A tall, athletic woman, who was most likely a coach, considering her age, wore a team jacket and was the first to welcome them to the event.

"What the heck are you doing here, slummer?"

Ben dropped his head to avoid seeing their faces transform into raw unfiltered ugliness. He followed on Coach's heels through the crowd, then out the other side. They cut through a row of trees, around a parking lot, and behind a large dormitory named Clark Hall. Behind the building was a secluded strip of grass. In the distance were three distinct towers jutting into the air, also looking like dormitories. *How many people live in this place?* he thought.

"Okay, hang out here for a bit. You shouldn't see too many people over here, and I'll come get you when you need to do a warm-up." Coach looked around, as if to confirm that the place was safe to leave them alone.

Maya scoffed, then said to Ben, "Don't worry, we'll be fine."

His head bobbed in acknowledgment, but his eyes told another story. The truth.

Coach headed back in the direction from which they had come. DNA manipulation had been in its infancy when he was born. Skin color was predominantly based on the family genes passed down, elite or otherwise. It wasn't until years later that a family could choose from a catalogue with hundreds of skin tone variants while designing their baby. At his age and with his old jacket, he could pass-off as a poor elite, similar to Ben's former boss at the foundry. In reality, his jacket was thirty years old. He selectively wore it for special occasions to ensure it lasted. Occasions like today.

"This is crazy," Ben said as he gazed off at the three towers. "I *really* don't belong here."

Maya glared at him silently until he noticed and looked back. "Ben. After today, your competition is going to feel like they got run over by a high-speed train and that *they* don't belong here."

Ben appreciated the effort. But he knew that two slummers hiding behind a building discussing how they would be accepted on the basis of a fast race was simply laughable.

***

Almost an hour had passed, which felt like half a day. Coach reemerged from around the side of the building.

"Okay, guys, go get a warm-up in. Stay fresh . . . Don't get lost."

Don't get lost? Ben thought, as if it was almost a good idea. A plausible excuse for not racing today. Nerves rattled his bones. His legs were heavy, and his entire body felt lethargic. His mind oscillated between one horrible thought process and the next. All of which hinged on his performance and an entire stadium enjoying the sight of his failure. *Schadenfreude*, he thought. A word he learned from an old German lady from his building, who'd passed on years ago. She said that it was a single word used to describe someone who enjoys it when something bad happens to another. Often when it's someone who deserves the consequences, but not necessarily. A single word that could summarize human nature.

Maya popped up and grabbed Ben's hand to pull him to his unassured feet. "Come on, stud. Time to put on the war paint."

The two of them glided off toward the main campus. The large pathways, designed to support thousands of students winding from one class to the next, were eerily quiet on the weekend. Ben hadn't been to a campus like this before. Truly a sight to be seen. It looked like an entire city without cars. Walking paths meandered through nice settings with small gardens and fountains. Interesting eclectic architecture. Some buildings looked old, others looked as if they had just been constructed and featured in *Architecture Weekly* a few months prior.

The warm-up was mostly silent, beyond occasionally pointing out one thing or another. The sound of the track event grew louder as they approached, with cheering, starter pistols, and announcements on the loudspeaker. With the track looming beyond the trees, Maya tugged his arm to stop, which he did.

"I am with you. Anytime you feel doubt creep in." She jabbed her elbow into him. "Just remember that there is no doubt that I will kick your butt if you don't show these DNA kids that *you're* the man."

Ben laughed. "You're crazy."

"I know," she said. "That's why you love me. Come on, let's bang the drum and let everyone know you're here. The general has arrived."

***

He saw Coach in the crowd, waving his hand in the air to signal for Ben and Maya to come over. They waded through the masses. Ben ignored the destructive comments and hurried fast enough to ensure a mob did not form ahead of him and block his forward progress. His wake was another story.

"Ben, good. Here's your numbers." He handed Ben the race bib as well as two stickers with the same number that needed to be adhered to each hip.

"Number Twenty-two?"

"Yup, that's your starting position. There are twenty-two runners competing today. You will be in the second row on the outside."

"Oh. Okay, where do I . . ." His eyes caught something that blew his world apart. "Is that?"

Coach twisted. "Yeah, Samantha Bell is here . . . She was asking about you."

"What?" His stomach dropped out.

"She heard that Kent was letting a slummer run the 5k today, so she came out to see for herself. I guess the news circle is light this week. Don't worry about it; it's nothing."

"Oh, crap, Coach. I can't run with her watching. What do you mean, 'it's nothing'?"

Coach grabbed him by the shoulder and shook him a single time. "Listen, Ben. Why don't you tell her your story over the next five thousand meters, huh? She won't have anything to say after that. Besides, she is going to be at the championships, as well as at Penn Relays. You're gonna have to get used to it. Better now than when it really matters."

Ben nodded to confirm that she was going to be at the other events, but not that he was going to get used it.

The announcer in the background said, "Men's 5000 meters, please report to the waterfall starting line."

"That's me," Ben said with an awkward smile. Worry wrinkled his forehead.

Coach obtained his attention. His eyes looked wise and calming. "Just do your thing, Ben. Everything is good. You trained for this, and your new shoes are going to conserve a huge amount of energy . . . You got this."

Maya looked as if she couldn't grasp the whole situation. Ben's rock, his confident and trustworthy girl, looked as if she, too, had been run over by a truck.

"Hey, don't worry Maya. I got my war paint on."

He offered a nervous chuckle. *What was I thinking?* Ben stepped under the railing onto the track and, with a quick burst, sped toward the official and the other runners. He couldn't help but notice how fast everyone looked. These guys were nothing like the mobs of road racers he had been competing against. They also didn't look as cheerful as the road racers. They were intense. Cold. Focused.

The official took attendance, and eventually got to him. "Benjamin Brandt."

"Here," he said, raising his hand.

Everyone glared, including the official, who paused before proceeding. *Enemy territory without camouflage.*

Ben looked up into the gray skies, then back to the blue track. He looked anywhere to not catch the eyes of the others. Anything to not increase the tension of being on their oval.

The official began his instructions. "There will be one verbal command and then the gun at the start. Please line up three meters behind the starting line, and on the command, 'On your marks,' come forward quickly to the starting line, checking to make sure your toes are not on or over the line. When everyone is still and in control, I will fire the gun. If anyone goes down because of contact in the first hundred meters, we will fire a recall gun and bring you back to start you again. Are there any questions?"

The runners remained silent. Ben had many questions, but not for the official.

After the instructions, they moved toward the waterfall starting line. An arched line allowed all runners to cut in as soon as possible.

"On your marks."

The group simultaneously stepped forward to the white arching line. Ben had seen it a million times on TV.

BANG. White smoke billowed into the air.

Twelve and a half laps. Ben progressed from the back row on the outside to the middle of the front pack. Two shoulders wide of the rail. Already within the first lap, he felt his competition was rather pedestrian compared to how they appeared. He maintained within the pack, letting the leaders guide the way. He saw the time tick off, lap after lap, and cruised effortlessly and anxiously. He saw coach jabbing his finger toward the clock. His expression shouted to him, "What are you waiting for?"

Today's objective had nothing to do with winning or giving Samantha Bell a nice show. Today was about one thing only. He had to run a fast time to qualify for at least the Penn Relays. His pace, until now, wasn't going to cut it.

Ben momentarily closed his eyes. *War paint,* he thought to himself.

On the backstretch, he moved wide into the third position from the rail. His jostling was met with a few choice words from the runner he had cut off. He burst into the lead through the final meters of the straightaway, then pulled back to the rail just in time to hug the turn. Down the homestretch, he was greeted with a fantastic silence. The flip card revealed that he had four remaining laps. His new pace quickly split the pack into a thin line of runners, slowly stretching the gaps until breaking points emerged. The pace still felt good.

Three laps to go. Ben's stride was long, quick, and powerful. He was still not fast enough to achieve his goal. He ratcheted into a new gear, which had already built a ten-stride gap on number two. Third place was now leading a distant cluster behind him.

Two laps to go. The crowd was horrified, as if they were watching their city being razed by hordes of barbarians. Helplessly witnessing their army be decimated by the enemy's savagery. Their silence was Ben's battle cry. He could hear exactly two things. The gentle, rhythmic thumping of his feet propelling around the oval. And his heart, pumping oxygen into his pulsing muscles. He was floating on eagle's wings. The pace quickened again.

The bell lap approached, and he was now commanding a sixty-meter lead, more than half the entire length of the homestretch.

DING DING DING.

A fury of passion, inspired by the sound of the infamous bell lap, surged through him. A sound he had never heard. A sound he'd imagined in thousands of workouts over many years. The adrenaline rushed into his veins, which launched him like a rocket into the stratosphere. *One lap is nothing,* he thought.

Ben's final lap was one of the quickest quarters he had ever posted. Nothing short of a four-hundred-meter finishing kick, vanquishing any would-be competitors into vapor.

As Ben crossed the finish line, breaking the tape, he saw that his time was still short of the national championship qualifying time. However, he had easily qualified for Penn.

What he also acknowledged was that the stadium was silent. Awestruck. His heart pounded as he bent down, attempting to catch his breath.

All eyes were trained on him. Other runners finished. Nobody noticed. Athletes, coaches, parents, kids, even the guy in the hotdog stand stood still, gaping.

Breaking the silence from behind him was a familiar voice. "Excuse me . . . Benjamin Brandt, I am Samantha Bell."

He turned toward her and smiled in response.

"Hi, I'm Ben."

She laughed. "Well, after today, I don't think you're going to need to introduce yourself anymore, Ben."

He was shocked at how friendly she was. He figured that she was just like the rest of them. Perfect in every way, full of charm and warmth, until a slummer was in her midst. She was different. She wasn't faking it. He had met several runners from the road races who were also genuine, but this was Samantha Bell. The thought of her standing before him sent an involuntary chill down his spine.

"You have a few minutes for me?"

Ben looked at the enormous camera resting on top of the cameraman's shoulder.

He inhaled deeply. "Yeah, of course."

She winked at him, then turned back to the camera with a million-dollar smile. "Good afternoon, America. I am Samantha Bell from CSUS sports news. Today I am reporting to you from Ohio, at Kent State University. Today, it is my distinct pleasure to introduce you to the next rising star in the 5000 meters. Coming from Cleveland, Ohio, Benjamin Brandt."

She turned toward him and asked, "So Benjamin, now that you have won the Kent State Invitational, what are your goals for this track season?"

Ben froze. He hadn't prepared how much information he should share. The entire country was watching. After a painfully long pause, he realized it didn't matter what his answer was; they would all laugh at him anyway. "Um, well. Um, I am going to run at Penn Relays, where I hope to qualify for the national championship."

"Your time today will require some improving to make the cut. Do you think you are ready for such a blistering pace?"

Ben smiled. "Oh, that?" He used his thumb to point backward over his shoulder to the blue track. "That was nothing."

Her smile told him everything. She was a fan. "Well, Benjamin, we are all rooting for you."

A man on the bleachers shouted, "No, we aren't, asshole. Go back to your tent."

She turned back to the camera, "Benjamin Brandt has overcome the adversity of growing up in Cleveland's ghetto. Rising through the local road race scene and today winning the Kent State Invitational with an alarming time. Today, he earned the respect of his competitors and is a champion of his hometown. What's next for this young man? If you ask me, anything he puts his mind to. See you at Penn Relays, everyone. It is promising to be quite a show."

The cameraman shut off the feed and lowered the camera.

She didn't report him as some shock news case or some slummer who had scammed his way into the event. But rather as a young man who had overcome adversity in the face of hatred. A hero among his people. Ben had met a champion for his cause.

"Thank you," Ben said.

She smiled. Eyes soft. "It's going to be a hard road, Ben. Not the racing. I think you've got what it takes. But the other stuff. I wish you the best. Sincerely."

***

"What was she like?" Maya asked as they jogged back through campus to purge the lactic acid from his muscles.

Ben inhaled deeply. "I don't know. She was so unbelievably nice. I really didn't expect her to show such compassion. Off-camera, she also told me that she will be rooting for me."

Maya bit her lip, then said, "You know, you qualified for Penn."

Ben nodded, then looked to her, fighting back tears of joy, fear, and a raw emotional hurricane. "Holy crap."

"I know." Her eyes welled, too.

"I qualified for Penn!" he shouted into the air with his fists pumping, startling the few unsuspecting students walking along the pathway.

A solo runner Ben recognized from his race, who was also cooling down, approached them wearing his Kent State jacket. "Hey, you're Benjamin Brandt, right?"

Ben nodded, unsure if he would receive a beating from a surprise attack. Sucker punch in the face, perhaps. He trusted nobody here. He trusted nobody outside the ghetto, and even within the ghetto he had to be highly selective.

The runner looked over his shoulder, then pulled out a T-shirt from his jacket pocket. Printed on it was an eagle's head swooping over the letter *K* with a lightning bolt trailing. It read, *Kent State Cross-Country*. He handed it to Ben. "Here. You're one heck of a runner, man. I'm from Westlake. Cleveland rocks."

The Kent runner darted off in the opposite direction.

Ben shrugged to Maya, who did the same in return.

"Guess you got your own fanboys now," she said.

Chapter Twenty-Three

Tap tap ... tap. The sound smeared a grin across Ben's face. His guest had arrived. He closed his well-worn running diary, where he was taking notes about his latest workout, and placed it back behind his socks in the top drawer of his dresser.

As he entered the living room, Maya had already let herself in. She had the day off due to a special event in the city, which forbid slummers to be present. At the same time, Ben's dad and brother were at the foundry. A rare opportunity to spend some time alone at Ben's place with no chance of interruption from either of their families.

He leaned in for a hug, but Maya pretended to punch him in the stomach, then laughed like she was as crazy as guano.

"What happened to you?" Ben asked.

"Nothing, *dude.*" She continued to laugh.

"No, seriously, why are you in such a good mood?"

She stopped laughing and scowled at him. "You *really* can't let people's emotions go, can you?"

Ben shook his head with a sense of humor but realized that she was right. Emotions struck Ben hard, positive or negative. If he didn't understand them, his first reaction was that they were bad. He didn't run because it pleased other people. However, if it displeased them, it wore heavy on him. Not enough to cause him to stop, but enough to zap the joy from his depths.

Maya reached around his waist and squeezed. She whispered in his ear, "Everything is good. I am just happy to see you . . . I'm happy."

"I know, I don't know why I do that. I just . . ."

"Shh. I know."

She did know. He thought that she probably knew him better than he did himself, and somehow it still surprised him.

She pulled back and hopped on the couch, pulling her feet beneath her. "So, what are we going to do today?"

Ben joined her and placed his hand on her knee. He liked her legs. "Don't know, didn't really plan anything."

She flipped over and sat on him, placing her forehead against his. "You and Coach can plan workouts a year in advance, but you don't know what *we* are going to do in the next five minutes?"

He shrugged.

"Should I call Coach over and ask him what we should do?" Her laugh throttled back to life.

Over the next four hours, they talked. About everything. Her job, running, and life. Everything about their relationship was built on shared experiences, living through the hard life. Even when they disagreed on a subject, they sincerely understood each other's point of view. Both of them were stubborn enough to not change their opinion, but flexible enough to allow discreet adaptations. Every time Ben was with her, he felt like they were wrapped up in a cozy blanket beside a fire tucked deep within their den. The outside world was the enemy, and together, their defensive shields amplified one another.

As the afternoon rolled along, they discussed what they expected to see at Penn Relays. Especially considering the protesters.

From outside the apartment, they heard loud voices approaching. It wasn't an argument, but there was anger. As the voices drew nearer, Ben realized it was his dad and brother. He looked toward the kitchen clock.

"They shouldn't be home for at least three more hours," Ben said.

The door opened and banged against the wall, further caving in the indentation from the handle.

"This isn't possible. When are they going to call?" his brother asked. He was revved up, and neither him nor Dad noticed Ben and Maya on the couch.

Ben looked at her and shrugged.

Their dad placed his hand on his brother's shoulder. "Come on, we need to take a deep breath. Prepare a plan. We got to be smart about this."

As they turned, it was the first time they noticed the couch was occupied. "Oh, I didn't see you there," Dad said.

"What happened? Why are you guys home already?" Ben asked.

His dad inhaled slowly with his eyes closed to compose himself. "Well . . . Um . . . They announced today that they will close the foundry by the end of the month."

Ben looked at Maya as the air escaped him. This wasn't a hardship; it was the end of the road—falling from the fragile ladder they had climbed. Already, the housing authorities were snatching back homes at an alarming rate. With the closure of AluMag, the largest employer in Cleveland, there would be more than 2,500 additional jobless residents—entirely consisting of slummers. Every one of them would be desperately seeking employment, which was scarce as it was. Tent City was about to get its own zip code.

Daniel, who hadn't calmed down yet, added, "They're gonna cut us to four hours a day until then, just to clear out the last orders received. It's all over."

"How can they do that? Just shut down a factory of that size?" Maya asked.

Dad crossed his arms. "The company is going to close at a time when the shareholders can still walk away with a nice check. Invest in another company elsewhere, or maybe lounge in their pools filled with coin. This isn't bad news for anyone except the employees. The same employees who have no say in the matter. In the dark from the beginning."

Ben faded away in thought. He lightly followed the conversation, however the discussion became muted. He thought of the cash sitting in the family safe. Coach had agreed to spend some of his own money, but it was the cash tucked within the wooden box in his dad's room that was the foundation of his attempt to chase the championships. The paperwork, drug testing, and immunizations were already taken care of, but travel was still outstanding and expensive. He couldn't ask Coach for more help, and even if he would be willing, spending money on anything except survival, at a time like this, was unimaginable.

Ben leaned over to Maya, kissed her. "I am sorry. I need to get some fresh air."

"Where are you going?" she asked.

His dad and brother anticipated his answer as well.

He looked at each of them with a long face as his eyes began to burn. He went to his room, pulled on his running clothes, then walked by his family without making eye contact. He slipped out the door.

Maya shouted, "Ben?"

Already on the steps, he heard her, but didn't respond as the door closed.

Ben ran for thirty miles that evening. Almost three and half hours rolling through the dreams that he had conjured throughout his life. All of them were no more than figments of a wild imagination.

At the end, he had made the hardest decision he'd ever made. Road racing was the only way to keep his family afloat. His dreams would have to come later, if at all. Sometimes life got in the way of your dreams. In fact, it usually did.

It was already dusk, but instead of going back to his own apartment, he headed to his coach's.

Logan had been called in by his mother just as Ben arrived. She waved to Ben and offered a kind smile. Ben pulled the door open for the boy as they entered.

"I wanna run with you someday. When I'm big like you, can we run together?"

Ben did everything he could to fight back the tears, but it wasn't enough. He wiped the streams from his cheeks as rapidly as they came. "Yeah, kid. I would love to run with you."

His heart ripped in two as he considered how naive this child was. A horrible life lay in front of him, and he was oblivious to the intensity of pain that it would cause. At that moment, the idea of being a runner seemed laughable. Useless. His dad was right from the very beginning. Dreams didn't belong in the slums. They were reserved for the privileged.

Logan went toward his own apartment and Ben climbed the stairs. His legs ached from the hefty long run.

As he entered, Coach's expression transitioned to mimic the sadness of Ben's.

"I heard about the foundry," he said softly. "Come. Let's sit down."

Ben collapsed onto the couch. "I made an adjustment to our training plan," he said, "but I don't think it matters, really."

Coach cocked his head.

"I moved my long run to today . . . Got a new distance record, though." He forced a smile through the agony.

Coach sighed. "I guess you did some thinking?"

"I decided that I need to get back into road racing. I can't be running for free anymore. All the track races are on the same days as the road races with purses. We can't afford to waste the time when I can help save my family from losing the apartment."

"Ben, there are a couple races in between that we could squeeze in. I will replan our workouts to consider this, but you can't give up on this dream. Not when you are this close."

"But I can't spend our family money. If it were free, I would consider it, but it's not."

"I already paid for Penn Relays, including the car. Let us see where that takes us, okay?"

Ben wanted to race with every fiber of his soul. He sighed and dropped his head. "Okay, I will run Penn, but I think that's the end. We could never afford flying to Oregon."

Coach grabbed his shoulder and squeezed. "Okay, we will do Penn. But we will do everything as if we are going after the championship. Even if we decide not to, at least we won't regret it if something miraculous happens."

Ben had never experienced anything miraculous before, and there was no reason he would now. He agreed anyway. "Okay, Coach. Just in case."

Ben ended up sleeping on Coach's couch that night. He didn't have the emotional strength to see his dad. His dad had done everything for the family, and because of some decisions from the high-horsed elites, despite everything, they forced him to fail in the most catastrophic of ways.

That night Ben dreamed of a demented shepherd, laughing wildly as he drove his flock over the cliff's edge.

***

Penn Relays wasn't some run-of-the-mill race. It wasn't just a highly sought-after competition for the most talented elite athletes. Penn was the oldest and largest track and field competition in the United States. The first race had taken place on April 21, 1895, and now, in 2085, Ben had a chance to race against his longtime heroes for the first time. His race would be a blip on the event's storied history. But to Ben, it was everything.

"Cyrus, Eric, and Archer have all announced that they will be competing at Penn," Maya said.

It had been four days since his victory at Kent State. Despite his decision to not run in Oregon, he agreed with Coach to push the subject aside and race through Penn as if it were a midseason steppingstone. There was no harm in pretending that he was preparing for the big show, just in case. He knew that his coach still maintained the expectation to see it through, and Ben chose to not interfere. After all, it was what he wanted, too.

It was imperative that if he did find himself at Hayward Field, he would need to peak then. Risking the qualifying time was a gamble, but Coach and Ben agreed that they weren't here to play games. Ben had nothing to lose.

The lopsided bicycle thumped along behind Ben and Maya as they jogged toward Edgewater Park. Rain clouds threatened.

Ben knew that he had all the supporters he could ever dream of. Loyal, passionate, and, above all else, aware of all the other nonrunning messes that confronted him.

Without them, Ben knew that he wouldn't be brave or confident enough to even show up to Penn. Coach prepared him physically, and they both did mentally. Both of them played a role in boosting his confidence. Ben may have been the runner, but it was entirely a team effort.

"These guys are gonna go out quick, huh?" Ben asked over his shoulder.

Coach said, "Typically. But both Eric and Archer have already qualified for Oregon, so they won't push it. Cyrus, on the other hand, will need a fast pace to get on the list for the national championship. He is the guy you need to focus on. You stick on him, and he will pull you through."

Cyrus was Ben's favorite. He had just been handed an assignment to specifically target and hang with his greatest idol. Everything was surreal. A boy from the slums running with genetically enhanced elite athletes. What was even more surreal, although he floundered back and forth on the idea, was that he actually belonged there, too. He deserved to be on the track with them. He'd earned his way through endless miles of training and intense workouts.

The bitter wind pelted rain at them from across the lake. He and Maya stretched at the bottom of the hill in the wet sand. Water dripped from his brow; eyes squinted to shield off the stinging drops. He looked out into the gray mess of the lake. The water crashed into scattered whitecaps. The same water that had nearly consumed him throughout the previous autumn.

It reminded him of how far he had come. He'd become a man in those depths. Few could pinpoint exactly when their trajectory shifted course, but for Ben, it was abundantly clear. Breaking his foot was the best thing that had ever happened to him. It was only then that he had the opportunity to prove his grit. Not to Coach. Not to Maya. Not to the seagulls swooping around attempting to crap on his head. He proved it to himself. On the horizon, the gray waters transitioned into the gray sky fluidly, as if it were a single homogeneous entity, limitless. He knew that he was unstoppable. He, too, had no limits.

"Let's do this," Maya said.

Startled by her words, he hadn't realized how long he had been staring out into the gray abyss. He nodded, then took position.

That cold, rainy afternoon represented another workout in the bag. Every run, good or bad, was added to that infamous bag collecting the sum of his training. Every workout built on the last. Intensity workouts allowed him to train faster, stronger, and longer. The next workout would be built on a new standard that perpetually created a storm of progress. Without the effort, without pushing through the wall, Ben would reach an invisible barrier. Training would stagnate and his limits would be met.

Ben didn't just push through the wall, he obliterated it, his effort only comparable to that of the Romans overcoming the meager defenses of a barbarian horde.

Chapter Twenty-Four

"Franklin Field," Ben whispered to himself. Their rental car glided in a whirl along the length of the stadium. A series of brick arches marked the structure, which stood like an ancient Roman coliseum. Gladiators would fight to their death at the sounds of cheers from the crowd. Blood would be spilled to the sound of laughter and jeering.

An athlete had to be at their peak physical condition, however the performance during that precise moment was the only thing that mattered. They didn't weigh your bag of workouts and choose a victor. Not here. They measured how you swung that bag and annihilated your opponents with it—or not. A hefty bag swung at the inopportune moment would result in failure.

Ben looked at Maya sitting beside him. Her eyes also hadn't blinked since they arrived.

He said, "Wow, this is nothing like Kent."

She slowly nodded. "This is a full-on stadium, with tens of thousands of fans. Kent just had some bleachers along the homestretch."

"Fifty thousand," Coach interjected. A smirk accented his face, as if he had looked forward to this very moment when his young disciples would catch on to the gravity of the situation.

Ben leaned forward as the car slowed to a stop in front of the main gate. "What?"

"Yup. Lot of people."

Ben took it all back. He didn't belong here in the slightest. His confidence, which he had earned at Kent and fantasized about for weeks, eroded immediately, and before he had even stepped out of the car. He was quite sure that he preferred to stay in the vehicle. It was a much better idea than racing in front of fifty thousand elites booing at him from every seat of the stadium. He could already see protesters at the main entrance. Their signs and banners were raised, anticipating his arrival. Ben just wanted to run.

"Come, let's find you a quiet place outside the stadium," Coach said.

Ben looked at Maya, who also looked as if she was seeing phantoms circling. Coach, on the other hand, was a natural. He had a smile as if he had seen an old friend.

Behind the stadium, along the cinder block wall of a neighboring building, Coach had found them a sheltered place to hang out until the warm-up. The place was buzzing. Races went off in rapid succession. Sprint qualifiers hammered through the walls. The crowd was thunderous. Race after race was filled with the most enthusiastic spectators Ben had ever imagined. The atmosphere was something that simply couldn't be felt through the TV. He had watched the event once at Maya's a couple of years back. It had done nothing to prepare him for the real thing.

They huddled together, away from prying eyes.

"Ben, time to warm up," Coach said as he returned around the corner with a white packet of information. "Don't get lost."

Ben snorted. There was no way on earth he could lose track of this place. He thought he could run all the way back to Cleveland and still hear the fans chanting.

Ben and Maya did their rounds. Not a word was spoken as they glided through Penn Park along the Schuylkill River. Ben focused on the race. *Shadow Cyrus*, he thought.

It was getting warm and muggy, which would not help anyone's performance. Ben knew this, which in turn upped the challenge for a fast time.

"Last chance to qualify. Is this even real?"

Maya pinched him on the side below his ribs. Hard. "Yup. Deal with it."

Ben jumped in surprise. "Ah, what you doing?"

She laughed. "Just go run. Stop thinking."

He scowled at her but knew that she was right. He had enough to overcome and didn't need to worry about worrying as well. The act of worrying in and of itself could plague a performance.

Ben entered the stadium for the first time. Not only was it packed to the gills, he knew that his presence had already been publicized. It was newsworthy that a slummer would compete among the elites, and that drew a dire criticism across the national track and field community. There were certainly people who cheered for his progress, which from their perspective was progress for the country, but they were few and far between. They didn't and wouldn't unify behind him. They were nothing more than whispers of praise such that nobody else could hear. They had the luxury of being an elite and the luxury of a good night's sleep with the pride that they were humanitarians. Ben had neither of these luxuries. Far from it.

His arrival at Kent was mostly unexpected, apart from the few in-the-know media personalities, but not this time. Everybody knew.

Just inside the gate, a group of about fifteen protesters, who apparently hadn't run in the past hundred years, stood there with signs. *Slummers not welcome*, one sign read. Another, which for some reason people kept repeating, *Say no to performance-enhancing drugs*.

They seemed to believe that the only way a slummer could ever run with the elites was if the slummer had been using illegal substances that somehow slipped through the intense drug screening. Somehow, his natural genetic composition, passed down to him from his parents, grandparents, and great-grandparents, could not possibly compete with a genetically enhanced designer baby. Handcrafted to race. It was incomprehensible to them that nature could produce something more elegant than mankind could create. Ben was a freak of nature to them and must have been boosted by something unnatural, illegal. The world now believed that manmade was better than nature-made, because it must be that way.

What Ben found most laughable was that even if he did desire the support of performance-enhancing drugs, he didn't have the bankroll. He could hardly afford the car ride to the races, let alone the extraordinary costs of treatments.

Independent from all of that, he would never in a million years touch drugs after the things he had seen in Tent City. He would prefer to lose a leg to some flesh-eating disease than to lower himself into that dark and ugly cavern of self-deceit and addiction. If these protestors knew him, they would know ... But nobody cared to challenge their own prescribed diagnosis. That would take more effort than simply hating someone.

The news cameras followed him like bloodhounds sniffing the trail of an escaped convict. Howling in the hunt. The cameras panned between the protesters and him, pushing deeper into the bowels of the stadium.

His race had been called for final check-in. Coach already registered him beforehand, and everything was prepared. His race number was attached to his shirt.

He looked back to Maya. "Wish me luck."

Ben darted onto the track. Finally, he was thankful to have a barrier between himself and the people. He was relatively safe among the other gladiators, even if they didn't like him or want him there. They were all preoccupied with their primary objective of racing.

The sounds in the audience shifted from the typical rumbling of fifty thousand people to the strangeness of thousands whispering. A haunting noise that followed him everywhere. His appearance was what they had all been looking forward to. They couldn't wait to hate him. They couldn't wait for the beast to be slayed.

Ben snapped back to reality as he saw Cyrus dash by him in a stride-out. Much taller than he imagined. He looked like the perfect distance runner. Shoulder-length sandy hair bobbed behind him. He was fast. Really fast.

Ben had chills shoot up his spine at the mere sight. *I'm supposed to run with him?*

He proceeded to the official for check-in, where both Archer Sinclair and Eric Richardson were laughing. They had both already qualified for Nationals, and today was just another race to prove their might. As Ben approached, their eyes went cold, as did Ben's blood.

They turned to each other, and Archer said, without a hint of subtlety, "The slummer has arrived. Now we can really get the party started."

Several other athletes laughed as well.

Ben was the joke.

Once he confirmed with the official that he was there, he charged down the track for a final stride-out. He was abruptly cut off by two other runners intentionally.

"You don't belong here." There was no laughter.

Ben kept his mouth shut. He knew he didn't belong here. He knew it much better than those two designer babies. Everything about this place was wrong. His dream was wrong. In the deepest chambers of his heart, he knew undeniably that he was the biggest fool of all. He was indeed the joke. His eyes darted around looking for an exit. He had to escape. Fifty thousand pairs of eyes watched him squirm under their microscope—waiting for him to fail. Schadenfreude.

They were called to the line. "Runners on your mark."

The only escape was through a 5000-meter course wrapping around the oval. Entirely exposed. He stepped forward to the waterfall starting line at the end of the backstretch.

BANG.

This was not Kent State. These guys launched off the line like jet fighters. Ben went straight to the back of the pack. Within the first turn, his legs already felt heavy. The fans were going to have a great time watching him flail like a fish in the final muddy puddle of an evaporating lake. Flopping and suffocating.

He had to find his pace. Quarters till death flashed through his mind. He needed to find his sixties. He needed to find that burned-in pace he had been training for. Everything else began to fade away. The stadium quieted. His mind blocked it all out except the feel of a rhythm. A cycle of motion. He had to dial it in, and he knew precisely what it would feel like when he hit it. It wasn't mental. It wasn't physical. His pace had become instinctual.

He rounded out the first full lap. He was there. Exactly where he wanted to be. Right on pace, which positioned him in exactly last place. His coach trained him for this. Time is the most inflexible natural force. Ben knew the math worked out. If he maintained this exact pace, he would go from last place to a national championship qualifying time. Probably somewhere in the top five positions. It was simple. The math, not the execution.

His coach had warned him of the occasional hot starts, but this was beyond his expectation. However, already within the second lap, he had picked off two runners. His pace was locked in. A machine. Tick. Tick. Tick. Tick.

Another runner slipped backward while rounding out of turn one. He ran wide to the line, dividing lane one and two all the way around as he grazed through the field.

Finally, as the mile split came, Ben was right on pace and in the middle of the field. He could see the truest warriors ahead. His former heroes were now his adversaries. They glided around the oval, just thirty meters ahead. For a split second, he was awestruck, but a moment later he transformed into something else. As a runner, and for no other reason, he belonged there. All the other stuff disappeared, and he was Ben the runner. Nothing more, nothing less.

Lap seven, Ben tried to move between two others, and at their realization that he was there, one hedged out and intentionally slammed his elbow into Ben's chest. It knocked the wind from him. He staggered a few strides, then caught another elbow from the other runner, directly into his upper arm.

Adrenaline surged into his veins. Ben broke from his pace trance. *It's time to start racing.*

He looked ahead. It wasn't these two chumps he needed to meddle with; it was those three, thirty meters farther up. He saw that Cyrus had broken into the lead; however, Ben needed to get past the more immediate numbskulled obstacles.

He huffed a hard breath and came up behind the two who had blocked him previously. Even pace wasn't the matter any longer. The track straightened out of the second turn. He prepared for elbows and dropped the hammer. He blew straight between them without allowing them a chance to interfere. He succeeded in getting past. He succeeded in making them look like fools in the wake of a slummer. A grin appeared on Ben's face. He was starting to have fun.

From here on out, in ninth place, the rest of the field was strung out into a single-file line.

Two miles clicked through. Ben had lost ground on his goal. He needed to qualify. Number one objective: time.

The air he sucked in was not enough to replenish his muscles with what they desired. His legs grew heavy. The adrenaline he had received just a lap prior had accelerated a physical degradation. The fight was on, but he had been to this battle before. This was nothing different than the towpath, besides the crowd, stadium, and competition. All of which had nothing to do with overcoming the pain.

Three laps to go was coming up quickly, and the large fluorescent-green numbers clicked by rhythmically. Six seconds behind his qualifying time.

Stop the bleeding, he said to himself. His pace was worse than he thought. It hurt more than he expected. Much more.

He could feel his dreams slipping away into a small footnote of the Penn Relays' historical records. *A slummer once ran here,* it would read. No name, no picture, just a slummer who came and went as a gentle breeze passed a meadow. He was certain that he couldn't regain pace, let alone bring back his lost six seconds.

Nobody wanted him here anyway, but he couldn't quit. Quitting wasn't in *his* DNA.

Hovering above the inner lane was a square metal rail to prevent runners from shortening the lap by stepping on the line.

Ben's thoughts had drifted from qualifying to self-sabotage. He knew that at his speed, if he landed his left foot halfway onto the rail, his ankle would surely break. At least cause severe damage, forbidding him from ever running again. He was optimistic. *Nobody would blame a runner for failing to finish with a shattered ankle,* he thought.

A competitor came up beside him, positioning for a strong final mile, and whispered to Ben between strained breaths, "Come on . . . finish this thing."

Ben was fading, and someone, a runner among the elites, believed in him. Hidden within a whisper, but he was there encouraging him. He looked over, made eye contact momentarily, and gave the slightest nod.

Flashes back to his training. His hands rode high with too much side-to-side swing crossing his chest. He dropped them and shook his hands to free the rigidity. Thumbs tapping his hip bone, tap, tap, tap.

His stride was weak. He lifted his knees to elongate it. Pushed his hips forward.

His leg muscles failed him, so he pulled his arms into the game to push the pace.

He charged into the bell lap, which had rung out well before his arrival, the clock informing him that he was still four seconds in the hole. He had successfully recovered his pace, and now he had a debt to pay. Too much debt.

He needed to start his kick from here. A 400-meter kick. This was it. Ben had one chance. He'd dragged his butt through a year of heavy training. Broke a foot, ran in the lake, lost his job, and had exactly fifty-six seconds of pain to take it to the next level. Fifty-seven wouldn't cut it.

The backstretch was a blur; he taxed his legs more than he had ever done before. He focused on twenty-meter stretches. Short, achievable goals, back to back to back.

The elite motivational whisperer had followed him and was a couple strides behind him. He, too, benefited by the encouragement, riding on Ben's rising wake.

Ben hit the final turn at a breakneck speed. He passed two more runners, which left Cyrus, who had broken free and already finished with an unbelievable time, and Eric and Archer with thirty meters till the finish.

His legs were meat on sticks. Numb beyond recognition. He flopped them one giant stride ahead at a time. He was made from jelly.

Ben blasted out of the curve, drifted out to the lane line separating lanes one and two, and it was there that Ben left his body. The bright blue sky and red track began to fade to shades of gray. His vision turned monochrome and wavered. His sight narrowed. He saw just one thing. The clock at the end of the track. Brilliant fluorescent-green numbers ticking by relentlessly. Tick, tick, tick.

Everything was on the table. His dreams were now controlled by the most uncontrollable element known to man: time.

His last few strides had shifted into an elongated stagger. Arms windmilling. Ultimately falling across the line into a heap of waste.

He barely kept his legs beneath him and had no idea if he had qualified. To his right, he saw frantic arm-waving on the sideline. It was Coach and Maya. They were bursting at the seams with excitement, screaming into the enormous stadium. Not words but archaic sounds of emotion cutting through the noise of the mob. He had assuredly qualified.

He couldn't find his way to them. He wanted to but needed to kneel. Gravity sucked him further until he was sprawled flat on his back on the track surface. Arms overhead, and knees propped up by his feet. His chest heaved.

A shadow shifted over him, blocking the bright sky. It was Cyrus. His hero. The champion of today's event, who also had just qualified for the big show.

He reached out his hand, which Ben reciprocated. "Gotta keep those legs movin', or you'll be in a world of hurt tomorrow."

Cyrus pulled him back to his feet; fifty thousand people watched one of the greatest distance runners America had ever produced help a slummer to his feet. A slummer destined for Eugene.

Cyrus left as quickly as he'd come. He didn't hide in a whisper. His support was broadcast across the world, even if it was just a fleeting moment. He had no shame, in the very best of ways.

Ben made his way back to his courageous support group. Coach Sands looked twenty years younger. The gray, dull soul, which had gradually oxidized year after year in the ghetto, had brightened. His hair was a wild mess from frequent pulling but looked youthful and manic. Maya was in tears. She swept them away as quickly as they came, but the irreparable dam had broken.

He extended his long arms and embraced them both into a single mega-hug. He leaned his full weight on them. Not because he wanted to, but because he needed to.

Physically and emotionally. He had accomplished something today that hadn't been done in more than forty years. A natural birth, a slummer, had qualified for the national championship.

Ben thought to himself that his coach had won. Coach knew it all along—that once Ben qualified, there was no way on earth that he wouldn't find a way to get to Oregon, even if Ben had to sell off his organs. He smiled for a moment, thinking that selling his organs could not only pay for the trip, he could also shed some weight, saving a few hundred pounds over 5000 meters.

As Ben embraced his team, he could hear angry jeers from the crowd. There was obviously no room for progress in this world. Backsliding was much easier. Effortless.

***

The athletic director of the national committee was on the turf preparing an announcement. He gathered himself beside the standing microphone as his image splashed across the large stadium screen. It was Harvey Woodard. The man who had defined US track and field. He'd catapulted the sport into the highest-grossing event in the country. He had become an icon in the world of sporting, and his relentless effort for perfection knew no bounds; however, it did have casualties.

His voice boomed into the stadium. Full, deep, and solemn. "I bring you news about the 5000-meter results."

The stadium was silent. "Due to a rules violation, racing without an approved sponsor, the fourth-place finisher, Benjamin Brandt, has been disqualified." His eyes twinkled in self-proclaimed victory.

Immediately the scoreboard rolled Ben's name out, and the people slower than him slid up one position. Scratched from history.

"Congratulations to the competitors in today's race."

A wave of cheering emerged throughout the stadium, steadily growing in volume. The few who had booed were drowned out.

Ben didn't know what had happened. "Did I not qualify, Coach?"

The life bled from all three of their faces. Coach bit his lip. "Seems so. Come on, I need to sort this out. I need to get you out of sight."

He pulled them along, beneath the stadium grandstands, and left them in a dark corner while he hustled off.

Moments later a large man turned around the corner and made eye contact with Ben. He lifted his massive video camera to his shoulder. "Found him."

Samantha Bell had arrived and waved the camera back down. "Benjamin. Independent of this ridiculous rules violation, you have done something here today. I am sincerely your biggest fan."

As people started to fill in behind her to gawk at the fallen runner, she hurriedly waved to the cameraman, who lifted the camera again, and a red light began flashing.

"Benjamin Brandt, today you legitimately qualified for the 5000-meter national championships, which you previously told me was your ultimate dream. Within a breath, your dream was stripped away by the track and field committee's decision to disqualify you due to an obscure sponsorship rule. Can you tell us what is going through your mind?"

Ben looked at her, then into the camera's domed glass lens. The red light flashed signaling that this moment was intended to circulate the country if not the globe.

"I don't know how I feel." He exhaled. "Maybe I feel that America has lost its soul."

At that moment, Coach came around the corner. A mob of people followed close behind him. "Come on Ben, we gotta go . . . quickly."

Ben nodded to Samantha Bell, then ran off with Coach and Maya. Their car was waiting outside. As they climbed in, he realized that a lady was already in the vehicle waiting for him. Once their car pulled away and Ben could regain focus after the whirlwind escape, he recognized her. He had seen her at many track and field events in the past, on live TV. She worked for the track and field committee, and Ben thought she might even work for Harvey Woodard. He couldn't remember her name.

She stretched out her hand. "Benjamin, I am Julia Turner."

Ben shook her hand but wasn't sure what this was all about. His thoughts ranged from underground support to an assassination attempt. Hoping for the former, but he would have accepted the latter as well. It was the in between that he actually feared the most.

"First of all, Ben, you really did something today. I *know* that you belong here and also that you belong in the national championship. I also know that Harvey Woodard, my boss, has it out for you. He sees track and field as a cash machine, and you are a threat to his empire. The broken cog. He is truly brilliant but determined to a fault . . . as you can see."

"I don't understand. How does he lose money with me? How could *I* be such a problem . . . I'm nobody."

"He believes that you will deter many viewers from watching the championships in protest. Maybe at first, it brings in the wrong crowd and cheapens the experience for the elites. He would seem like a sellout in their eyes. Sleeping with the enemy. Perhaps sponsors will find somewhere else to invest, where they know their advertisements can reach the customers who can afford their products. Ben, we live in an ugly world. In the television business, once Harvey's ratings begin to slip away, a relentless avalanche is inevitable. Desegregation means economic failure."

Ben sat there. Eyes wide open, mouth agape and unaware of it being so. He shook his head. "That's what all this is about . . . ratings? We are just actors in his game show?"

She shrugged. "From his perspective . . . Exactly. Sorry, Ben, but I don't have much time. I just wanted to say that you are a true hero to some of us, and I will always do everything I can to help you . . . Please, Ben, don't give up. There is always next year. We need time to organize."

The car had parked on the side of the road at some point during the conversation. He only recognized it now. She stepped out of the car.

"Good-bye, Ben. Never give up. If you do, he wins. Not you, not the other runners, not the sport. He and he alone will be the victor."

Chapter Twenty-Five

Ben gazed into the murky mirror. The edges were tarnished, and the top-left corner was missing a triangular piece. It was a proper frame for his reflection, which hedged to the fleshier side of skeletal. Intense training for months had dropped his body fat to ultra-low levels. However, the devastating events from earlier in the day had created a dull, pasty finish to his skin, almost grayish, lifeless. His body temperature would be the only indication a mortician could rely on to not lay him on the slab. Even his pulse would hardly register.

He didn't know how long he had been there. Coach knew a few people who had decided to throw a big party on Ben's behalf on the east side of the slums. The party was going to happen with or without him, though.

A slummer from Cleveland had competed against the elites today. Not much to celebrate throughout the year, so this event was quickly latched onto. The gathering primarily consisted of the slums intellectuals. In another life, they would be doctors, lawyers, and engineers. However, in 2085 and without papers, they were janitors, factory workers, or, more often than not, unemployed. At least the ones who endured. It was well known that the traits that inspired someone to be successful were the same ones that made the chains unbearable. Many of the smartest and most ambitious slummers ended up drinking heavily to take the edge off the pain, which was frequently a one-way street toward self-annihilation.

Not everyone in the slums thought that bringing the spotlight down upon them was wise, but then again, how much worse could things really get?

Despite not feeling like there was much to celebrate, Coach thought it was still best to make an appearance. He said that the enthusiasm from his fellow slummers might put a little extra spite in his step against the machine. Maybe it would encourage him to fight on.

"The battle at Penn doesn't represent the entire war," Coach had said. "Unless *you* make it so."

He was tired of the questions, though, which drove him into the confinement of the restroom. It was the same ones, over and over again. Why would they ask how he felt? *How do they think I would feel?* This entire day was a hurricane, and he just wanted to escape into the eye for just a moment. Everything was bullshit. He didn't want to party, he didn't want to be seen at all, and he absolutely didn't want to answer any more stupid questions about his experiences swinging with the elites. Within fifteen minutes after arriving at the party, a girl in her twenties had actually said it was quite an accomplishment that he ran more than three miles without stopping. She explained that her uncle had also run that far once, but he did stop a few times along the way. Turned out that the cops did eventually catch up to him, though.

There was only one question Ben *did* have to answer, and that was a question of his own. Gazing into his reflected sunken eyes, he whispered, "Will I ever run again?"

A knock on the door broke him from the trance.

A sweet muffled voice penetrated the rickety door. Her voice was strained. "You okay in there? Can I come in?"

Ben looked into his eyes one last moment, the greenish-yellow strands of his irises twisted together in a complex weave. He then turned to unlock the door.

Maya entered, then closed it again behind her. "We shouldn't have come here tonight."

Ben nodded. "What the heck are we celebrating, anyway? Are we celebrating how we are slummers and that no matter what we do, they will just change the rules to keep us slaving away? Seriously, what would happen if all the grunt workers started to demand equal rights again? It would be the end of the elite's glory days, wouldn't it? No matter how sympathetic they might be toward a slummer, they can't handle a change like that. It is bad for the economy."

Maya moved in close and held Ben tight.

Ben dropped his head into her petite yet mighty shoulder. He could feel her shirt become soggy with the slow release of tears. He didn't care. He was breaking into a million pieces.

"I'm a loser," he whispered. "I never should have been so naive to think that this was going anywhere. There was never a chance . . . My dad already knew it, too."

She didn't answer, just squeezed him tighter.

"I am not a runner. My bones break when I train too much." He paused for a moment. "Did you know that I considered breaking my ankle today on the lane rail just so I didn't have to finish the race? What kind of person would hurt themselves just so they didn't have to lose properly? Neither a gentleman nor a slummer would be such a loser."

She pushed him back. Her eyes sought his as she wiped his cheek. "Ben, you *are* the single most heroic person I have ever known. If you think you are a loser for what you have done, then I do think you are also the biggest idiot I have ever known."

He snorted a laugh. "I really hate this . . . this feeling. I have no control over anything. Everyone is expecting something from me, and most of them are expectantly waiting for me to fail."

"I know. But do you know what I saw today?"

"What?" he said, not wanting to hear her say more about him being a hero.

"I saw Cyrus Cray, one of the best American distance runners in history, reach down to you, to pull you up . . . as an equal."

He scoffed. "Equal? Hardly."

"Something changed today, because of you. Tens of millions of people all over the country watched that moment. Cyrus grasping the hand of a slummer. I don't think we fully appreciate what chain reaction that started. I don't think anyone can."

Ben nodded. She isolated the single most exciting moment of his day without hesitation.

"That was pretty great, wasn't it?" A smile warmed his hollow face. "If it wasn't for all this political crap, that may have been the best moment of my life."

"It still is one of the greatest moments in your life. You know, besides the day you met me crying beneath our tree. You just need to break the events down to smaller pieces. If you only look at the big picture, you will never have enough things to celebrate. It's the little things that turn us into the people we are."

He understood what she was getting at, but he also knew that it was easier said than done.

Maya nodded toward the door. "Okay, come, let's get outta here. Nice walk in the night air will be good for both of us. Besides, I want to be alone with my man. I already shared you with millions of people today, and I got no more room to share you with anybody else. Not tonight, not any night."

She led the way and found Coach standing by the kitchen. Maya softly spoke in his ear, "We're gonna head out now, okay."

Coach looked at Ben, whose eyes were swollen and red, then nodded in approval. "You made me proud today, son. Let's sit down together soon, whenever you're ready. Just to talk."

Ben leaned in, grasped his coach behind the back of the neck, then whispered in his ear, "Thanks, Coach."

It was not just a casual thank-you. It was an appreciation beyond words.

***

At almost 1:00 a.m., Ben and Maya strolled along the streets of Cleveland. Not directly home, but in that general direction. It was late April, and the night air couldn't have been nicer. Cool yet comfortable. The streets were damp from a light rain a few hours earlier, which brought out the scents of nature. Scents that were reminiscent of places far from the ghetto. The best part was that it was silent. Nobody was out on the streets that night. They had the city to themselves, which made it surreal.

"Want a coffee?" Ben asked as they walked by a small corner store. "I'm really not ready to go home yet . . . Maybe we can watch the sunrise together."

Her eyes brightened. "I would love to stay up all night with you. That's a great idea . . . Get some snacks, too. I'm dying for some potato chips."

They crossed the street toward the corner store, which had inspired the idea. The two of them made their way through the narrow shelves stacked high overhead, toward the back of the shop. Just as they hoped, between the doors to the restrooms a small self-serve coffee bar was nestled, which was nothing more than a small machine with paper cups stacked beside it.

Ben grabbed two cups and placed the first under the nozzle.

"I'm gonna go find some chips," Maya said as she headed back toward the front.

"Hey, get those cheese puffs, too. I want to splurge tonight," Ben said with the first sound of brightness in his voice.

The machine made some strange noises, and a thick, sludgy black liquid, loosely resembling coffee, half filled the first cup.

The front door flung open, followed by loud shouting. Ben couldn't place it at first. He tried to peer around the shelves but couldn't get a view.

"Give me the cash," the newcomer shouted. The voice was angry and nervous.

Ben moved to the side, where he could see the man behind the counter pull out a small handgun from beneath the cash machine. He still couldn't see the perpetrator.

Red mist filled the air, simultaneously with a deafening popping sound, echoing through the small store. At least two of the many shots had splashed through the clerk's chest.

Ben ran to the front of the store to get Maya out of Dodge.

The voice cried out, "There's someone else in the back."

The door flung open again, and all Ben could hear was a wheezing sound. Once he reached the front, the wheezing came from beyond the counter but quickly faded—the store clerk. Lying at his own feet was Maya. Silent. Contorted. Very bloody.

Ben dropped to the floor and pulled her body up into his lap. Her head cradled. His heart pounded, but it ticked alone. She was gone.

***

At first, he was frozen with Maya in his lap, then moved over to the clerk, who was also lifeless. He rejoined Maya on the floor and sat in her pooling blood. Blue and red lights flashed through the front window of the store. He had been there for almost two hours, but it felt like a month, and just seconds at the same time. Two hours surrounded by two corpses was unbearable.

Later, Ben found out that it was a gang initiation gone wrong. This exact same store had been hit repeatedly in the past several months. The owner, who had been working double shifts for years, was a known pushover. Tonight, he stood up to his tormentors and fought back. He was no longer going to stand idly by as he gradually lost his business. His wife had already left him due to his never-ending work hours. His kids, whom he hardly knew, had grown up and moved out of the house, which he hadn't realized for almost a week. He chose tonight as his last stand to fight back for a little human decency. Rules of the ghetto. Eat or be eaten, and tonight he was swallowed whole.

Ben was informed that Maya had died instantly. A shot penetrated her chest and tore a large piece from her heart. It tore an even bigger piece of Ben's heart. However, unlike Maya's, the void in his heart refilled with a helpless and aimless fury. He was already teetering on the edge, but now it had become all-consuming. He hated the world and everything in it.

Ben decided that same night that he would never run again. In fact, he knew that somehow he would never really live again. There was nothing purer or as perfect as Maya, and without her, he had no hope. He felt lost within the riptide, being pulled out to sea quicker than he could swim if he tried. Land still in sight, however he already knew that it could never be reached. Sinking. No need to fight it. No need to embrace his survival instincts. Wherever she was, was better than where he was. He intended to join Maya, and the sooner the better.

Chapter Twenty-Six

He jerked the covers over his head as the alarm screeched. A sound that had only recently been heard on race days, the last being for Penn Relays. His stomach groaned as the emptiness inside folded together. He rolled to his side to turn it off. Three days of no food, no running, and a mind drained by both. A wreck of lifelessness. He floated through in a haze while reality washed along beside him unnoticed.

There came a point where what he wanted simply didn't register as a consideration any longer. As a child, his first obsessions sparked life in every step, like being an astronaut hurtling through space to a distant solar system, with the mission of colonizing a new frontier. Later, his dreams became more reasonable, such as running against the elites despite the birthmark of being a slummer. But once all the cards were revealed, a moment of clarity occurred. The glass ceiling was in fact made of concrete with rusted rebar jutting through from above. Ben's dream of competing for the national title avalanched into a raw and primal survival mode. He had still not decided how much he really cared to prioritize his survival. An instinct that can easily be overridden by one's will. This capability was what set humans apart from the animal kingdom.

The sun came up each morning and set in the evening. Besides that, there was no real reason for Ben to consider the time of day any longer. He had no job, nor any willingness to find one. His running career was over, which eliminated any reason to meet Coach Sands. There was no more reason to trod down the short trail from his street to the next to visit Maya.

While brushing his teeth, Ben couldn't even look into the frightfulness of his reflection. He chose to blankly stare into the basin, watching the small doses of water chase down the white foam into the shadowy depths.

Today's alarm clock represented the only task remaining on his annual calendar. Today was the day he would lay his beloved Maya to rest. He wasn't ready and wished to sleep until he was, however, there were no options available to him. His toothbrush reminded him of her for no particular reason. Perhaps fresh breath held no great benefit any longer. A frown pulled on his sullen face. An emotion tugged at him in every waking moment, as if gravity had intensified tenfold.

He stood beneath the shower; tears streamed over his face. They stopped, then started again without warning. His mind drifted through the memories of her, and he could not imagine this day would possibly end, let alone getting past this feeling that dragged him to the dirt.

He hadn't realized how long he had been in the shower until the water began to run cold. Even this, at first, didn't register.

He wrapped the towel around himself, missing swathes of skin still dripping. It really wasn't so important.

"Ben," his father called behind him as he slogged toward his bedroom to get changed.

He must have been in the kitchen. Ben didn't notice him, either. He turned at a speed of the sunflower twisting its head toward the morning sun, but he found no warmth. His hand still on the doorknob to his room.

"You okay, buddy?"

Gravity pulled relentlessly. The burn returned to his eyes. *I will never be okay.* "Yeah, Dad . . . I'll be okay."

His father moved toward him. "Listen, Ben. When I laid your mother to rest, I also thought the world was over. To be honest, it *never* was the same. But many other things in life moved on. These other things can also be wonderful and fulfilling. What I'm trying to say is that today is the hardest day of all. If you want to talk . . . anytime. I understand what you are going through in more ways than you may realize. You were just born when I lost your mom . . . Every day I still think of her. My one true love. But until now, I never *wanted* you to fully understand what I went through. I was in a dark place for a very long time."

Ben nodded. It was inevitable that he'd talk to his dad about this. But not now or anytime soon. They finally had something in common, but sharing sorrowful stories would not improve matters. Ben was concerned that if the conversation didn't play out well, it would tip him off the fence to the more permanent and destructive side of things. He didn't need more variables but also knew he needed to give his dad hope that the conversation might happen.

"We'll see."

He pulled the door open and slid into his bedroom to get ready.

Ben had walked the half mile to Box Row alongside the freeway. It was a corner of the city allotted to the slummers. More specifically, a corner dedicated to dead slummers. A mass grave for the have-nots. Fully funded by the generous city to ensure bodies weren't discarded in the park or dumpsters, which still happened often enough. Affording a funeral was not in the cards for any slummer. In former times, the burden of dealing with one's own losses could set families in financial ruin, ultimately increasing the suicide rate. A death spiral that did not bode well for the morale of the workers. Death was bad for the workforce, which was bad for the economy.

He walked by the small excavator, which stayed on the premises permanently. It opened up plots so close they touched. Pine boxes were lowered in side by side. Ahead was a dreary gathering of the few people who were making an effort to say good-bye to Maya. Death was so common in the slums that besides the immediate family and the very closest friends, nobody else was in attendance. Maya's world extended greater than most, with exactly eleven visitors. Her father was too weak to stand and was the only one sitting on a nearby bench.

Coach was there; he also looked like he had a rough night, with bloodshot eyes and white stubble aging him a decade or two.

Ben's dad and brother huddled with Amy together at a distance, and simply nodded as Ben approached.

"Hi, son, come join us." His dad placed his hand on Ben's shoulder, pulling him into the huddle.

Ben's emotions had already run dry for the day. His well was empty, and he said nothing.

The resident priest, who operated the small chapel as well as the excavator, stood in his threadbare ceremonial clothes. Next to him was a small wooden sign at the edge of the trench where her box had already been lowered.

"Please everyone, gather around."

The people inched forward, but the effort was languid. Her father never left the bench.

"Maya Ramirez was lost so young, at the age of just twenty, to the violence that encumbers our daily lives. This shameful society has taken her to a better place where she will no longer suffer in the cruelty of the slums. I would like to offer a moment of silence."

He lowered his head, as did most others.

With just a short silent moment, a slurred voice from behind them announced, "I wanna say somethin'."

Ben inhaled deeply. Maya's dad had some wisdom to spread upon the day. Her father was wasted, as usual.

"I hate all those gang bangers for taking my only pride. She did everything for me, and now I need to do everything myself. I am lost without my little Maya." He slumped back onto the bench.

Ben had no need to say anything. He spoke to Maya every minute of every day, which was much more meaningful than trying to share his thoughts with the others. She was *his* Maya, and that conversation was between her and Ben, and them alone.

The priest concluded with a few words, but Ben was no longer listening. His eyes were glued on the small wooden marker.

Typically, the plaque contained the deceased's name, birth date, and death date. If the name or birth date were not known, which happened rather often, it simply had the date of departure.

Maya's marker was prepared with all the trimmings. Although Ben knew that she wasn't entirely sure of her birthday, it was certainly in the middle of October of 2065. She chose the eighteenth because she liked the sound of it.

Maya Ramirez
10/18/2065–5/5/2085

That was it. Her entire life summed up. Two words and some numbers. Everything about Maya was somehow captured within Ben. Her passions, personality, and oddities. A soft smile creased his face as he recalled her process of perfecting the snot shot. A talent any runner must master, and a talent that is utterly unknown outside the running community. Runners learned to press closed one nostril to blow out the contents of the other—the snot shot. The learning curve for those not naturally gifted but determined proved for gross memories. Maya was not gifted.

She was his Maya, and he was hers. Their wedding date had already been set.

Before leaving, Ben tossed a single red rose on the plain pine box. It bounced from the top, down the crack between it and the previous box, onto the dirt. He couldn't even get that right.

Her eternal neighbor could have been the guy behind the counter at the corner store. Cleveland had more than five hundred murders per year, and two times as many deaths triggered by "natural" causes in the slums. Ben didn't want to know who and specifically chose not to look. It wouldn't change anything.

The priest moved over to the excavator and began hooking up another box to be lowered. Two people stood by, waiting for their ceremony to begin. *A busy day for the priest,* Ben thought.

Ben walked away from Maya's mourners without saying a thing. He didn't make eye contact with her dad, who probably wasn't coherent enough to catch it anyway. Ben hated him for tarnishing her short life and knew that if he tried to say anything, it would most likely be catastrophic.

He didn't have a plan where to go, but he wasn't going home. He wasn't going anywhere anybody knew him. As he walked, he decided that maybe Lake Erie would share its infinite wisdom, as it often did.

He meandered through the factories and headed toward a fishing area beside a marina lined with rich people's boats.

His weight was relieved by an empty green bench positioned to look straight out over the water toward Canada. The water was choppy with a moderate onshore wind cooling the otherwise warm humid day.

He gazed off into the infiniteness of the lake. Not capable of seeing the other side. For all intents and purposes, there was no other side.

His thoughts ran in circles as he tucked his knees up to his chest. Partly to shield himself from the wind, but primarily to hold onto something. Anything.

There was not a future in which Ben could be happy. He thought back to his naïveté about his running injury. How could he have known back then that getting hurt would ruin his life? How could running in the championship be important at all? He cherished her all the while but at the same time took her for granted. She was always second to his running. If he'd known he would lose her, he would have done everything different. He didn't know how, but he would have done better. Dragged her out of that house she lived in. Worked harder at his job to give them the possibility of a family together. She deserved everything. More than he was ever capable of providing.

He now knew there was only one important thing in his life; however, he realized it after it was already gone.

Chapter Twenty-Seven

A loud knock rapped on his door, jolting him back into awareness. Ben had been sitting in his bed peering into the ether, wafting through memories of all sorts—about Maya, his childhood, a life with the mother he never knew.

He hadn't left the room since the funeral, and his brother had gone to stay at Amy's to give him space. Or, more likely, to escape the morbid atmosphere.

The door opened despite Ben's lack of response. But it wasn't such a surprise, since he didn't respond to much of anything these days. Every day his dad tried to give him a sandwich or bowl of soup, which went untouched until the next effort. Thoughts of self-destruction were at the forefront of his mind, not swapping stories with his dear ol' dad.

He inhaled deeply as he watched his dad enter with a shoebox-sized package in hand, wrapped in a brown paper.

"Hi, buddy," his dad said. "This just came in the mail for you."

Ben looked at it. His facial muscles didn't respond. They were exhausted.

"Here, I'll leave it on the nightstand . . . Er, you need anything?"

Ben's eyes drifted to the box, then back to his dad, then he shook his head ever so slightly to not disturb the settling dust.

The box sat there beneath the yellowish lamp for almost an hour. As much as Ben told himself that he didn't want to open it. That he didn't deserve anything. That he didn't want sympathy. He realized that he was *intentionally* wallowing in his sadness. This infuriated him even more, knowing that he had become such a sack. It was the same quitter mentality that reared its ugly face while deciding if he should sabotage his last race. His shame bellowed, so he reached for the package as the curiosity won over the fight. He was indeed very curious about its contents.

He groaned as he reached for the box.

Handwritten in a thick black ink was his name, *Benjamin Brandt*, with his address below. Postage claimed it had come from New York, New York. He shredded off the paper, and it was a shoebox indeed.

He grabbed a pen from the nightstand drawer, then punctured a few holes in the tape so that he could easily pop it open.

The contents were wrapped in the same brown paper, with a letter on top and his name neatly printed.

The envelope was tucked inside, and within it was a letter. Folded twice, into thirds. It read.

Dear Benjamin,

It was a great pleasure to have met you at Penn Relays in your "escape" vehicle. I have not slept since our meeting and have finally found a solution to your situation.

As a part owner of a small running shoe store in New York City, I have rallied the team. We unanimously decided that we would like to sponsor you as our athlete. You would be our first sponsored athlete, which is a great pleasure for all of us. If you do accept this sponsorship, I have also retained a vote in the committee, against Harvey Woodard's wishes, that would reinstate your results of Penn Relays. This would in effect automatically qualify you to run at the national championships in Eugene, Oregon.

Our limited sponsorship will cover travel costs for you, your coach, and manager (a.k.a. girlfriend). Also included are four free running shoes per year, our team uniform, and other running gear. Enclosed within this package are the best racing spikes available, as well as your race singlet. You may keep these, independent of your decision. If you do agree to this sponsorship, a formal contract is included, which would need to be signed and returned to us promptly. Postage has been prepaid.

Personally, I truly hope that you join our team. I know that we would have a very bright future together.

Yours Most Sincerely,
Julia Turner
Sole's Runner co-owner

Ben tossed the letter on the bed beside him. He pulled the brown paper from the package, which slid off the edge of the bed to the floor.

The uniform was folded on top so that the design was on full display. It was all green with a white racing shoe in the middle, spawning wings on either side like a Pegasus. He pulled it from the box, and the smooth material was of the highest quality, at least compared to Ben's limited experience. Beneath the image of the winged shoe was the sponsor's name, Sole's Runner.

An image of him racing down the homestretch at Hayward Field, carried by the wings of Sole's Runner bolted to his chest, flashed before his eyes.

Still holding onto the shirt, which he was not ready to put down yet, he pulled out the pair of race spikes hugging each other, inverted front to back. They matched the same green color as his shirt with white strips along the side. He was set back by how light they were. He thought that they were even lighter than his socks. And he knew that they were lighter than the duct tape and adhesives that he had once bound his old trainers with.

Ben closed his eyes, inhaled deeply, then lay back down in his bed. The uniform draped over his chest. Shoes still in hand, he gingerly caressed the tip of a spike with his finger.

He needed to think, and for that, he needed blood circulation to clear the haze.

Sprawled across the bed were the package's contents. Ben pulled on his running gear. As he passed through the living room, his dad was in the kitchen and brother was on the couch, visiting for the afternoon.

Ben mumbled, "Be back later."

He didn't wait for an answer as the door closed behind him. Ben needed to search for his own answers, and the only way for him to think clearly was to go for a run.

***

His training shoes felt nostalgic. It had only been a week and a half, but his feet missed the feeling. He wound his way toward the old trusty towpath. He often chose this route for his long runs, and rather quickly, he remembered exactly why. Minutes from the dreariness of the slums, he was teleported into a natural and breathtaking pathway along the ancient creek. His muscles still ached, but they slowly returned to normal. He never performed a proper cooldown after Penn Relays, and other than the funeral, he'd sat like a rock in his bed for much of the time since.

As the kinks loosened up, Ben ratcheted up a solid yet sustainable pace. He glided along the trails. However, today wasn't about training. He was searching.

His face crumpled each time he remembered Maya's laughter, her targeted jokes at his expense, or her soft lips. She was everything to him. He recalled that he had nothing to look forward to in his life before he met her, even though he was still just a child. She was his inspiration. Not just in running, but in living.

In some way, he ran to make her proud. He didn't believe he had much to offer her, but his running was something she admired and something unique that only he could provide. What was the point of running without a muse? Self-driven accomplishment could bring one far down the road, but without sharing the thrill of it all with someone who understood, it was all kind of meaningless.

A biker came toward him on the trail and as he approached, his face transformed by anger. "Go home, slummer."

Ben stopped in his tracks, turned around, and shouted after him, "I have a disease that you certainly just picked up riding that close to me. Good luck with that, Slummerphobe."

The biker stopped pedaling and looked over his shoulder. His face had changed once more from anger into fear, with an aftertaste of disgust. He returned to pedaling and sped off into the distance. He would probably call his doctor just in case.

Ben walked over to the stream beside the path and found a bench to rest upon. Maya would have laughed her head off at that, he thought. Maya would have chased him, making crazy noises to really startle the man so much so that he might have a coronary. Maya would not have found it hilarious that Ben was preparing to quit his running career, especially because of her. She would downright beat the sense back into him.

Maya wasn't there on that bench beside him that day, but she spoke volumes to him anyway. His mind was made up. He wasn't going to race again because the people expected him to. Or because it was his dream. He decided on that bench that he was going to race at the national championship because that is what Maya would have told him he must do. Even in these extreme circumstances. Her spirit wasn't drifting around him in some mysterious fog, it was his memories of her that told him how to proceed. He extrapolated everything she had ever said or ever done and applied it to the current situation. She would have been ashamed of him for the very first time. This man who was sitting on the bench wallowing in sadness was not the man she intended to marry.

Ben continued on his run for several more miles before turning back. He was at ease. Every streaming thought from that bench forward bolstered his decision. No doubts remained. He was going to enjoy the beautiful nature as he paced down the path. Then it was time to see Coach.

Chapter Twenty-Eight

Still damp with sweat, Ben climbed up the flights of stairs to Coach's apartment. The package from Julia Turner was tucked beneath his arm, which he retrieved as soon as his run was finished.

Coach opened the door, and his expression switched into one of surprise, gratefulness, and empathy, all tucked within the folds and lines around his puffy eyes.

Ben stood just outside the door. Happy that he had found a turning point today. He noticed the redness of his mentor's eyes.

Without grace, he waved Ben in. Coach scurried toward the table and chairs by the window to quickly clear the dozen empty beer bottles, which were haphazardly strewn around the apartment.

"Son, it is good to see you," he said between the clanging of bottles as they dropped into the trash can.

Ben sat by the window and placed the folded letter on the table. His hand gently rested on top.

As his coach slid into the chair opposite him, breathing heavily from the unexpected exertion, the afternoon light cast a deep contrast over his face. He looked as if he had aged another decade since Ben last saw him at the funeral, just days before.

"I've been thinking," Ben said as he peeked out the window, mostly because he didn't like seeing his coach this way. "I just went for a run and really burned out all of my wasteful energy. I've made a decision."

Coach inched forward in his chair. "Yes, Ben."

He returned his gaze toward the broken-down man. "I am going to run in Eugene."

The weathered fold lines softened around his eyes, and new creases formed horizontally across his forehead. "Oh, that is wonderful news, Ben. We've got an entire year to get you ready. We're gonna bring the fight to their doorstep."

Ben pushed the paper across the table, then retracted his hand.

Coach looked toward the paper, then back up at Ben. "What's this?"

Ben nodded for him to proceed.

He opened it, and his eyes darted back and forth as a typewriter would. His brows lifted further with each passing line.

Ben couldn't refrain from smiling as he watched Coach read the letter. "She got us reinstated for *this* year."

He snapped his head upward and slammed his hand on the table. "Wow, Ben!" he shouted. "Yes, yes, yes."

"We gonna do this?" Ben asked in sincerity. He needed to share the weight of this unmeasurable challenge. Without Maya, his support group was all on Coach's shoulders. "I can't do this alone."

His coach bobbed his head. "As long as I am around, you will never be alone. You were destined for this, Ben."

"Well, I don't know about that. But check this out." Ben opened up the box and placed the race singlet and spikes on the table. His heart rate fluttered each time he saw the race shirt. "It's awesome, isn't it?"

Coach reached out to touch the fabric. "Oh, I am so proud of you."

"Before we go too far. I am not really so good at writing. Can you help me write a response to my new sponsor?" Ben got chills as he said it. It was the first time he had said it out loud.

"Gladly." Coach heaved himself to his feet. "I'll be right back."

Ben looked at the singlet laid flat on the table. He wished Maya could see this thing. He wished she could be celebrating with him right now. After all, this moment was because of her.

Coach came back into the room with a piece of paper and a pen.

The two of them crafted a response to Julia Turner. As they reread her letter to ensure everything was covered, they agreed to add a postscript.

P.S. Only Benjamin Brandt and Coach Martin Sands will need travel and lodging arrangements. Our manager will not be available to attend.

Ben signed at the bottom of the contract and placed both papers into the prepaid envelope.

They looked at each other and began laughing.

"You okay, Ben?"

Ben swallowed hard and nodded. "Yeah, kinda. It still hurts, but I got a new perspective on things, you know? It's just gonna take some time. I don't think it will ever be *really* okay, but it's getting better."

"Good. That makes me happier than everything else. It does take time and I am here for you if you need anything."

***

Ben arrived a few minutes early to the bench. His young friend Logan was playing with an old plastic dump truck, which was missing the dumper as well as both front wheels. His face lit up when he saw Ben.

"Hi, are you going to go running?"

He laughed, then said, "I am. We are going to the track so I can do a repeat workout."

"Repeat?"

"Yeah, I will run four-hundred meters fast, then two hundred slow, and repeat them until I can't any longer. It helps me practice my speed and makes me quick. I am getting ready for a big race."

"Can I go watch your repeats . . . I have never seen you really run?"

"I would love for you to come, but I don't think your mom would be okay with you going with us."

From the balcony, his mother interjected. "Hey, I would love to see you run, too. If it's okay with you, I have a bike and Logan can sit on the handlebars."

Ben shrugged, "Yeah, that could be fun."

Coach had come up from behind him. "Hey. Good morning everyone."

Ben turned. "You mind if they watch the workout today?"

"I think that would be a wonderful thing." He patted Logan on the shoulder. "Have you ever seen a cheetah running wild through the Savannah?"

He shook his head, looking bewildered.

"Well, you're gonna see one today."

This was a turning point in Ben's life. He had once been a runner with a dream. Everything was on the surface, focused on competition, and nothing else. Now, he was racing for something greater than himself. Something much deeper and more profound. He was racing not just for Maya, but for what she believed in, too. He was racing on behalf of the very slums that took her life. He was racing for a better and more tolerant future for all those who had no choice but to be born as natural births, who would then pass that very same fate on to their kids, grandkids, and beyond. An unbreakable chain growing more cumbersome with each generation. He was going to race for every Logan in the world, and more specifically, the one sitting on his mom's handlebars riding behind him on the way to the track.

Ben's intensity breached limits that he didn't previously believe possible. It was a Tuesday afternoon in the middle of May, and he found himself back at the old cinder track in front of the closed steel plant. The ominous smokestacks loomed overhead—a symbol of the dysfunctional corporate world.

"Today, it's quarters till death," Coach said. His sadistic grin was alive and well as he winked at the young boy and his mother. He went on to explain the intricacies of the workout to Logan and his mother.

Everything that Ben held dear was laid out on the line. He crossed over to a new dimension on that particular Tuesday. Over and over again, Ben maintained the grueling sixty-second pace. Exactly on target, never wavering more than a half second plus or minus. He had become a machine. A mechanism of war driven by the power of everything.

He had the most authoritative weapon of all. With Logan and his mom watching, Ben's destiny was finally clear. He was the champion of all slummers.

After the workout, he stooped down to Logan's level. "Wanna run with me?"

His eyes nearly popped from the sockets. No words. He nodded in the way only a child could.

Ben winked, then tilted his head toward the track. "Come on, let's crank out a quarter mile together."

He and Logan headed into the first turn. Playfully exchanging surges as Ben shouted out like an announcer might. Everything in the world evaporated.

Logan would never forget that afternoon. Ben wouldn't, either.

Chapter Twenty-Nine

"Hi, Amy. They aren't home yet, but come on in." Ben grabbed the cardboard box from her arms as she entered their apartment.

"I think this place could use a lady's touch. What do you think?" She winked at him.

Ben laughed as he looked around his family room, not seeing a trace of color. "Yeah, actually, you're probably right. Maybe some pink doilies over there."

She smacked him in the shoulder. "Pink doilies? Really?"

Ben laughed at his own joke.

"I know it's going to be a bit crowded, but if you ever need a little space, please Ben, let me know."

Ben shrugged. "It's good. Your parents are moving in with your brother, right?"

"Yeah, with the foundry closing, it is better to downsize a little. I am actually looking forward to spending more time with you. We don't talk enough."

Ben agreed. He liked Amy and was glad that his brother had found someone who was completely the opposite of him, someone who was actually nice.

"Hey, Amy." Ben's dad and brother arrived back from the last day at the foundry. Permanently shut down. "Welcome home."

She giggled. "I was just telling Ben how much I am looking forward to this."

"Us too." Ben's dad reached in for a big hug. "Have you got more things to bring over?"

"Um, yeah, I got two more boxes, just some clothes."

"Boys. Help the young lady out. I want to spend some time with her."

Ben and Daniel headed out of the apartment together.

"I can't believe you are really going to Oregon," Daniel said. "I've never even left Cleveland."

"Until a year ago, I hadn't, either. On one side, it is really cool to see a new city, but I gotta say, the people are horrible. I am getting more used to it, though."

"I don't say this much . . . um, I mean never. I am really proud of you. I know how hard it is without Maya, and I think this will help you move on. Are you sure having Amy around won't be a problem?"

Ben had never seen this side of his brother. "No, I like her very much. Besides, them getting rid of their apartment will help cover costs. Who knows when everyone can find work again?"

"At least Amy still has her job, but her dad isn't handling losing his job at the foundry well. It doesn't look good. I went to three different factories after my shifts this week, and even in the afternoon, there were a hundred people lined up outside of every one of them."

"Things are getting bad, aren't they?"

His brother nodded. "It's going to get worse around here. For the entire neighborhood."

***

His legs felt like springs wound so tight that they might explode at any moment. Ben jogged along the street, heading to the towpath with Coach riding beside him. It was six days until the championship, and for the first time in his life, he was going through the process of tapering.

Unlike Ben's legs, Coach's bike had picked up a peculiar squeak.

"What did you do to that thing?" Ben asked. He shook his head. "And I thought the lopsided wheel was bad enough."

"Not sure. I just unlocked her this morning, and she started crying. Maybe it's starting to fear you."

Ben laughed. "I don't know, I thought we were friends after those days taking me over to the lake for swimming workouts."

"Maybe she just longs for you."

Ben nearly had to stop running to catch his breath from laughing. "Are we still talking about your bike? No wonder everyone stares at us."

While discussing the crippled bike, they cruised into the park entrance.

"Come on, Coach, let me blast one out a little. I can't control myself anymore."

He laughed. "Ben, we need to save it for the big race. You're tapering. Nothing we do now is going to get you more prepared for next weekend. All we can do is keep the joints moving, do some stride-outs at race pace, and, above all else, rest. We are in a preservation mode."

"I know, but come on, I need a hot mile or something." Ben was losing it. He had so much built-up energy already, he would never survive another five days without opening the release valve a little.

"Okay, okay. One hot mile . . . Not too hot, though. Warm, lukewarm."

Ben winked at his coach as he began to accelerate. "Inferno hot . . . Be back soon."

He leaned forward and started to roll. After days of rest, he felt like a lion being released from the zoo. Absolute freedom. Wind in his hair, quick, rhythmic padding of his feet down the trail. His muscles had never felt so powerful in his life. Effortlessly pushing off stride for stride. His forward motion was restricted by absolutely nothing. He knew no bounds. Ben knew that he was ready. Not just ready to race, but to contend for the title. He thought, *Maya would be proud of me if I won the whole damn thing.*

He smiled at the thought, knowing very well that Maya would already be proud of him, whether he won or not.

Chapter Thirty

Ben clenched the armrest. He looked out the window, and the engine thundered away as he was pushed back into his seat.

"You good?" asked Coach.

"Oh, yeah, you know." At that moment, the plane lifted from the ground, but Ben's stomach remained below.

"Woah," he whispered. "That is some serious acceleration. I need to get myself a set of these jet engines."

Coach smiled, entirely relaxed and clearly enjoying the sight of Ben squirming.

Ben stuck his nose to the window and looked down as his Cleveland shrank away from him. "This is really amazing. I had no idea what it would be like."

"Yeah, I remember my first time . . . but it wasn't so pleasant."

Ben looked back. "What do you mean?"

"Well, I was heading to New York. It was before the high-speed train line was installed. And we flew right through a thunderstorm." His face whitened from the mere memory. "I thought we were going to fall straight out of the sky at one point. The dumb thing kept dropping at unexpected times. Crew members all buckled in. You know it's a bad flight when the crew members lose all color and their fake smiles attempt to show confidence where there clearly is none."

Ben looked back out the window, appreciating the turbulence-free flight. He could see the entire coastline of Lake Erie, and truly how massive the body of water really was. "Yeah, I am happy with the current weather situation."

Coach patted his hand on the arm rest. "All right, I am gonna try to take a nap. Not as young as I used to be."

"Okay." There was no chance for Ben to take a nap. He was wired.

As the plane broke through the cumulus clouds, the skies became a rich blue, with the brilliant sun rising in the east. *I can't believe I am really doing this.*

Almost 2,500 miles from home and just a two-and-a-half-hour flight. The time zone shifted by three hours, which meant that he would arrive before he left. As a distance runner obsessed with time, this perplexed Ben in the most curious of ways.

After they landed and left the airport, their car pulled up to the Best Western by the Willamette River. His new sponsor had arranged everything. It was three days before the showdown, and he had nothing to concern himself with besides resting and getting his mind in the right order. The ghetto was far behind him but not forgotten.

While grabbing their bags from the car, Coach said, "Okay, let's go check in, then you can go for a very short and slow run to loosen up your legs after the flight. Then we just lay low. Got it?"

Ben nodded.

It was the nicest room Ben had ever seen. They had adjoining rooms so that they could convene together as they wished.

Ben flopped onto the bed, which absorbed him like the clouds they had just flown through. It was as if the bed was an enormous pillow. His bed at home was more like boards with a thin stuffing on top, hardly superior to sleeping on straw.

Once settled in, he pulled on his shoes and headed out the door. The air smelled fresh and was scented with nature. It was mesmerizing. Every city had a certain smell, and this was, without question, Ben's new favorite. The slums had a more disparaging odor, even though it did smell of home.

Coach had already given him directions to the stadium. He headed south, and within just a moment, he could see the massive stadium with an enormous tower looming overhead. Contrary to Franklin Field, which was an historical landmark, this place was a modern high-tech marvel. Rebuilt twelve years ago, it was the gem of American track and field. So much so that they'd held the national championship there every year since.

He jogged straight up to the gates and could look through at the track. *Beautiful.*

A man came up to him from the other side of the gate. His face was serious and he wore a security uniform. "What's your business here?"

Ben smiled. "Oh, I'm racing here on Saturday. Can I come in and look at the track?"

He pulled his head back and laughed. "You kidding me? Get out of here, slummer."

Ben leaned forward and looked him in the eye. Holding on to his anger as best he could. "See you Saturday."

The man scoffed as Ben looked back at the track one more time. He whispered to the track this time, "See you Saturday."

He ran a couple circles around the outside of the stadium, then jogged through the campus before returning to the hotel. They ordered in a pizza, which turned out to be the best dinner Ben had ever had.

Despite the time difference and staying up three hours longer than normal, he lay in bed staring up at the dark ceiling. Everything was racing through his mind, and he couldn't for a moment think that he would ever fall asleep. Sometime around three in the morning, Ben grabbed the duvet from the bed and moved to the floor. He slept like a baby.

* * *

With just a few hours of sleep, he woke to his alarm at 8:00 a.m. The exact same time he planned to wake for the big event in two days. A routine had to be established.

He laced up his running shoes and went out the door.

An easy six miles was on the agenda.

He was tired, but not as much as he thought he would be with such little sleep. His interest was piqued, which helped overcome the weariness.

The town was beautiful. Nature and civilization intertwined. He loved it already.

Ben found himself on a hilly, windy road with houses clinging to the rocks and an assortment of tall trees everywhere. He ran along Birch Lane, then took a left onto Skyline Boulevard.

On his right was a cliff wall alongside the street. Nestled into the rock was a monument. Running shirts lay on the nearby stones, and miniature American flags were stuck in the ground. The dark-gray marble marker had a picture of a guy with a mustache. Ben vaguely recognized him. The text read.

"PRE"

For your dedication and loyalty
To your principles and beliefs . . .
For your love, warmth, and friendship
For your family and friends . . .
You are missed by so many
And you will never be forgotten . . .

It dawned on Ben that this was a monument to Steve Prefontaine. An American running legend and the namesake for the championship race in just two days. He was also the runner Samantha Bell had profiled just one year ago. A lifetime ago.

Pre was a natural blood, as everyone was in that era. A warrior of running, a legend who would endure forever. No DNA enhancements, just guts. Raw and brutal guts. Ben respected that.

***

The last day before the race, Ben felt refreshed. The previous night he had skipped over the bed altogether and slept directly on the floor, where he fell into a deep and necessary slumber.

Coach had returned from the grocery store with an assortment of food. They had a small kitchenette in the room with a stove where he prepared dinner.

"It's an old runner's tradition to have spaghetti the night before the race," Coach said as he filled a pot of water.

Ben laughed. "That's why I became such a good runner. Noodles are the only thing I can afford."

"Well, I got a little surprise for you while we eat."

Ben stood from the sofa and headed toward the kitchen area. "I like surprises."

"Well, I got this at the front desk earlier." He pointed to a small package on the counter that had already been opened. "It was sent from Samantha Bell."

His eyebrows lifted. "From Samantha Bell?"

"Yeah, check it out."

Ben reached into the yellow packet and retracted a letter. As he opened the letter, he noticed that Coach was smiling from one ear to the other.

Dear Benjamin Brandt,

Welcome to the 2085 National Championship. Since capturing my attention at Kent State, I have become one of your biggest fans. It brought tears to my eyes when I heard that you had been disqualified at Penn, and again when I learned, with joy, that you were reinstated.

I have never looked forward to a championship as much as I have this year, and I cannot wait to watch you compete for the title. I believe in you.

One hour before your race, I will be profiling an athlete, as I do each year. Who they are, where they come from, and what makes them a competitor who strives for greatness? This year, I have chosen to feature you. The young man from Cleveland.

Below is the video QR code, which you can scan from your hotel television since you will certainly be warming up tomorrow while it runs live across the United States. I hope you enjoy it.

Yours Sincerely,
Samantha Bell
CSUS Sports News

Ben hurried over to the TV, turned it on, and placed the black and white block code over the scanner. This was nothing like Maya's old dinosaur of a television.

The media player opened on the display. "Hurry, Coach, let's watch it."

"Hold your horses. Let me finish making dinner first."

Ben scowled at him.

He laughed. "Okay, okay. Fine. I never should have assumed a runner could be patient."

He turned off the stove top just as the water began to boil and moved over to the sofa with Ben.

Samantha Bell looked into the camera as if she was talking directly to them. Her famous smile oozed charm. "Today's much-anticipated showdown of the 5000 meters has been written up as the race of the century. Eric Richardson, Cyrus Cray, and Archer Sinclair—all of them will be gunning for the title. All of them have won major races this very season, and they hold multiple national records between them at the 5000- and 10,000-meters.

"However, I would like to introduce you to a fourth competitor. A young man from simple upbringings. A young man who has waged war against poverty and qualified for the main event amid a storm of controversy. I would like to introduce to you, and to the world, Benjamin Brandt."

Ben looked at his coach. "This is freaking unreal."

Coach was stunned, silent.

The documentary began to roll.

It was Ben's life story sprawled across the screen. Tomorrow, it would be broadcast coast to coast, across tens of millions of televisions.

The video contained interviews of people from his neighborhood. A clip from Maya talking about Ben as a poet who writes with his interval workouts. She'd never mentioned the interview to him. Another clip of him crushing the competition at Kent State in the final lap, as well as the angry words shouted at him from the stands.

A still photo of when he crossed the finish line at Penn Relays as the clock showed his qualifying time. The narrator explained his disqualification while the photo stood frozen. It dissolved and switched to his quote from after the race: "Maybe I feel that America has lost its soul."

Ben winced and sucked in air between his teeth. He instantly regretted saying that, now knowing that everyone was going to hate him even more.

Next was a still photo of him and Maya, with their foreheads together in a tender moment just before Penn Relays. The photo remained, slowly zooming in until their high-resolution faces captured the full screen.

The matter-of-fact narrator's voice turned somber. "Just four weeks ago, Benjamin's fiancée was brutally murdered in the slums. Gang violence knows no boundaries on the tough and cruel streets of Cleveland. Despite this most devastating travesty, or perhaps because if it, Benjamin Brandt is here today to represent his people, his city, poverty at large, and the love of his life, Maya Ramirez."

Samantha Bell broke back in. "Today, Benjamin Brandt will contend against some of the fastest 5k runners this world has ever designed. Benjamin is the first natural birth to qualify for the championship in more than forty years, and in just thirty minutes from now, he will toe the starting line among the giants of the track and field world. And for this, it will truly be the race of the century."

Chapter Thirty-One

He looked at the bedside clock with its glowing green numbers. The alarm was set, but it was just 6:30 a.m., an hour and half before the thing would sing in the new day.

The edges of the window, around the thick drawn curtain, began to glow a faint orange.

He exhaled, switched off the alarm, preventing it from going off later, and pulled on his shoes.

There was no chance for more sleep anyway.

As he opened the door, a rush of fresh damp forest air charmed him with scents of pine. He had fallen in love with the mornings of the great Northwest.

Today marked the inconceivable. The odds of him even being in Eugene, Oregon, were impossible to calculate. However, it was upon him. He had been officially obsessed with this goal for one year, but in many ways, he'd had his sights on it ever since his birth.

He propelled himself forward into a three-mile morning warm-up to shake everything loose. These weren't the final anticipated moments of Christmas morning. There were no gifts spread out below the tree ready for the taking, ready for effortless gratification.

This wasn't anything like that. This morning was more like waking up anticipating the final surge of a battle in Old England, prepared to storm the castle. Odds stacked against you. Chances of survival were slim, but the rewards were unimaginable.

This was a day that promised monumental results, one way or another. It was medieval in its very nature.

Ben trotted along the Ruth Bascom Bike Path, then across the Willamette River to Day Island, where he found a well-maintained dirt trail, Pre's Trail it was called.

As he passed the occasional jogger, without fail, they welcomed him with a warm "Mornin'."

He was surprised by the quantity of joggers at this early hour, and more so by their demeanor. Although Ben didn't look as much like a slummer, wearing the new running clothes his sponsor had left for him at the hotel upon his arrival, he still expected some taunting. *Maybe they are still half-asleep*, he thought.

His legs had been bound springs for days, but this morning, they felt heavy. His stomach was unbalanced, and his energy was lacking.

He wished he could have raced any day this week, but not today. Today was one of those days where he just didn't feel like a rocket.

Ben tossed in a few thirty-yard stride-outs to see if he could get the machine to kickstart, but no luck.

As he came back to his hotel, the sun had already risen over the trees. He stretched while basking in its warmth.

He looked at his watch. His race started at 1:13 p.m., and it was still 7:00 a.m. Ben headed back to his room so he could put his feet up. A banana waited on the table for him.

***

Coach knocked on the adjoining door between their rooms, then entered. Ben's side was already left ajar in anticipation.

He looked good. Dressed like a gentleman, clean shaven, and with a glow that radiated into the room.

"I feel like crap, Coach," Ben said. He had been waiting to discuss it with Coach all morning. He figured Coach couldn't do much about it, but maybe there was a trick or something that could rid him of this weariness.

"Of course you do," he said nonchalantly as he sat on the couch.

"What?"

"I would be worried if you didn't . . . It's just nerves. Everyone gets them."

"Yeah, but my legs felt so powerless and heavy on my morning run."

"Come." He patted the couch beside him, enticing Ben to join him. "Listen, it's the circle that you must master. A mental game."

Ben sat. Tuned in.

"You feel heavy because you worry about your race. Worrying makes you feel out of sorts, so then you worry about feeling out of sorts. You get it?"

"Um, you're saying I need to stop worrying?"

Coach winked at him. "Good. Problem solved, let's move on."

A half smile came to his face. "Okay, Coach. I'm moving on."

Ben had been holding his race singlet since before Coach entered the room. He placed it on his lap and admired the stenciled shoe with a wing. "I can hardly believe it."

"It is a special day today, Ben. For me, too." He looked to Ben, then squinted his eyes. "Hey, I got an idea . . . One moment."

Coach bounced off the couch and went into his room, leaving the adjoining door open. A moment later he returned, and halfway across the room, he tossed Ben a black permanent marker.

Ben nearly caught it as it bounced from his fingertips and landed beside him.

"What's this for?" he asked as he picked it up.

"Write her name . . . There on the wing."

He warily looked back to Coach.

"Go ahead. She is here with you today. That's all you have to remember. She is with you through everything. Especially at the grittiest of moments."

He laid the shirt flat on the coffee table and wrote along the top arch of the wing in capital letters.

MAYA

He looked up again. "Gosh that's stupid. They're gonna laugh, aren't they?"

"Who? Who cares, Ben? This is between you and Maya. Any fool who laughs at that isn't half a man."

Ben snorted a single laugh. "Yeah, Coach. Got it."

"Ready to go?"

Ben wanted to either stop time or catapult forward until after the race. His preference was for the latter. His nerves told him he wasn't ready, but his body was in the best condition it had ever been in. He sucked in a deep breath, then blew it out again. "Okay."

Together, side by side, athlete and coach walked the four hundred meters down Agate Street to the famed Hayward Field. They could already hear the sounds of the event hanging over the city. It was called "The House That Pre built." Despite being rebuilt twice since then, Ben wanted to believe that it was still Pre's house, and he had the honor of being there. A tribute to the natural bloods. Perhaps a sacrifice.

Two hours before the race, they arrived to the sound of thunder. The stadium roared as events ripped the fans into a frenzy of cheering. Above, dark clouds had moved in.

They walked through the crowded stadium until they found a covert corner tucked beneath the grandstands. A place he could hide out until it was time for his warm-up.

It was the first track race he had ever been to without Maya. In fact, since she was the one who owned the TV set, he had never even seen a track race without her beside him.

Watching the national championship on TV was a very different experience than sitting in the shadows, preparing to strike. The anticipation to see your favorite runners compete for the championship was nothing like attempting to chase them down yourself. A distant spectator who became the center-stage gladiator.

Coach had wandered off to ensure the registration was all in order.

Ben closed his eyes and envisioned the strategy he and Coach had agreed on over the past few weeks. Steady pace, conserve energy, glide up through the field at the mile mark, maintain mile two, and come into the third and final mile with guns blazing. *I'm going nuclear today.*

"Benjamin?" asked a man's voice.

Ben opened his eyes and looked up at the person looming over him with shoulder-length hair and a smirk that brimmed with confidence.

"We haven't officially met. I'm Cyrus Cray."

Ben knew exactly who he was; the only question was, why he was there?

"Hi. Yeah, I am quite sure who you are. I'm a big fan."

"Just wanted to wish you the best today."

Ben nodded. "You too, thank you."

"You know, my mom grew up in the slums of LA . . . Skid Row, they call it. Dad found her singing on a street corner panning for money. He couldn't believe that an angel could be trapped with bound wings, so he freed her."

Ben's face muscles contorted in a wave of awkward emotion.

"Thank you, Cyrus."

"No problem, man. See you on the oval of misery."

Ben chuckled as Cyrus disappeared as quickly as he had appeared.

"Okay, Ben." His coach returned just minutes later. "Time to get in your warm-up, then onto the track for check-in."

Ben rolled out for a quick jog, then returned, still feeling heavy.

"You good?" Coach asked.

Ben just nodded as he stripped down to his official racing uniform and pulled on his ultra-light racing spikes. He whispered to himself, "Hardest part about running is lacing up the shoes."

His singlet wore Maya's wings.

The small quarter-inch spikes clattered on the concrete floor until he reached the track surface.

As he emerged through the tunnel, every fan in the stadium had their eyes on the pole-vault pit, where the long-standing women's world record was being threatened. She was fearless as she launched above the pole with a poetic arch, twisting her body in perfect harmony with the cross bar. Her hip touched the bar, causing it to wobble as she crashed back to earth, into the squishy blue mattress. The bar's bounce slowed and settled back into position. The stadium went into a frenzy, a thunderous sound as the new world record had been set. Ben was shocked that the crowd's rumble hadn't inadvertently sent the bar off its perch.

All of them were there. His competition sprinted into short stride-outs along the backstretch. The race was moments away. "The race of the century," they called it. Their disposition was different than it had been at Penn Relays. They had a different level of focus and concentration. No joking around. No slummer jokes. No direct eye contact. They were all preparing to storm the castle.

Cyrus, Archer, and Eric were each expecting to destroy one another. Everybody on that track, in the stadium, and in homes and bars across America where the tens of millions of fans watched, knew that two of these three would fail to accomplish what they had been training for. *The cruelest sport ever*, Ben thought.

The current world record had been picked away at for years. The second generation of genetic engineering competencies had finally matured into their twenties. The designer athletes ruled the show. The world record currently stood at 12:14. Ben was nowhere close to that, but his competition was certainly capable of pulling it out of the hat.

Cyrus shot by on a gust of wind.

Ben checked in with the official, then jogged up to the wall beside the track where Coach stood.

"Ben?" He twisted his head to capture his attention.

His eyes were up in the stadium, then returned to Coach's. "Yeah?"

"Destroy them."

Ben pulled his head back, surprised that he wasn't offering any specific advice. He smiled, placed his hand behind his coach's neck, and pulled their foreheads together. Absorbing his energy. Eyes closed, silent. It was time.

Ben turned back toward the track and ran to the starting line. *Lucky jerk . . . his job of coaching is already done, and he gets to enjoy the show.*

The dark clouds stacked overhead. A breeze from the stratosphere came through, chilling the air. The storm was coming.

The official got everyone in line.

Over the loudspeaker, the announcer named the participants, as the stadium reciprocated with cheers.

Midway through, it was his turn. "Benjamin Brandt, from Cleveland, Ohio."

The sound changed to something less welcoming. He glanced over at Cyrus, who was three positions from him. He was absorbed in his own thoughts.

After the following two, the announcer said, "Cyrus Cray, from Los Angeles, California."

The stadium thundered to life. Ben distinctly heard a young lady scream out, "I love you, Cyrus."

"The former American record holder in the 5000 meters, Eric Richardson."

Fans electrified the air again.

"And the current American record holder at the 5000 meters, at 12:18, Archer Sinclair."

By now, everyone in the stadium was on their feet, and they wouldn't sit down for the following twelve-plus minutes. This was the most anticipated race of the year, and for good cause. Never had three nearly equal and ferocious competitors toed the line together, shooting for the national title.

Despite Samantha Bell's story about Ben, which would have aired just moments ago, he would be just a footnote on this epic event. This thought put his mind at ease. He realized that he wasn't what everyone would be focusing on anyway. He had already accomplished his dream, standing here inside Hayward Field. He had nothing more to prove; he just had to not screw it up. He could just take it easy, run a good time, and celebrate his accomplishment. That wouldn't be enough.

"Runners, on your marks."

Flashes of the past year raced through his mind as he stepped forward.

The cannon in the infield shot a mighty puff of smoke. BOOM.

He felt the percussion in his bones as he launched forward. The sound echoed around the stadium.

Within the first twenty meters, the heaviness in Ben's legs evaporated. They glided along the track effortlessly, just as Coach had predicted.

Pace, pace, pace, he repeated to himself.

Ben was caught up by the event and had found himself directly in the middle of the pack. His pace seemed fast, but he didn't trust the accuracy of his measurement. Not with so much adrenaline. As he came through the first half lap, he was right: three seconds too fast already. He felt good. Great.

The pack was tight with at least eight people. Cyrus led the main group. Eric and Archer found themselves even farther ahead. Their own paces had already earned them ten meters ahead of Cyrus.

Perhaps it was for the sole purpose of running beside Cyrus, but Ben edged through the field to join his idol. Shoulder to shoulder, stride for stride. Tied for third place with a pack of hungry wolves behind him. All of whom were also just footnotes of today's event.

On the next turn, Ben tucked in behind Cyrus to shorten the distance of the long arch. He planted his eyes directly on a small logo embroidered between Cyrus's shoulder blades. A blue *M*, but he didn't know what it stood for. Over the next two laps, he pondered its potential meaning without removing his eyes from it, not thinking of the race he was running at all.

As the mile marker approached, Ben was much too fast. His even pace, energy conservation strategy was already out the window. Eyes locked. Legs on cruise control.

This is fun.

The field was close behind Ben; however, it was thinning out. A string of elite runners formed into a serpent, with Cyrus as its head.

Both Eric and Archer widened the gap. Now almost thirty meters ahead of Cyrus.

Ben thought they must have been going after the world record, and he had the best seat in the house.

His eyes returned to their lock on Cyrus. A sharp pain slashed into the side of his right leg above the ankle. Searing wet blood chased the spikes that had gouged him from behind. Ben stumbled to the ground as his attacker huffed out, "Slummer," to him as he passed. Ben slammed his knee on the ground but kept his hands in front. With a quick roll, he rebounded to his feet. Four more runners passed him without sympathy. His natural-born blood sprayed onto the backstretch. The crowd responded with an, "Ooo," as if a beast had just been wounded in the colosseum.

Bloodied and wounded. A surge of adrenaline pumped into his veins.

There was no more cruise control.

Ben launched himself forward, back toward the few who had passed him. His energy conservation was long gone. He knew that this surge was going to hurt worse than the wound in just a few minutes. Exactly how many minutes was the question he couldn't answer.

A few cheers emerged from the stadium to applaud his resurgence.

Lightning flashed in the distance. Three seconds. Thunder clapped from the deepest pits of the universe.

Ben found himself two positions behind Cyrus, split only by the jerk who had spiked him.

Five laps to go. Ben's pace remained tight behind his nemesis, but Cyrus started to pull away. The leaders had maintained their healthy gap, side by side, but hadn't increased it for several laps. Thirty meters.

Ben recognized that Cyrus was going after them. He was going to contend for the title. He thought about Maya and surged once more as the turn straightened out into the backstretch. His leg was burning, seeping blood, but it felt good. He felt alive. With a burst, he maneuvered into fourth place again; more cheers brightened the audience.

Are they rooting for me?

The sky opened up as another lightning flash blasted through the cumulonimbus clouds. They darkened to something wicked. The thunder was immediate . . . deafening. Large raindrops slashed through the runners. The stadium had the show of a lifetime. Zeus and Thor had even joined the party.

His eyes retrained on Cyrus. One stride at a time, he reduced the gap. Ben was already a good twenty meters back from him.

One mile to go, four laps, and his original strategy was guns blazing going into the final mile. *Going nuclear.* Ben didn't even look at the time. There was no need, as it was now irrelevant. He was racing, and he had less than four minutes to engrave his tiny mark on the national stage.

He dropped his head for a moment to compose himself for the fight of a lifetime. He lifted it proudly again. Stride after stride, inch after inch, he began closing the gap.

With three laps to go, Cyrus had closed in on Eric and Archer. Archer maintained the lead. Ben was just fifteen meters back.

Coach yelled as Ben screamed by, "Come on, Ben. Got a great one going."

Eric overtook Archer on the backstretch. Cyrus maintained. He was poised like a cobra ready to strike.

Ben turned onto the straightaway as a gust created a tail wind, pushing him faster. He accented it with a surge into a breakneck speed. Driving toward the lap marker, with two laps to go, Ben found himself immediately on the heels of Cyrus. The pack of the legends was tight, and Ben hung on.

Coach was frantic. He jumped up and down at the wall. He screamed, "Tough as nails, Ben. Tough as fucking nails."

Ben held it through the turn. Directly into the wind, drenched by the heavy drops.

Cyrus broke out of formation and against the wind, laid out an unbelievable surge. He overtook Archer and Eric in a moment. Ben, without thinking, followed.

Ben drove into second place. With a lap and a half to go, the field was lined up for the second turn.

As they rounded into the wind-aided home straightaway, the line tightened back into a pack, ready for the bell.

Everything hurt. His backstretch surge was punishing him now. He was drained, his tank was empty, and he knew that the wind behind his back at the moment was going to end soon. Flashes of Maya running with him through the towpath surfaced. A short clip played of him churning up Lake Erie in a downpour worse than what he was running in now. A final image of Maya's wooden box at the bottom of the trench. A rose in the dirt beside it. His visions were interrupted by the clang of a bell. The final lap, and his competition had found themselves in a dead heat with four hundred meters to go. Every warm-blooded human in the stadium was on their feet. The entire nation, at home watching the race, was inching closer to the screen. The race of the century was living up to the hype. Ben was not a spectator. He was center stage.

As he rounded into the backstretch, the wind had eased but was still burdensome. He struggled to hold pace. Cyrus, too, had fallen back to third place. Archer had regained the lead, Eric tightly behind.

Ben surged again to close the gap. It was futile. Each surge took away from his base pace. He was slipping backward, quickly. The four of them had left a large void between them and the distant fifth place. Almost an entire straightaway had separated the men from the boys.

Cyrus punched into the final turn with a surge that would be reshown for decades to come. Running wide, he pulled into the first position again as he began his wind-aided homestretch charge.

Archer, who had led most of the race, was breaking apart. The wheels were falling off, and Cyrus's final push had broken him. He slipped behind Eric and faded back toward Ben.

Ben felt an animalistic instinct overcome his body. A charge inspired by Thor's hammer itself. He became the cheetah who smelled the blood of a wounded antelope in the tall grass. As he came out of the second turn, Ben let his limbs fly. Legs, arms—all of which were numb beyond recognition. He could hardly lift them, but his will carried him. His gut wrenched. He refused to listen to his body cry out in pain. Maya whispered to him, *Archer is yours.*

The crowd roared as Cyrus crossed the line, setting the American record in the process. Just two seconds off the world record.

Eric followed narrowly on his heals, also with his personal best time, which would have been an American record as well.

For a single moment, Ben wasn't some kid from the slums. He belonged here. He knew at that moment that he'd always belonged here. The only thing between him and the finish line was Archer. He dug into a reservoir that had been unknown to him before. It was bottled and under immense pressure. The hatred spewed at him for a year—his whole life. The hatred he saw from the crude guy on a bike swinging down the towpath. The hatred of the gang violence that ripped a hole through his fiancée's heart. Ben spat that hatred back at them.

Archer's wheels were long gone, and he was in survival mode, only attempting to maintain his third-place finish. In the final ten meters, Ben gunned him down, passing him at a pace Archer couldn't react to.

The stadium hadn't stopped roaring since Cyrus finished. Drenched by the torrential storm overhead.

Staggering to a stop, Ben grabbed his shirt and pulled the image of the shoe with a wing to his face. He kissed Maya's name, then collapsed to his knees. Chest heaving for oxygen.

***

"You're a stud, Ben. You're a stud," said a familiar voice. It was what Maya used to call him.

He stood from the track, where he had been sucking air, drawing from his own exertion. It was Cyrus, the new American record holder, national champion, and fellow son of a slummer.

"Wow, Cyrus. You got some serious wheels at the end there."

He laughed. "It was otherworldly, wasn't it? That wind and rain made it surreal. Come. Let's stretch out those legs; otherwise, you will be a pile of hurt for a week."

Ben grabbed his extended hand once again, which pulled him back up to his feet. The two of them jogged side by side down the final straightaway. A wave of cheers followed Cyrus's every move. He wasn't just Ben's idol; he was the nation's.

"Benjamin Brandt," shouted a man from the side of the track.

Ben looked over and saw a tall, well-dressed man who had another person holding an umbrella for him.

"Go on, Ben, you earned it," Cyrus said.

Ben stopped his jog just before him. The rain had turned into a mist.

"What a show you put on today." He extended his hand. "I'm Jason Bryon. I represent Tyger Sports."

Ben grabbed his hand, which returned a hearty squeeze. Ben knew that Tyger Sports was the up-and-coming sports apparel brand in the country. "Yes, sir, it is nice to meet you."

"You really impressed a lot of people out there today."

"Thank you, sir."

"I just got off the phone with our executive committee, and they told me to do anything it takes to get you to sign with us. Right here, right now."

Cyrus smacked his shoulder in a *you made it now* encouragement.

He placed his hand on his chest where the winged racing spikes adorned Maya's name.

"Oh, this is an unbelievable offer." Ben knew that even the lowest figure they could offer him would be a hundred times what his family made in a year. He also knew that Sole's Runner couldn't support much more than travel arrangements and a few pairs of free shoes.

Jason Bryon looked bigger than life. Perfect hair, perfect teeth, and an aura of unbridled success.

Ben looked down as his finger caressed Maya's name. "I'm sorry, sir. I owe my life to Julia Turner, who took an outrageous chance on me. And no matter how excited I am that you are making this offer, I will never leave her side."

Cameras flashed all around.

Ben turned and winked at Cyrus, whose mouth hung agape. "Thanks anyway, though."

Cyrus surged back up to Ben. "Now I know it for sure."

Ben looked at him.

Cyrus blurted out "Ha. You're gonna be a livin' legend."

As they jogged along the track, he could see the perplexed faces of the fans. Cyrus, the runner of the century, America's darling. And Ben, tarnishing Cyrus's image. He knew that they would hate Cyrus for even touching a slummer, let alone befriending one. The prejudice was as ruthless as it was ignorant.

"Ready?" Cyrus asked.

Ben looked at him. "For what?"

"A victory stride-out down the homestretch. You know, stir our fans up a bit."

Ben didn't want to draw more attention to them. He could handle the abusive comments, but he didn't want Cyrus to hear them, or feel pity for him.

"Nah, you earned it man. Enjoy."

"I'll only go with you, Ben."

He inhaled deeply. *Welcome to the other side of the tracks.* "Okay, let's do it."

Cyrus grinned and ripped into a fast clip down the homestretch. Directly on the middle lanes of the track.

The crowd stood in a wave as they approached.

Ben surged right beside him. His legs hurt so good.

Cyrus raised his hand in the air to thank the fans, which returned the gesture with thunderous cheering.

"Come on, give them a show," he said to Ben. "Wave to your fans."

Ben raised his own hand, expecting to prove to Cyrus that the people hated him, but something miraculous happened. The cheering grew instantly louder.

"Living legend," Cyrus repeated.

Further competitions were temporarily on hold due to the thunderstorm that had passed within the hour.

Ben stood beside his coach at the winner's ceremony.

"You are a true warrior, son," Coach said. He reached his arm around his shoulders and squeezed with the might of a man thirty years his junior. "The whole world has changed just a little bit today . . . because of you."

"Come on, Coach, nothing changed. Not really."

The announcer interrupted their conversation.

"I bring to you the results of the men's 5000 meters."

Ben readied himself for a disqualification or some bogus trumped-up charges.

"In third place, setting a new natural-birth world record, at a time of 12:21, rising from the slums of Cleveland, Ohio, Benjamin Brandt."

The crowd erupted. Coach's hands shot into the air with a battle cry leaping from his depths.

A tear charged over Ben's cheek. His emotions were a wild mess. They entangled him in a fragility that could break at any moment. Through the haze of watering eyes, he watched thirty thousand people on their feet begin to chant. "Ben, Ben, Ben . . ."

Ben climbed onto the lowest platform, designated for third place. His knees wobbled.

Archer, who hadn't made the cut, stood beside Eric and Cyrus, who had. All joined into the chant.

The announcer said, "And in second place . . ."

He paused as the fans refused to quiet.

Ben felt like an idiot standing there by himself. He waved his hand in the air as a thank-you for their support—their transformation.

He nodded to the announcer to continue.

He cut in again, this time louder. "And in second place, Eric Richardson."

The crowd reemerged with fresh cheers. Eric climbed up on the opposite side of the podium, winking at Ben.

"And I present to you the 2085 National Champion of the 5000 meters and the new American record holder with a time of 12:17, Cyrus Cray."

Cyrus hopped up onto the winners' stand, patting Ben on the shoulder in the process.

Although he knew it was temporary, he felt like he belonged. He felt like he was an elite athlete. He now understood what Coach had said. Something had indeed changed.

As the ceremony ended, a large camera moved in front of Ben. Stepping in front of him was Samantha Bell. He smiled at her, and she returned the smile with a note of pride.

She waved the camera down, stepped in closer, and said, "Not bad, huh?"

He laughed. "That was nuts ... I am gonna need to watch it on TV to even remember what happened out there."

"I think I can get you an exclusive copy." She winked at him. "Something truly magical happened out there today. You have captured the hearts of the nation, Ben. In all my years of broadcasting, I have never felt so proud of what I do as I do right now. An opportunity to interview the young man who turned America on its soggy head. Ever since Kent, I was hoping for you, for this." Her hand waved toward the crowd.

She looked to the cameraman. "Ready?"

The red light flipped on.

"So, Benjamin Brandt, what do you have to say to your fans back in Cleveland?"

Ben laughed. "Well, I'm not sure many people from my neighborhood even knew I was running today."

She smiled like she had a secret. "I would like to show you a clip that we took during your race."

She produced a tablet with a video. The cameraman continued to roll while he watched.

"What's this?" Ben said as he hit the play icon.

"We took the liberty of setting up a large projector on your street. Your dad was there, as well as a couple hundred people, cheering you on."

Ben looked at the screen in awe. He had never seen his neighbors so full of energy . . . full of life. "You did this?"

"Of course we did, Ben. It would be a shame if what you did today couldn't be witnessed by those who care about you the most."

Ben looked up from the screen and laughed. "Gosh, I'm glad I didn't go down in flames."

"Ben, I have been in this business a long time. You have a spark that can never be extinguished. I knew that what stands behind your motivation is greater than anyone else's in this stadium. I knew that you were either going to have the race of a lifetime or go down valiantly until you had no more life. Either way, you would be celebrated for putting everything on the table." She turned to the camera. "Clearly, Benjamin Brandt ran the race of his lifetime today and has earned a place in the national track and field community."

Ben couldn't believe his dad watched the race.

Samantha returned to him. "Ben, I have a call for you." She handed him a mobile phone. "Go on, it's for you."

He hesitantly picked up the device and placed it to his ear. "Hello, this is Ben."

In the background was loud cheering, like a party that had gotten too rowdy.

"Ben?" came a voice from the other end of the line.

"Dad?"

"Ben! I can't believe it. I'm here with your brother and Amy. I'm so proud of you, son."

"I wish you were here with me, Dad. I miss you. I love you."

"We are with you. Your mom, too. I am so unbelievably proud."

"I will be home soon." The dam broke wide open as his tears raced over his cheeks. Samantha ensured that his gripping and raw emotion had been transported to every television screen in America.

Chapter Thirty-Two

Ten weeks had slipped by since Ben returned to Cleveland. He hadn't run a step. Most of the neighborhood received him as a hero. However, plenty blamed him for being a poser—wishing he would leave the community in exile for turning his back on them. Dreaming to be better than them was sinful in their eyes.

Ben just wanted to run and race against the best. He had no dreams of leaving the east side of Cleveland. This was his home, where he belonged. Besides, he didn't trust the outside world.

Throughout the weeks, his supporters faded back into their menial and dismal lives. Zombie-like routines of their never-ending survival mode. The effects of AluMag being shut down drove more and more families into Tent City. Crime rates and petty theft surged.

Ben had received a new contract from his sponsor, promising him a monthly payment that exceeded what their family had ever earned in the past. Included was a percent share of Julia's shoe store's growth, which later proved to be significant.

Ben also found out that Julia Turner had traded her position working for Harvey Woodard on the track and field committee in exchange for reinstating Ben's Penn Relays results. In anger, he had also revoked her access pass at the championship, leaving her without a ticket to the event, which was why Ben hadn't seen her in the stands.

Her decision to help a slummer out as an act of charity had turned into the best marketing campaign her company had ever seen. From just two stores in Manhattan, the company had turned into a franchise, slowly stretching across the country, and Ben became the store's branded image which flourished from state to state.

Ben spent almost every hour hidden within his apartment. Hiding from the snide comments, which were not only coming from the elites, but from his own people, too. He never intended to lead a movement against injustice, but nevertheless, he became the poster boy. Famous, and he wanted none of it.

The media often commented about how the only way Ben could have competed at that level was through the use of performance-enhancing drugs. This stung more than anything else. He despised unnatural advantage in sport, which was his top grievance against the elites. Being accused of the exact opposite of what you believe in weighed heavy. Nobody ever asked Ben about the truth. Nobody cared to get data to support their claims. It was the lies that everybody wanted to believe in. The lies were more palatable.

Together, Ben's dad, brother, Amy, and Coach stood by him through his darkest hours. He hated that his dad had to fight for Ben's integrity with the neighbors, which he was now forced to do frequently. Ben was a burden for those who loved him most. Caught in the crossfire of his fame.

Ben often asked himself if any of it was worth it. What unexpected consequences had prevailed, contrary to what his logic predicted.

There was no place for him, not any longer. He was stuck directly in the middle, between two sides of the most polarized society of modern times. Liked by neither and hated by most.

Today was marked on Ben's calendar, which was the singular reason he planned to leave the house at all. It was the first time in almost six weeks, despite his dad's constant nagging to get some fresh air.

He pulled on his running shoes for the first time since his cool-down with Cyrus. They felt good . . . great actually. He decided to wear his race singlet, which had gained him iconic photos that were now being used on the covers of not just running magazines, but some of the biggest publications in the country. Some of which heralded him, while others demonized him. He left a letter in an envelope on his bed. *Dad* was scribbled on the front.

It was a hot summer day, and Ben gradually increased his pace as he ran toward Edgewater Park. He was a complex creation of his accumulated life experiences, yet resembled nothing of the man he was just six months prior. His own character had been crossed out and rewritten. He was everything and nothing.

He took off his shoes and socks at the edge of the sand and headed across the beach to the water. Quite a few swimmers had been splashing around, but nobody noticed him or recognized him.

This was a day for him and Maya. It was August 23, his planned wedding day, and he stood there alone. No friends. No family. No bride.

Ben collapsed into the ankle-deep water and sat there as the water lapped against him.

A tear streaked over the creases of his face, dripping its salty taste into the freshwater below.

The lake sprawled off into infinity. From this perspective, the lake had no ends. A body of water, eternal.

The same body of water he'd spent hours upon hours thrashing and churning in as it grew colder heading into the winter months. It felt like decades ago.

He had no place on this earth. No desire laid before him.

"What should I do, Maya?" he whispered to himself. "What the hell am I supposed to do now?"

He stood and waded into the silky water, then began to swim out toward the horizon. The beachgoers, cheerfully splashing in the water, were now fifty yards behind him. He continued to search for answers. *I miss you, Maya. I'm coming for you.*

Ben swam for almost an hour until he lost sight of the shore, then began treading water. He dove into the greenish-yellow water streaked with sun beams as far as he could, then returned to the surface.

He had decided that he would join Maya today. Swimming until he could no longer. Slowly sinking, without the capability to reverse his decision. Exhausted physically, mentally, and emotionally.

He was only lightly tired and realized that he could probably cross the lake before he sank. He underestimated his own fitness.

For a half hour, he was alone, treading the water rhythmically, thinking of Maya the entire time. His eyes welled, and the tears streamed again.

"Don't you want me to join you?" he said into the empty air.

A wave of shame and guilt washed over him.

If there was a heaven and he somehow reunited with her there, both of which were long shots, he thought, she would turn her back on his cowardice. She would tell him to return to the shore and finish what he had started. *Stop crying like a child,* she would say.

He knew she was right. He'd started a transformation in the world, and without finishing the job, he would leave the world a worse place than when he had entered it. He would have to bear the burden of the movement upon his shoulders. Absorb the world's anger even though he was emotionally ill-equipped. He wished he could just be a runner and nothing more.

Such a simple sport, he thought, *how could it be so complicated?*

Ben splashed the cool water over his eyes, then pulled his singlet off. He kissed her name, then let it sink to the bottom of the lake. He started back for the beach.

He had at least an hour to consider his decision to continue forward in life, and although he was still unsure how to do it, he knew it was exactly what Maya would have wished for him.

Finally, he dragged himself back onto the beach, and basked in the sun to dry off. The warmth of its rays was encouraging. His journey ahead would be long and unforgiving. He now accepted that. Not with confidence, but with determination.

Behind him, a voice shouted, "Hey, it's that guy."

Ben turned, and two young upper-class teenagers pointed at him.

One of them, who had unkempt sandy blond hair and a few strands of a desperate beard, and who looked as if he were a well-trained runner himself, said, "Hey, you're Benjamin Brandt, aren't you?"

Ben inhaled deeply, "Yeah, that's me."

"Woah." He stepped forward to shake his hand. "I'm Kevin, I'm a runner from Avon Lake High School. Dude, you are freaking awesome."

Not once in Ben's life had a Clevelander from the West Side greeted him as an equal, let alone as an idol. He had never even shaken one's hand before.

"My buddy and I are here to do a hill workout. In a running magazine, you mentioned that this was your favorite place to run hills."

Ben smiled, stood to his feet. "It is indeed. Hey, mind if I run a circuit with you?"

"Holy crap, absolutely," said the second boy. This one's voice cracked under the torment of puberty. Even elites couldn't escape that fate.

Ben walked to the starting line with the boys in bare feet and bare chested. "Ready, guys? Go."

He maintained a gentle pace, staying side by side with the two kids. As he crested the top, he said, "Dig in, back to race pace for thirty yards to the tree. Push it all the way in."

The three of them crested and flew to the finish line. It felt great.

Ben ran the entire workout with those boys. He had never felt so honored in his life.

***

Coach had been contacted by Samantha Bell for a follow-up interview. Despite dragging his feet, Ben eventually agreed to schedule the event. It took place directly in the middle of the slums, outside his apartment building. As usual, the word got around, and the street was full of onlookers hoping to get a chance to be on TV.

"Hi, Ben. How ya doing?" she asked while waiting for the camera crew to set up the equipment.

Ben was happy to see her. "I'm doing good. Real good, actually. It has been quite a tough few months, but the worst is past."

"Glad to hear it . . . The media can be ruthless. I'm sorry you got dragged through so much. I have been following closely, and most people couldn't handle so much pressure. You have done very well."

"It's okay, I got good people with me." Ben looked at his dad and coach, who stood beside each other. She didn't need to know how not well he actually was back then. His dad had found the note Ben had left for him. It made for a long and complicated conversation about his mental health. His dad in turn shared it with Coach, and they formed a support team for Ben, to do a better job of protecting him from the unwanted fame. He was indeed in a much better place now, though. Family, which included Coach, held him up and running carried him through.

"Okay, shall we get started?"

Ben nodded.

The red light flipped on.

"Benjamin Brandt. It has been four months since your spectacular debut at the national championship. What's next for you?"

A month ago, in the lake, followed by running hills with the high school kids, he decided that he would get back into competitive running. It was a wake-up call, and he in fact had run every day since.

"Well, Samantha, with the best coach in history beside me, I have decided that there is only one place where I belong. The oval of misery is calling me." A quote he picked up from Cyrus.

"The oval has certainly called you," she said. "And to your fans everywhere, do you have anything to say?"

Ben thought about it for a moment. Then nodded. "I am a runner, nothing more, nothing less. I have just one dream, and that is to be faster than the guy I was yesterday. Many people have been affected by the fact that I am some natural-blood slummer from the east side of Cleveland. Some of those people had a chance to put their judgments aside and support me. Others allowed their hatred to get the better of them, spreading lies to justify their misconceptions. Some people have even become inspired." Ben looked at his dad, who stood just beside the cameraman. "I have one thing for my fans. I am a runner, and that is what gets me out of bed every morning. Find out what wakes you before your alarm goes off. Allow it to burn like a wildfire that nobody could ever extinguish. Not even yourself. Especially yourself."

Ben swallowed the growing lump in his throat, then gazed into the glass dome of the camera, where he could see a fish-eyed reflection of his apartment building behind him. "I love you, Maya."

***

The cameraman stayed behind packing up his gear as Ben took Samantha on a tour. As they arrived, she looked pale and frightened. Her radiant glow had dissipated.

Industrial Valley had once been the location of multiple steel plants, which had shut down decades ago. The barren parking lots had come back to life in the form of an overpopulated mass of desperation. Tent City, as Clevelanders had come to call it, was row upon row of cardboard boxes, tarps tied up to rusted-through fence posts, and corrugated sheet metal leaning against crumbling walls of the factory. Inside the abandoned buildings were cities of rat-infested dwellings of the poor. Ben would never dare venture within those walls. A unique social order within Tent City took hold there. The premium weather-protected locations in the old buildings were coveted by all and claimed by those who could defend them. A social order molded by terror.

"This is it," Ben said. "This is where we live if we lose our job or the City declares that we are no longer fit to stay in a house or apartment. My dad, brother, and I all worked at a foundry, which shut down earlier this year. If I wasn't sponsored by Julia Turner, we would be living here right now."

The smell turned Ben's stomach. The onlookers were curious about the visitors, however they cowered under cover.

"I don't know what to say, Ben. This … this is atrocious."

"This is what we slummers fear every day. There is no climbing back from Tent City. Once you arrive as a resident, it is guarnateed that you will die here."

Chapter Thirty-Three

Ben went on to train for the following year's championship, but as winter rolled around, he was plagued by injuries. His right knee gave him problems, which migrated to a left hip issue due to his inadvertent overcompensation.

Three consecutive years of battling his body's natural limitations. Three to six months of progressive training crashed into another injury, repeatedly. He finally gave up chasing the continuation of his dream, never racing again after his miraculous 5000 meters at Hayward Field. His fans faded away, and his foes used his failure to jab sticks into his ribs.

Schadenfreude, he thought.

He had learned that alcohol softened the edges of the pain. Not the pain of his injuries, but the emotional toll they burdened him with. Wooden crutches allowed him to move around with a bum foot or a faulty knee, and the bottle was the crutch that allowed him to sleep at night. Gradually it became a daily routine, with or without an injury, to have a few swigs of whiskey in place of breakfast. The light buzz was a welcome gift to begin the day after a night filled with dreams of misfortune and calamity. He had once been addicted to running, but it was more that he was addicted to whatever he set his mind toward.

One morning, while he was at the corner store to replace his depleted stock, he saw Logan. The inquisitive boy from outside Coach's apartment who had joined him for the final workout before the championships.

"Ben. Wow, I haven't seen you in forever."

The boy had grown. Now probably twelve years old.

"Hey, Logan, good to see you. What have you been up to?"

"I started working at the scrapyards this year. Some extra money is always good, right?"

"Sure is." Ben looked at the boy, whose eyes were eager and full of life.

"I run sometimes, too. I don't have too much time, but whenever I can. I love it."

Ben had once loved it ferociously, long before ever dreaming of competing. More than anything else the world had to offer. It helped him cope with the life sentence of being a slummer—before all the drama that came when his dream transitioned into a nightmare. As he looked into Logan's vibrant eyes, an idea leaped from the shadows.

"Hey, do you wanna meet me at the track once a week to do a little workout?"

The boy's eyes grew. "Absolutely."

The idea alone brought life back into Ben, life he had long since forgotten. A moment of sobriety.

It was in that insignificant corner store that something had changed within Cleveland. The most miniscule idea of running together started an unexpected chain reaction.

Logan had a couple of friends who started to show up, too. Ben spent some of his stockpiled sponsorship money and bought all three of them running shoes and running clothes.

Within a year, on every Wednesday evening, the cinder track beneath the abandoned steel plant became a hotspot. Over a dozen kids and a few adults joined him for his favorite pastime. The same cinder track where Ben had laid his life down for his infamous quarters till death workout.

With a little help from Julia Turner, who maintained her sponsorship of him despite his lack of racing, Ben opened the first slummer-founded track club in the United States. Gradually, over the following few years, they began cropping up in other cities, too. Mostly following the expansion of Julia's franchise, where she donated the necessities to the local clubs.

Although Ben didn't change society at large, he had changed these individuals in the most profound ways. He gave them a reason to get out of bed in the morning.

***

Samantha Bell received a phone call while attending her friend's five-year-old son's birthday party.

"Sam, um, I got some terrible news . . . your guy Benjamin Brandt . . ."

She froze at the tone of her boss's voice.

"Um, he died last night. He got knifed by a gang member who tried to squeeze Ben's track club."

The life ran out of her, and the phone almost slipped from her fingers.

"Sam, you there?"

A torrent of moments rushed through her mind in rapid succession. Ben's life flashed before her eyes.

"Sam?"

"Uh, yeah . . . Cory, I am sorry, but um . . . I quit."

"What? I don't think I heard you right. I hope I didn't, anyway."

"I just woke up, Cory."

"It's the middle of the afternoon. I thought you were at some kid's birthday party."

"No, that's not what I mean. I just woke up." She wiped her tears away. Her voice wavered. "You heard me right. I am handing in my resignation."

Samantha hung up the phone and thought, *He found his Maya at long last.*

She headed to her car without saying good-bye to the hosts of the party. Within hours of that phone call, she sat at her kitchen table with her laptop, writing. Over the following months, she made hundreds of phone calls, researching the deepest and darkest corners of Ben's existence. With every new piece of the puzzle, she become even more motivated to tell the full story of Benjamin Brandt, and not just the life of an athlete in the slums. The life of a natural blood.

It wasn't Ben's life that brought a significant change to America, it was in his death. The mayor of Cleveland, amid much controversy, erected a bronze statue of Ben in the middle of the Cleveland Public Square, not far from the Civil War monument where Maya had once worked. It showed Ben in the final stride of the national championship, including his winged shirt with the name *Maya* etched on to it.

The statue was so controversial that for twenty-four hours a day it required a standing guard to protect it from vandals. It stood as a symbol of promised reform and the struggles it takes to initiate change. The base of the statue had a simple identification, similar to one from Box Row, but it had a short quote from Coach Sands at the bottom.

Benjamin Brandt
2/4/2064–10/21/2090
Greatness teeters on the brink of tragedy . . . Relentlessly.

He was twenty-six years old when he died, and he accomplished more than ten times what a typical elite could.

It took more than a year before Samantha released her book. However, it was the most meaningful work she had ever done. On a November morning, the first copy arrived at her house. *The Slummer: Quarters Till Death.*

Dear Reader,

The Slummer is a work of passion which materialized from my experiences as a former competitive runner at Kent State University. Writing the training and racing scenes transported me along a nostalgic journey through those years—Friendships, PRs, and broken bones alike.

As a self-published author, I rely on word of mouth and bookstore ratings. If you enjoyed the story, and could spare a moment, I would sincerely appreciate your feedback and recommendation to others.

Warmest Regards,
Geoffrey Simpson

P.S. Check out my website for status, because a spin-off novel to **The Slummer** is in development.

www.BarkingBoxerPress.com

Books by:

BarkingBoxer Press
The Future of Sports Fiction

- ***The Slummer: Quarters Till Death*** (Slummer -Book 1)
  by Geoffrey Simpson

  An impoverished runner, from an era of prolific genetic engineering, chases his dream of the 5000-meter national title.

- ***The Farmhand: Dante's Ladder*** (Slummer -Book 2)
  by Geoffrey Simpson

  Coming Soon

- ***The Humiliation Tour***
  by Jeffrey Recker

  A humiliated cross-country runner makes a redeeming comeback in this hilarious coming of age story.

- ***The Three Hares (Bloodline) (Reynard's Dream)***
  by Geoffrey Simpson

  Their discovery of an encrypted code entangles them in a centuries-old struggle between warring secret societies. They must save Winslow Falls; however, it may already be too late.

Ready for more sports fiction?
www.BarkingBoxerPress.com

Acknowledgements

Lili, Jonathan, and Henry—My family who tirelessly support me on my life's journey. Writing in the morning, working through the day, and family time in the evening is the balance we have achieved together. Forever thankful!

Mom and Dad—From the first pages of my first novel and millions of years before when I struggled with reading in school, you have always been there. Your suggestions, critiques, and editing support runs thick through *The Slummer*. I am proud to be surrounded by such wonderful and encouraging parents.

Tom Barko—My dear Kent friend who forged more memories together with me than we ought to have. I thank you for your enthusiastic and critical support with *The Slummer*.

Derek Griffiths—From intervals on the blue track at Kent State until now, I am proud to have you as a friend. Your support on this project is sincerely appreciated, and your ongoing effort of progressing the world of running through *Colorado Runner* magazine is inspiring to all.

Suzanne Kelly—I never dreamed of a better support team. Your enthusiasm, motivation, and honest feedback have provided a sincere meaningfulness to my writing.

Minette Antonucci—Thank you for your enthusiasm and urgent, tactical support on this project, especially when the hours were thin.

Jen, Dirk, Jayden, Alia, and Riley —Our time together in Florida, captive in our hotel due to the first round of pandemic closures and killer jellyfish, is where *The Slummer* took form. The power of family is inspirational and is never to be taken lightly.

Kent State Track & Field and Cross Country—There is no way to appropriately thank the teammates, coaches, and university for contributing so much to my life. Twenty years later, rarely a day goes by when I am not thinking about a fellow Golden Flash or a moment from those cherished days. A family from which we will always be a member of. Thank you!

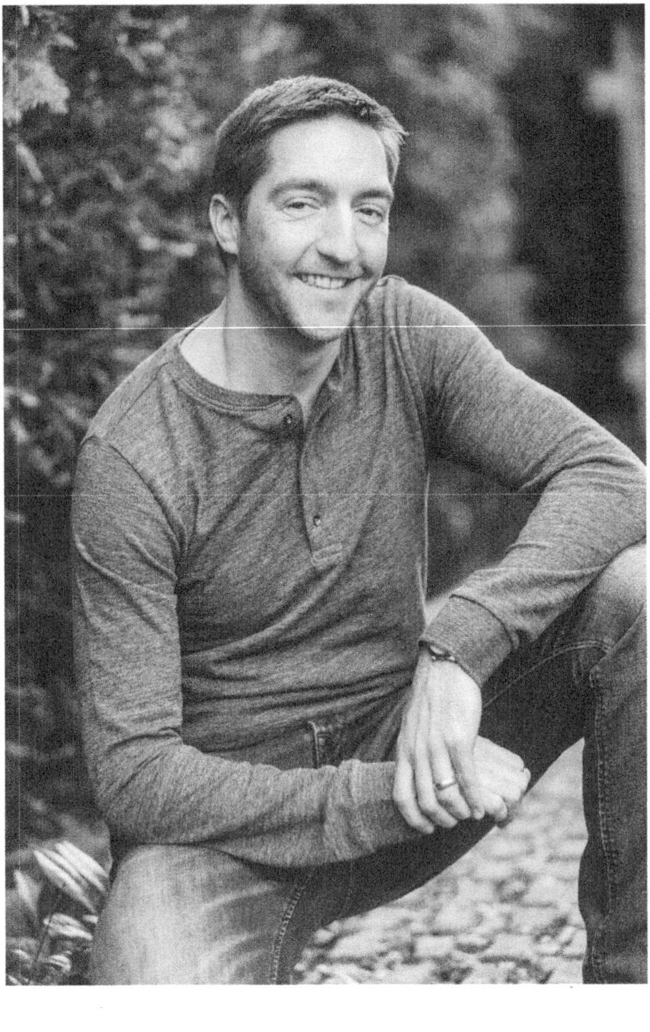

About the Author

Geoffrey Drew Simpson

Born: February 1978, Cleveland, Ohio.

    Geoffrey Simpson was born and raised in Avon Lake, Ohio, just outside Cleveland. He attended Avon Lake High School and competed in the state cross country and track & field championships on multiple occasions.

    At Kent State, he graduated from the School of Technology and was a member of the Track & Field and Cross Country programs. His primary events were the 5,000 meters (14:57) and 10,000 meters (31:14).

    After releasing *the Slummer*, he created BarkingBoxer Press to publish other sports fiction titles by talented authors.

    His family of two boys, Jonathan and Henry, and his beloved wife Lili, impassion his craving for adventure. An adventurous spirit which is passed down to his sons. Now living with his family in Minden, Germany, in the pre-dawn hours, he is an author.

    Geoffrey is the author of the middle-school aged adventure-mystery series, *The Three Hares,* and the near-future, speculative fiction novel, *The Slummer*.

Check out his website to further explore his many passions and intrigues.

www.BarkingBoxerPress.com

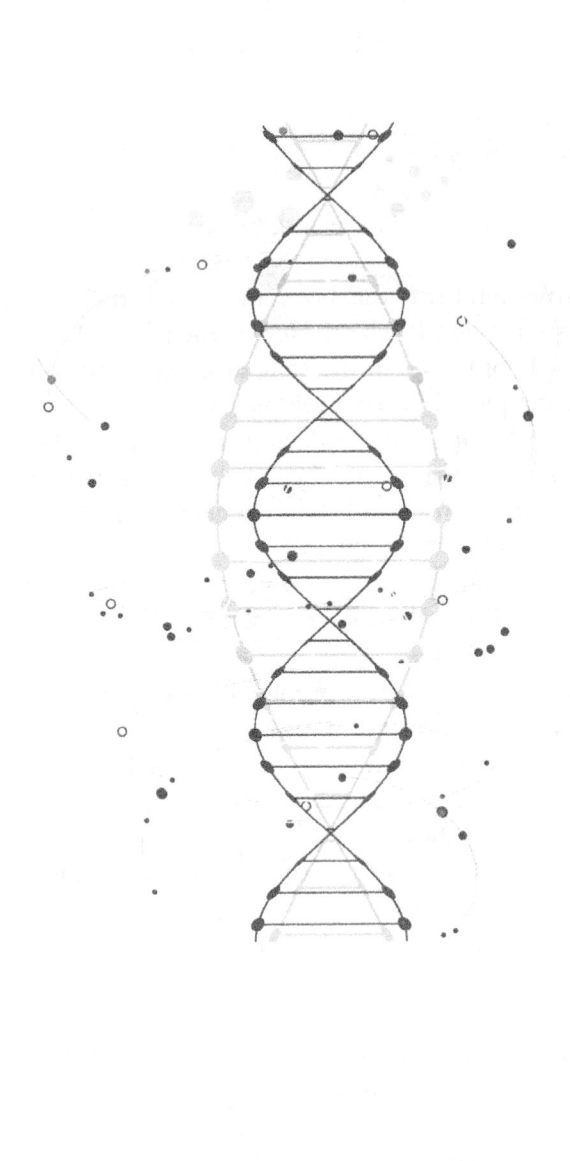

Made in the USA
Monee, IL
22 December 2024